ED
For Love and Hope

BOOK 2 OF THE BAND 4 TRILOGY

BY MARGUERITE NARDONE GRUEN

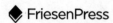

Suite 300 - 990 Fort St
Victoria, BC, V8V 3K2
Canada

www.friesenpress.com

Copyright © 2017 by Marguerite Nardone Gruen
First Edition — 2017

All rights reserved.

No part of this publication may be reproduced in any form, or by any means, electronic or mechanical, including photocopying, recording, or any information browsing, storage, or retrieval system, without permission in writing from FriesenPress.

Portrait Photographer: Brittany Bahner

This book is purely fictitious—stemming from the authors' imagination. Resemblances to actual people or events are purely coincidental.

ISBN
978-1-5255-1078-6 (Hardcover)
978-1-5255-1079-3 (Paperback)
978-1-5255-1080-9 (eBook)

1. FICTION, ROMANCE

Distributed to the trade by The Ingram Book Company

I am once again dedicating my book to my sister, Jeanine, and my brothers,

Joe and Frank, for always being there for me, along with my parents.

I would also like to dedicate this book to my three friends, Lisa S, Sarah D, and Roseann B, for their continued support and advice during the whole writing process.

Thank you, Roger, for giving my card out to everyone you meet!

Thank you to my best friend, Judy, who has been my

best friend since the beginning of time.

Thank you for helping me promote the first book and for helping me with 'Ed'!

A PRIVATE NOTE TO ALL OF MY READERS!

When looking up the definition of fiction, I have found many meanings. My favorite descriptions are 'fabrication,' 'untrue,' and 'fantasy!'

Having said that—please remember—this trilogy is totally fictitious. The characters and circumstances surrounding their stories were totally invented by my imagination. When you imagine a story, you can go wherever your thoughts take you. If I wanted to give Chase and Marguerite two heads each, I could very well do that, because it is fiction.

So, whether or not you think some of the story-lines are not believable—please remember—it's fiction. It basically isn't supposed to be believable, as much as some of us wish some things in all fictitious books could actually be possible. It is a fantasy. 'Fantasy' is my absolute favorite definition of fiction.

Please keep an open mind and enjoy the characters and the story-lines.

I wrote this for all of my family and friends who wanted to read more about Chase, Marguerite, and their 'family.'

Enjoy!

1
Life Changing

The sun was shining brightly, and the warm air swarmed around her. However, Lilli didn't feel a thing, nor see anything in front of her. Her legs were moving, but she didn't know where they were taking her. She felt numb. If someone had randomly bumped into her, she wouldn't have even realized it, as she was oblivious to her surroundings.

She exited the cancer hospital in L.A., her worst fears confirmed. It was as though she were living in a nightmare. Multiple surgeries, and countless months of treatment, and none of it had made any difference. She was dying. There was nothing more that could be done for her. She had a few weeks, or possibly months, but that was all they could promise her. She refused any additional treatments since they weren't going to help, and she was tired of being sick from them. All that she wanted now was what the doctor had suggested: to try and live as normally as possible, in the short time that she had left.

Lilli needed to be at the production studio right after her hospital appointment, to meet a new up-and-coming singer-songwriter named Ed Mehan. She had handpicked him to write the music for a movie she had produced and written the screenplay for. She had written the book too, *Waiting for Love*, and had insisted that she be the one to adapt it for the screen, thinking that she was the only one who could capture the love story as it had been written. The studio had taken a chance and given her the job, and so far, they were more than pleased with her work.

The director was also fascinated with her work, and understood everything she was trying to do, in order to communicate to both the fans of the book and those who would be seeing the story for the first time in the theater.

Lilli now needed killer songs to add to the movie. That was why she'd enlisted Ed. She'd begged him to review the movie and see if it touched him emotionally. If so, she hoped he'd be able to write some love songs to accompany the events that happened in the script. She was thrilled that he had agreed, and was now going to finally meet him in person.

Lilli thought Ed was brilliant with his music. His songs were very soothing and touched every person that had ever been in love or were just falling in love for the first time. When someone listened to his music, they always felt like he wrote that song just for them, or with them in mind. She was hoping that he would be moved enough to write something for her, and was secretly hoping that he would be able to distract her from the horrible news she had just received.

Lilli didn't know how she was going to be able to concentrate. She had waited a long time for this meeting though, and it was finally happening, so she had to pull herself together.

She decided to wait in the private theater for Ed, rather than meet him in the office or the lobby. Her legs were wobbly, and she couldn't really stand at the moment, so she sat in one of the big theater chairs in the private viewing room. Lilli just sat there waiting for him, trying to stay focused, but her mind kept wandering off to the news she had been given and how little time she had left to live.

She heard the door open and saw a light coming into the dark theater. She finally calmed down enough to stand, anxious to meet him, and she wasn't disappointed. He looked just like all the photos she had seen of him, and his smile was just as infectious when he saw her. It went from ear to ear; his face lit up and flushed red, just like the color of his hair. His eyes were bright blue and really stood out when his face flushed like that. He walked over to her the moment he saw her and greeted her with a huge hug, which took Lilli by surprise. At that moment, with the news she had just received, that hug was exactly what she needed.

Ed didn't understand why she melted into his embrace like that. He immediately felt the tenseness in her body and decided to hold her until she was ready to let go. Lilli finally relaxed a bit and held back tears. No one knew about her condition, although she'd had to work hard to squash a rumor that had started after an interviewer had picked up on some physical weakness and nausea she'd experienced after one of her first treatments. She didn't want to tell anyone. She didn't want anyone know. There was too much work to be done on the movie, and she wanted this to be her distraction.

Ed felt instantly that something was up. He didn't know just what but did know something wasn't right. He sensed that she was distraught about something, but didn't know if he should even ask. He had just met her.

She let go of him and just smiled at him, as if to say, *thank you,* and Ed looked back at her, as if to say, *you are very welcome.*

Lilli got down to business, explaining the love story and the connection between the two characters. That was the main message she wanted to communicate with the story-line and the music. Lilli wanted to make sure that the love between the main couple was conveyed to the audience, and for it to be the best love story ever written.

Ed understood what she wanted and agreed to watch the movie with her. He warned her that, if he didn't feel anything about the story, he would not be able to write anything about it. Ed was going to keep an open mind though, and that is all Lilli could ask of him. They sat down and both pulled out notebooks to jot down anything they felt or thought about while they watched the movie. Lilli went to sit in a different aisle, so that she would not disturb Ed, but he stopped her and asked her to sit next to him. This surprised her, but she obliged. She found some comfort, sitting next to him. He was very down-to-earth, and Lilli just knew he would love the movie.

It wasn't far into the movie before Ed began writing. She watched him for a moment. He was really writing away! She was thrilled. She felt that the story must have touched his heart and inspired him, for him to be taking notes that way. It was exactly what she had wished for.

By the end of the movie, Ed had written several pages and asked Lilli if she would mind playing the movie again. He wanted to make sure that he didn't miss anything—not a single glance, embrace, or kiss that was shared by the main couple. Not one feeling was left unnoticed.

Ed loved it, and didn't want to miss a beat with all that he was thinking about. His mind was just racing with ideas and thoughts. That is why he was writing so much. Lilli smiled with contentment and told the technician to start the movie over, as they both slouched down in the big leather chairs, watching it again.

As the movie played for the second time, Ed did something that surprised her. While leaning towards her in the big leather seat, he took her hand and held it, remembering the hug she had given him when they met. She tried to pull her hand away, but he looked at her, and said, "Let's watch the movie like this." He didn't explain why, but she couldn't refuse—not while looking into those beautiful eyes. She felt uncomfortable doing it though.

She was 35, and much older than Ed, who was only 23. Her illness had greatly affected her appearance as well, or so she feared. She could see it in her face whenever she looked in the mirror, and her body had so many scars from the surgeries that she felt she looked like the bride of Frankenstein. Her hair was short brown and thinned out from all the treatments she had gone through. She kept it cropped close to her head, so everyone would think it was just how she wore it. Her eyes were brown and seemed to sink into her face.

That was one of the reasons why she never dated. She hid all the reminders of her illness and would never let someone get close enough to her to see her body like that. It even grieved *her* to see it. Now, this was going to be a constant reminder that her time was limited.

As Ed watched for the second time, he kept thinking about how brilliant Lilli was. She had captured the heart and soul of the couple in the story, and knew that every person who went to see that movie would be as captivated as he was with the story-line. She actually *made* you feel their torment, sorrow, heartbreak, and above all, the love they felt for each other. In all the movies or books he had ever seen or read, he'd never felt what he was feeling now, watching her movie. It was magnificent!

The movie was over for the second time around. Lilli gently pulled her hand from Ed's, and he released it this time. He then began writing again and didn't stop for a long time.

When he was done, he turned around, smiled, and said, "I am taking you to dinner, because I'm starving right now and we can talk about what I saw and felt while we eat. I want to make sure we're on the same page with what I'm thinking and feeling about this." Lilli reluctantly agreed, since he wanted to discuss the movie.

Ed had an ulterior motive though; he had totally connected with the movie and the characters, and just wanted to get to know Lilli better. He knew how old she was. He had looked her up while flying over from London. He had researched everything about her, and had even uncovered one article that hinted at her being sick. It was only mentioned briefly, and it was very subtle, but he wanted to know if she was throwing herself into her work to keep her mind off of an illness, or if she was really just that passionate about the story.

After meeting her, he already knew the answer. It was both. She was definitely passionate about her story, which pleased him, but he felt sad not knowing what was wrong with her health.

At dinner, they spoke for hours about the movie, and he shared his thoughts and feelings with her.

"I have many thoughts and ideas swimming around in my head right now, about the lyrics and the music. If I don't sit and put them in order, the songs will sound incomplete and won't end up the way you might have envisioned them. They'll just come out all wrong."

Ed had not yet booked a hotel for his stay in L.A., so she offered to help him find a place to stay. He took her up on it, surprising her once again.

"I need to stay with you. I think it's important, in case I have any questions about the movie or the characters. I can't make a mistake on this. I can see how important this project is to you, as well." Secretly, however, he was hoping that it would introduce a situation where he would be able to spend more time with her.

Lilli could feel his intentions, but it confused her. For some reason, he was attaching himself to her, and she couldn't figure out why.

She protested, but for every excuse she came up with, he countered, begging and pleading with her, staking the success of her movie and its soundtrack on the arrangement, until he wore her down. With the day she'd just had, she couldn't argue anymore.

Lilli eventually agreed, but wasn't entirely happy about it.

Home

Lilli and Ed arrived at her house. It looked like a cottage. She was renting it while she was in L.A. Lilli actually lived in Pennsylvania, which she loved.

Her rental place was beautiful but small, and she knew it would be hard to avoid him in the close quarters. Ed loved it from the first moment he saw it. It was very comfortable and cozy. He just knew that he would be able to write song after song while he stayed there.

It was, of course, awkward having Ed in the house. Even during the brief tour, they kept bumping into each other, and this began to annoy Lilli.

"How do you want to do this?" she finally asked him. "Would you like to write in your room or somewhere else in the house?"

Ed shrugged. "I write anywhere I'm comfortable sitting, and right now, that's here at the snack bar, in the kitchen." Lilli gave a sigh as Ed continued, "If I'm in your way, just say something and I'll move. I promise, I will not disturb you."

Discussing that calmed her down a little, but she just wanted peace. She was still trying to process what had happened that day at the hospital, and she knew the tear-fest was going to start shortly. She was exhausted and just wanted to crawl into bed, feeling sorry for herself. *At least I can give myself one night to feel like this,* she thought. *I'll pick myself up tomorrow.*

Lilli said goodnight to Ed. She told him that she was tired after the trying day she'd had, and he fully understood. He could see it on her face, even though she kept trying to hide it. That was why he'd wanted to go to dinner, to keep her out of the house and have her talk about something that made her happy: her movie.

Ed stood up and walked over to where she was standing. He then grabbed her and wrapped his arms around her. He had a feeling that she needed a hug, and he was right. Lilli embraced the kindness for a long moment, and then broke free, saying goodnight to him as she looked into his beautiful blue eyes. She had to get away from him! She couldn't allow herself to have feelings for him. For one thing, she was too old for him, and for another ... she was dying.

Just like she had predicted, as soon as she went to bed, she began to weep uncontrollably. She definitely needed the release. It was overdue, and she felt that she deserved the meltdown. She just couldn't stop though, and continued crying for a very long time before she cried herself to sleep.

Ed sat in front of her bedroom door, worrying and listening, in case she needed him for something. He didn't leave her door until he stopped hearing her crying, realizing that she must really be sick. The buried article that had mentioned it was right. He was glad to have read it, and then began to feel a sense of urgency. He needed to write the greatest love songs ever for her movie, as soon as possible. He felt it was the only way he could help her. They would be her legacy.

Ed was up all night, writing and singing. He tried to be quiet, so as not to disturb Lilli. The thought of her coming out and yelling at him brought a smile to his face. He just had so many thoughts going through his mind; it felt like he could write a whole CD full of songs for her movie. He wanted to go over them with her, and pick the songs she loved, or just select the ones that were best for the movie.

Lilli woke up around eight in the morning, and saw that Ed had been up all night. She felt bad that he hadn't gotten any sleep. She also wondered if he'd heard her crying.

She politely asked, "Are you still writing?"

He nodded. "I have to keep it up while I have all of these thoughts or I'll lose them."

It was then that Lilli knew how serious Ed was about his music, and about writing for her movie. She made breakfast for him, because he had to eat at least or he would pass out. Ed was so touched, and seemed genuinely worried about her. They sat together at the snack bar and ate together, happily making small talk.

"Does the sun always shine so much here in L.A.?" Ed asked, smiling at her. "It barely shows up in London."

She returned the smile. "It shines more than in Pennsylvania, where my home is. I'm only living in L.A. temporarily, until the movie is finished." She suspected that he'd heard her crying last night, but she didn't want to talk about it. She felt relieved that he wasn't bringing it up.

After breakfast, she got ready for work. She gave him a key to the house and told him that she had to get going.

He knew that he would just be camping out, writing the songs going through his head, so he said goodbye to her and hugged her before she left.

Weeks went by, and Ed remained at Lilli's cottage, writing and composing. He was finally ready to submit the six songs he had written for her. The movie had really spoken to him, and he couldn't stop thinking of the story-line, which had inspired him to keep writing. He also couldn't bring himself to leave Lilli. They had dinner every night together, and she cooked him breakfast every morning. He touched base with her at least twice a day, while she was in the studio working.

Lilli was shocked and surprised at how much she liked Ed's company. She totally enjoyed spending time with him and looked forward to his calls during the day, but in the back of her mind, she was upset with herself. She couldn't lead him to believe that they had a future together. Even if she weren't dying, she was still too old for him, and thought a scandal like that would ruin his career, especially since he was just starting out.

Old Friends

Ed called to say that he would not be home for dinner, because he was meeting up with some friends in L.A. Chase Martin of The Band 4 was in town to record with his bandmates, Blake Thomas, Drew Bishop, and Quinn Howard. Chase was his best friend, and like a brother to him. They were very close, and because of his friendship with Chase, Ed had become great friends with his bandmates too. They were all like brothers to each other.

They met up for dinner, and when they were done, Blake, Drew, and Quinn left to be with their girlfriends, Abbey, Cara, and Jeanine. Chase was the only single guy in the group, and for some reason, had picked up on the vibe that Ed wanted to speak with him about something. He stayed with Ed, and they went to Chase's hotel to talk. Ed knew that they wouldn't be able to hear each other if they went to a club, so Chase was okay with going back to his hotel.

Ed told him about the movie, which Chase knew was going to be very successful. He explained how Lilli had captured the feelings of the main characters and how beautifully it was written. Then Ed told Chase all about Lilli, and about how drawn he felt to her. He then told Chase that he had written six songs for her movie, and Chase was blown away. He knew how long it sometimes took just to write one song, let alone six.

Chase could see Ed's face light up when he spoke about Lilli, and asked him directly, "Are you in love with her?"

Reality didn't hit Ed until that moment, when Chase had asked it out loud. Yes. He was in love with her.

Ed told Chase that Lilli was much older than him, and Chase countered, "No one can choose who they fall in love with."

Ed knew Chase would understand, but as he looked at his friend, his face turned serious all of a sudden, as if a cloud of darkness had just come up in his mind.

Chase instantly saw the change in him and asked, "What is it you're not telling me? Is she married?"

"No," Ed quickly replied. "She's not married."

"Then what is it? Her age?" Chase asked, trying to dig out the real issue. "Because she's really not that old."

Ed put his head down and tears started rolling down his face. He couldn't look at his best friend, and that's when Chase's expression grew concerned. He knew it had to be bad. He waited for Ed to share what was on his mind.

"I think she's very ill."

That was not what Chase was expecting to hear at all. "How ill is very ill?"

"I think she's dying!"

Chase was so taken aback by what Ed just revealed. His heart just ached for his brother. Tears welled up in his eyes, and he couldn't control them. He was just as sensitive as Ed, if not more.

"Are you sure? Did she tell you about it? Did you ask?" Chase asked, his voice shaking and filled with concern.

"No. I couldn't bring myself to talk to her about it, but I know it's the worst. I did some research on her on my way over here from London, and found an interview she did for a magazine about the movie. It briefly hinted at her being ill, but then I didn't find anything else regarding it. From the moment we met, I knew something was wrong. I just sensed it. There are little things ... like how she keeps me at a distance, like she knows we can't have a future together. I think the day I met her was when she got the news. I hugged her when I met her, and she just clung to me as if she needed me to save her. Then, that first night at her house, she went to bed and cried for the longest time. I just sat outside her door in case she needed me."

Chase was pale. He was distraught for Ed *and* Lilli, and he had not even met Lilli yet.

"Can I meet her? I would be so honored if you would introduce me to her."

Ed began to smile, hearing his best friend's wish. He was so happy that his brother wanted to meet Lilli, and he agreed.

"I'm going to the studio tomorrow with the songs and would love it if you could be there too. I'll clear it with Lilli. I can't wait for her to hear the completed songs, and I would like your opinion on them too." Chase nodded in compliance. Of course, he was going to be there.

Ed felt better talking to Chase about his concerns. Chase was only too happy to meet Ed at the studio. He was anxious to hear the songs and more than anxious to meet Lilli. He had never seen Ed look so excited about someone or about the music he had created.

4 I know

Lilli was home puttering around the house. She was finally alone after two straight weeks of having Ed in her home every day and night. She kind of missed him, and was starting to look forward to seeing him when she got home from work every day. Now that she didn't have to worry about supper and had some time to herself, she decided to pamper herself. Lilli was, for the most part, feeling pretty good. Although the bottom could fall out at any time, with Ed around, she rarely thought about her time being almost up, and she was so grateful for that—not wanting to dwell on it. She had to go on as if nothing was wrong.

Ed finally came home and yelled out for Lilli, but the blow-dryer was on and she didn't hear him. He walked to her bedroom and stopped dead in front of the bathroom door, which was open. That's when all the things he had suspected were confirmed. He turned white and felt weak in the knees, as though he were going to pass out. His heart just broke at the sight of her.

Lilli was standing in front of the mirror drying her hair when he saw her. There were big scars across both breasts, another huge line the entire length of her abdomen, and two more crossed on her back and under her arms, revealing the substantial number of procedures that had been done.

Ed quickly walked away, so she wouldn't see him, but she caught him out of the corner of her eye and was so shaken that all she could do was yell and cry.

"YOU SHOULD HAVE TOLD ME YOU WERE HOME!" Lilli screamed. "How could you invade my privacy like this?" she continued, yelling with pain, realizing that her secret was out. "I should have never let you in my house! GET OUT!"

Lilli was sobbing, but Ed wasn't insulted. He was just so shaken and didn't know what he could do or say to help her or apologize. But he knew he wasn't leaving.

He walked over to her and just grabbed her, pulling her into his arms. He had a tight grip on her and had no plans letting her go. She was struggling against him, trying to escape, but he wouldn't release her. Lilli was so tiny that his arms could have wrapped around her twice.

They both were now crying together. Without Ed even hearing what Lilli's illness was, he knew that it was bad. He picked her up and carried her to the bed, where he laid her down under her soft sheets. Then he got undressed and joined her. She was more distraught than before. All he wanted to do was hold her until she calmed down, so that they could speak about what was happening.

Once in bed, he wrapped her in his arms again, and this time she clung to him like it was going to be her last day on earth. She had a tight grip on him, like she couldn't let him go. Ed just held her, rubbing her back, and then stroking her hair, trying to calm her down. All the while, he kept thinking to himself, *I am so in love with her. I just have to tell her I don't care what's wrong with her!*

After a while she calmed down, and he took her face in his hand, forcing her to look at him. Her eyes lit up again with tears, and she was shocked because she saw that his eyes were watering too. They could not look away from each other.

Ed spoke first and chose his words carefully, trying not to push her, or force her to shut down on him.

"I know you are ill. I have known something was wrong from the first day we met. I hugged you and you just clung to me, as if to say, *'help me.'* I heard you crying that first night at your house, and just sat outside your bedroom door in case you needed me. You keep me at a distance ... I feel you pushing me away when I know you have feelings for me too."

Lilli was shocked hearing his revelations. "You know I have feelings for you?"

"Yes. The way you look at me and talk to me. How kind you are to me, letting me stay here and not asking me to leave. You cook for me and talk to me about your day. You bare your soul to me every day. Except for telling me what's wrong." Frustrated, he paused then, looking into her eyes for a long moment. "Please tell me! But whatever you say, do *not* tell me that we cannot be together because of our age difference."

Lilli started to speak when Ed interrupted her. "Wait. One more thing. I don't care how sick you are. All I know is that I am in love with you, and no reason on this earth can make me want to leave you... No reason, whatsoever!"

Lilli started crying, and Ed wondered if he'd pushed her too far. He pulled her in again until she managed to process what he'd just said. Once she calmed down again, she knew she had to tell him everything, and be real about it, or he wouldn't get what she meant. She couldn't give him everlasting hope.

Lilli looked him in the eye. "Here is why we cannot be together ... I'm dying. I don't know how long I have left. There are no treatments that could help me now. I have spoken to many hospitals and numerous doctors, but nothing can be done anymore." She took a deep breath and let it out slowly. "How can I do that to you or anyone? You saw my body. It's broken. I'm trying to stay in one piece, but there's no point anymore." She then paused to choose her words in a more compassionate way, "I do love you ... but you have to see how painful this would be for you. Just watching me die right in front of your eyes!" Lilli continued, as if trying to convince him. "Look at me, fading away to nothing! I can't do that to you. I can't allow it to happen this way."

Her heart was breaking, having to reveal all of that to Ed. And he waited, letting her calm down again before speaking.

His tone was more forceful this time. "Not you or anyone on this planet can tell me whom I can or can't fall in love with. I don't care if we have minutes, hours, days, or months left. I am not spending one more minute of that time arguing with you about why I can't love you, or why we can't be together. If you have a different reason, other than the ones we already spoke about, then let me hear it. I am not leaving you. Ever! Get used to me being around. Get used to me taking care of you. Get used to me loving you, even if it's just for a few days."

Ed tried to control his feelings, but it was very hard to contain all that had built up inside. "Think about this! Think about what you would be missing ... not experiencing this love before you die. Not being with the love of your life before you die ... because that is what I am, and will be for you.

I will be the love of your life. I will give you love, and I expect to be loved in return. Can you do that? Can you love me in return?"

Lilli just stared at Ed. She was stunned at what she was hearing. He surely did not comprehend what was happening to her, how much work it would be taking care of her towards the end, or how much emotional strain there would be for both of them. She tried to tell him and hoped that he would understand her better, but he was having none of it.

"Ed, I don't think you understand what will happen to me as my condition worsens. You want to take care of me, but do you realize you might be changing my diapers by the time the end is near for me. Do you understand all that? Do you understand what will happen to me? Can you actually look at me and say you'll be able to handle it? Can you watch me die?" She stopped, her voice fading away.

Ed was distraught, but undaunted. "Not only can I watch you die, but you will die in my arms and nowhere else. I will make that promise to you. I will never leave you!"

Lilli was speechless. Her jaw just dropped, as she tried to process everything. Had she just heard him right, or was she just dreaming?

She couldn't counter him with anything logical, aside from the arguments she had already mentioned, and she felt herself start to give in. Maybe it wasn't so bad to believe that Ed really did love her, and he wanted to be with her right up to the end. He wanted her to die in his arms! That statement alone was unarguable. She looked into his beautiful blue eyes, which were still filled with tears.

She hardly dared to believe. "Do you love me that much?"

Ed smiled. "You have no idea!"

Lilli wrapped her arms around Ed and held him this time, as he rested his head on her shoulder. She caved. She was going to let him love her, and she was going to love him back with everything she had. That is how special his words were to her. He was a fighter, and so was she.

Maybe she would live longer, if she were happier than before. Maybe he could help her be in a better state of mind. Maybe he could give her the peace she was looking for, allowing her to accept her terrible lot in life. All she could do was nod her head in agreement. She was going to accept his love, and with that, Ed kissed her very tenderly. Emotions spiraled for Lilli, and she didn't know how she was going to control herself.

He surprised her again by tenderly touching every scar on her body, and then kissing each one, as she lay there, tearing up. Then he came back up to kiss her lips, which were now wet from crying. She responded to his kisses with passion. They both could feel the love they were going to share from then on.

Ed hesitated then, not knowing how much further she was willing to go with him. He wasn't sure if she was ready, but Lilli instantly understood the hesitation. She just pulled him down, and that's when he knew that there would be nothing stopping them for the rest of the night, or the rest of her life.

Lilli was never going to forget that first night with Ed. The tenderness when he touched her body, the passion when his lips touched hers, and the love they felt when their bodies finally connected. She felt lucky and blessed after such a long time. Lucky to have Ed love her like he did, and blessed to have experienced real love before she died. She was happy and grateful.

At the Studio

Ed and Lilli didn't get much sleep that night, but they were up early and ready to start their day. As they were heading to the studio to listen to the songs Ed had written for the movie, he asked Lilli if it would be okay to have his best friend, Chase Martin, of The Band 4, join them there. She was absolutely okay with it. Ed told her that Chase was really like a brother to him, and after hearing that, she definitely wanted to meet him.

Ed then told her that he had spoken to Chase at length about her, and that it was Chase who'd made him realize how much he loved her. He also told her that he had discussed her illness with him. Lilli didn't want to show a reaction to the fact that Ed had discussed her private business with Chase, but it really bothered her. Particularly because he would not have even fully known, had she not told him about it. Ed saw the concerned look on her face, and reassured her that Chase would not tell a soul, and wouldn't look at or treat her any differently.

"Chase is my brother, and last night I needed to speak to him about everything. He's actually the one who noticed the distressed look on my face when I was telling him about you," Ed said trying to reassure her.

That made Lilli feel a little better, but she told Ed, "Please don't tell anyone else about my illness. I want to go about my life as normally as I can, for as long as I have. Can you understand that?"

Ed said that he would respect her wishes, until she was ready for others to know. "I do understand. Chase is my support system, and has been there for me whenever I've needed him. And I'm your support system. If this is going to get as bad as we both think it will, then I'll probably need his support." Ed looked into her eyes, seeking her understanding. Lilli did understand and nodded with a faint smile.

As they got into the studio, Chase was already there and looked very happy to see Ed and Lilli walking in together. Ed had the biggest smile on his face and Lilli looked happy too, walking along by his side. She was tiny and very beautiful. She was so tiny, in fact, that it was hard to see that she was older than him.

"This is my girlfriend, Lilli Parker," Ed said to Chase, with the biggest grin on his face. Once Chase heard that, he instantly realized that whatever had been holding them back had been resolved.

Lilli smiled widely as she heard Ed introduce her as his girlfriend. She felt very happy at that moment. She extended her hand out to shake Chase's, but he just grabbed it and pulled her into the biggest hug ever. Ed was beaming, and his face was flushed so red that he couldn't hide it.

"I heard all about you last night," Chase said. "Ed couldn't stop talking about you. I am so happy for you both."

Lilli was kind of star-struck. She'd felt that way when she first met Ed, and now she was meeting Chase Martin of The Band 4—the biggest band on the planet. It was a big deal. She couldn't help but just gawk at both of them.

The record producer, Robert Patrick, came out immediately when he heard that Chase was in the studio along with Ed. They were expecting Ed, but having Chase there was like icing on the cake. He just looked at Lilli, as if to say *How did you do this?* She just smiled knowingly back at him, even though she had nothing to do with it.

All of them got right down to business. Ed, Lilli, and Chase went into the recording room, where Ed started going over the songs he had written. He linked which part of the movie felt best suited to each song. Lilli and her producer Robert were blown away. Ed had everything mapped out.

They immediately called John Peters, who was writing the score for the movie, so that he could hear the songs too, and he was also blown away too. He asked Ed if he could use some of his music during the score, to keep the film all tied together and Ed was pleased with the idea. He didn't really know how soundtracks were created, so it was all new to him and Chase, who was smiling and very happy for his brother.

Lilli was also happy with what was happening. She actually couldn't believe it was going so smoothly. More importantly, she couldn't believe how beautiful Ed's songs were. They captured everything she had hoped for in the movie. She knew that Ed's songs would put the movie over the top. She had to contain the tears that wanted to spill from her eyes as she watched him. She loved him and her heart was overflowing with happiness.

The producer looked at Ed. "Let's begin recording these, as you're going over them."

Ed agreed and so they started. Not only were they going to record them but they were videotaping it too, for a behind-the-scenes special. Everyone was excited.

A problem occurred when Chase realized that his help was also needed. He got worried when they started to tape it, because he had never done anything without his bandmates. He wanted to leave the recording room, but Ed pleaded, "Ask your brothers if they would mind you being here with me. Then you can stay and help me out. I'm a little nervous about this, and would feel better if you stayed."

Chase could see how much Ed wanted him there. He excused himself and went out into the hall to call Blake, Drew, and Quinn. He told them what was happening, and they were thrilled for Ed. None of them had an issue with him being there, or Chase being recorded. Blake said that he would call their manager, Peter, and tell him what was going on.

Chase felt much better after that and went back to be with Ed. He thought Ed had everything so well thought out that there really wasn't much for him to contribute. He had everything covered. The songs were perfect. Chase ended up working out some harmonies for some of the songs, and suggested to Ed that he just record his own voice for the different parts. Ed and Robert thought it was a great idea and worked that out.

It was time for Chase to leave. He had to meet up with his band at a recording studio across town. Ed gave Chase a big hug of gratitude. Before they separated, Ed whispered a confirmation of Lilli's condition to Chase. Chase felt really bad hearing it, and felt hopeless, not being able to do anything about it.

"Don't be sad for me," Ed said. "We love each other, and that's something good that came out of this whole situation. I'll call you later, and we'll talk all about it. I have so much to tell you. Can you stay in L.A. or do you have to go back to London?"

Chase said that he would stay, and they would speak about what was happening. "I won't leave until you need me to." With that, they hugged again.

Then Chase went to say goodbye to Lilli. He told her that he was staying in L.A. to be with them both, and she was blown away by the kindness and genuine love he had for the both of them. Lilli blinked away tears, as it touched her heart.

Chase noticed Lilli getting emotional, so he just held her and said, "It's okay. I'll be here for the both of you. Ed is my brother, and now you're my sister. I won't leave either of you."

Lilli could not believe what she was hearing. The kindness in his voice, and in his embrace, was very endearing. She was overwhelmed.

My Wife – My Life

Six months passed and the film was completed. The score was ready and the soundtrack had come along perfectly. Lilli thought that everything had turned out flawlessly. She was over the moon and very pleased with the outcome.

Her relationship with Ed was something that she could never have imagined having. He loved her with all of his heart and kept his promise to never leave her side. She felt really good too. She credited her continued health to being in love and being happy. Lilli rarely thought about her illness and wanted to keep it that way. She felt that as long as she had Ed, she could survive anything.

Ed was happy as well. He took her back with him to London a few times, when he had to get back to business there, and she loved his townhouse. He even let her decorate it enough to make her feel welcomed. Lilli wanted to make it hers too, and she wanted him to have a few reminders of her … once he was without her. She was careful not to do too much though, for fear it would be too hard on him when the time came.

They were rarely without each other, but Lilli wanted to keep their romance hidden. She believed that people would talk, because she was older than Ed. Ed kept saying that he didn't care and wanted the world to know that he loved her. The matter really distressed her though, so they kept it a secret, telling all the paparazzi and gossip columns that they were only best of friends. They were caught being photographed everywhere, but they never held hands or arrived in the same car.

When the premier of the movie came out, they both attended separately. Then they met up inside the building. It was a smash hit. The CD that contained the six songs Ed had written for the movie hit record sales. Five of the six hits made it to number one, and the sixth song made it to the top ten. Everyone was so pleased and excited about what was happening. The movie was number one at the box office for six weeks in a row, racking up tons of money for all of the stars in the movie and everyone associated with it, including Lilli. There was even Oscar buzz for the actors and the music, including the score by John Peters. It couldn't have turned out better. Lilli had known all along that the movie was special, and she was happy to be able to see it.

Ed wanted Lilli to marry him. He wanted her to be his wife, but she could not say yes. She felt that she could not do that to him. She didn't want him hanging onto their life together when she died. She told him, time after time, "You have to move on and live your life to the fullest when I'm gone. Promise me you will. Say it out loud, so I know you mean it!"

Ed said the words, so she wouldn't get upset. But in all honesty ... he didn't know if he could ever find another love like hers, and didn't know if he ever wanted to. He didn't know how he could ever top what he had with Lilli.

"Do not grieve over me," she said one evening, as they lay in each other's arms. "Remember how happy we were. Please ... don't grieve over me. Promise me."

Subsequently, Ed reassured her multiple times, and promised her whenever she spoke about his future without her.

Then right after Christmas, she fell ill, and they both began to worry. He took her to the hospital and they ran some tests, saying that it was time. There was nothing they could do for her except keep her out of pain and try to make her comfortable. As Lilli lay in the hospital bed, with Ed at her side, she knew her time was up.

"Ed, please take me home to Pennsylvania," she told him after the doctor left them alone. "I don't want to die in the hospital."

Ed agreed and made arrangements to take her home. He hired a nurse to help care for her, but he still stayed by her side.

He called Chase to tell him what had happened, and he flew right to Pennsylvania as soon as he could. He stayed with Ed, in Lilli's house, to be with them both. Chase sat at her bedside and held her hand whenever Ed had to leave to take care of something. Ed was never gone long though and would come back quickly to be by her side.

Right before they knew the end was near, Ed said to her lovingly, "Will you do something for me?"

Lilli nodded her head weakly, "Yes."

"Will you marry me? Right now. Today?" He drew in his breath and held it, waiting for an answer, as tears streamed down his face.

When Lilli looked at Chase, she saw that he was crying, and through her own tears, she finally said, "Yes."

Ed already had the magistrate there and did not wish to lose a moment without her. He wanted to make her his wife. Lilli's agreement, however, came with a condition and she told him so.

"Anything," Ed said eagerly. "What's the condition?"

With tears in her eyes, she said, "You still can't tell anyone. No one can know but the people in this room. Don't do that to yourself. Please."

Ed lowered his head. "Yes. I accept your condition. I won't tell anyone."

She looked at Chase, and he nodded his head in agreement as well. Ed pulled out a ring and after a short while they were married.

7
A Future Plan

Ed and Lilli talked most of the night. Lilli felt that, with the love they shared, it just couldn't be the end for them. Ed was confused when he heard her say that. He didn't understand what she meant and didn't wish to pursue it. He thought that maybe the strong medications were taking effect.

"Do you believe in an afterlife?" she asked him, quietly. "Do you think we've all been here before in a different time? Do you think we could come back in the future as someone else?" Ed had no answer for her, but tuned in to her deeply and listened to what she had to say.

"When I die, I'm going to wait for you," she said. "I will see you again. I promise you! I don't think that God means to end this much love ... like we have for one another. I think we'll come back in the future as different people, and I'll wait for you. I won't be born again until you're ready ... no matter how long my soul has to wait in heaven. I'll wait for you, and we will both be born again at the same time."

Ed pondered what she had just told him for a long moment. But she wasn't done.

"We will have to figure out how to find each other," she said. "We won't be the same two people." Ed just looked at her amazed. She was actually plotting how they could be together again ... in a different time!

As it turns out, Ed *did* believe that he had been on earth before. He did believe in an afterlife and that he could come back again in the future. He was shocked that Lilli held the same belief. He kissed her hand and just adored her even more. Then he said, "How do you think we will be able to find each other?"

Lilli thought about it. "We should have a catch word. If we were indeed meant to be together, then when that word is said between the two of us ... it should act as a trigger. Maybe it will cause us, or the two people in question, to feel something—something that draws them in and makes them want to find out what's happening."

Ed smiled. "Your brain never shuts down with ideas, does it? I don't know how you come up with this stuff." The thought of it all just made them both laugh.

Lilli was still thinking. "Ed, I know this will work. I know we will be together again. Somehow! We just need a catchword to act as the trigger—triggering the memories of each other, so we'll know that it's us trying to reach one another."

Ed knew she was serious, and at this stage of the game, he knew he would do anything to be with her again. "What word do you want to use?"

She thought about it. "Prerogative! That will be our catchword."

The conversation actually made Ed feel better about the situation. He wondered if she was just saying all of that to get him to deal with her death better, but he went along with her and agreed that it would be their catchword.

"I'm not crazy, Ed. My body is giving out on me ... not my brain. I know I will see you again. I'm certain of it. I'll wait until the end of time to see you again. I will find you. I promise you. You kept all of your promises to me, and I believed you ... now it's your turn to believe me. Believe me, Ed. Believe my promise of seeing you again. We *will* be together again! I know it in here." She pointed to his heart and then hers.

Tears welled up in both of their eyes and Ed nodded in agreement. Somehow, he did believe her. He felt hope that they would be together again someday ... well into the future. He knew the catchword ... and only hoped someone would find their souls.

8
She's Gone

The next morning when Chase went to check in on Ed, he found him crying. Lilli had passed away. She died in his arms, just like he had promised her. In fact, Ed had kept all of the promises he had made to her. He was the love of her life, and she was the love of his. She died knowing that her project was a hit, and she had received all she could from Ed loving her.

There was some hope though, in the plan they had made to meet again someday and use the trigger word to wake up their former souls, so that they could be together again. Ed thought that, if he ever mentioned that to anyone, they would think that he had gone crazy. He hadn't though. He shared those plans with Chase, his brother, and no one else. And he told him about all the other plans they had made as well. They had spent hours, some of her last on earth, strategizing about how it all might work, and what they could do to help the process along. It was the epitome of wishful thinking, but it seemed to help her—easing her fears ... for him and for herself. She seemed to find some peace in it, and so did he as well. If his wife believed they would find their way back together, then somehow, they surely would.

The funeral was private, which is what she wanted. They wanted to have a memorial service for her, but she had left strict instructions that she did not want it. The press was hanging around her house, hoping to see what was going on and who was there. They did see Ed and Chase there, but with Chase being there, it really threw them off. They continued to release statements saying that her best friend, Ed Mehan, was at her side when she died, and he just let it go at that. They didn't understand why Chase was there too though. There was some speculation that maybe Chase and Lilli were dating, but that story died out quickly when no one could confirm it.

A month later, Ed won an Oscar for one of his songs, which had been nominated for Lilli's movie. During his acceptance speech, he was really shaken. He thanked the producers, his label, and Lilli, for showing him what love truly was and for allowing him to write the most amazing love songs for the most amazing movie ever made. He couldn't get any more words out, as his heart was breaking all over again.

Life went on for Ed. He won six Grammys all together in his career, and continued to write the most amazing love songs. Chase always suspected that he was still writing about Lilli. He could see Lilli in every song that Ed ever wrote.

Ed dedicated his life to his friends, especially Chase, who got married unexpectedly, less than a year after Lilli died. Chase asked Ed if he would sing at his wedding, and Ed willingly agreed. He was so happy for Chase, who had been struggling with some demons before meeting Marguerite, his wife. At that time, Chase didn't know if he wanted to be in the band anymore, and was totally distressed. He had spoken to Ed at length about it, but in the end, they both knew that the decision had to be Chase's. He was the only one who could make it. When Chase met his Marguerite, though, everything changed.

Chase always told Ed that his life got easier once he met "Mam", which was what he called her. It represented her initials: M.A.M. Marguerite Angeli-Martin. Ed was so close to Chase that he often referred to her as Mam as well, which never bothered either of them.

They made Ed part of their lives and included him in everything they did. Ed became godfather to their four sons, and they even named one after him, Zac Quinn Edward Martin. Ed was the one who took Marguerite to the hospital when she went into labor with their first set of twins, Zac and Zeke, because Chase was in the States at the time. Ed sat with her and held her hand until Chase got there. He couldn't help remembering when Chase did the same for him, years before, when his wife, Lilli was dying. Chase and Marguerite were truly like a brother and sister to him.

Ed now had four nephews and a niece, all of whom he had been there for from the moment of their arrivals. They all loved him unconditionally. The children treated him like he was the most special person on the planet. Ed never understood why they always clung to him so much. He was thrilled though, as it made him feel so special.

Dreaming

Forty-one years after Ed *lost the love of his* life, on a foggy London night in January, Marguerite had a dream—a dream that Chase felt her having, without knowing what it was about.

Marguerite and Chase had always had an unusual connection to each other and had discovered that their five children had that same connection, to each other *and* their parents. They all felt each other's feelings, and knew when someone was upset or happy about something.

Ed always said that it was "spooky!"

No one understood how it could be possible, but it was real. The feelings were real. Quinn had always told them that it was a gift from God—to all of them.

When their boys married, amazingly enough, they all found spouses with those same capabilities. The wives always felt what their husbands were feeling and vice versa.

Their daughter Sarah's husband, Josh, was the only one who didn't share that connection. Sarah had explained everything to him, because she would always "feel" her brothers, and she had to let Josh know what was going on so he wouldn't be worried when she was sometimes upset. Although he knew about it, it was something they never discussed in front of him, so as not to make him feel left out.

The connection never ceased blowing Chase and Marguerite away. They never talked about it to outsiders though. They felt that people might judge them or think they were delusional.

On that January morning, Marguerite woke up crying and could not stop. Her children were all married and had their own houses, so Chase was the only one home at the time. He felt her distress and woke right up with her. He grabbed her and held onto her until she could compose herself. Through her tears, she kept saying Ed's name, over and over. Chase was thrown by this. Ed was like a brother to Marguerite as well, and he thought that something bad might have happened to him.

He waited to let her calm down, then asked her, "What happened? Can you tell me about it?"

She was feeling something, but couldn't describe it to Chase. All she could say was that Ed was in her dream, but she couldn't remember much about it. Ed had appeared to be very distraught though.

Chase did not realize it at first, but it was January, and that was when Lilli had passed away all those years ago. As it occurred to him, he realized who he had to call.

Since Marguerite had been so close to Ed, Chase felt that it was the right time to tell her about Ed and his wife, Lilli.

No one knew about Lilli and Ed. Not even Marguerite. But he felt he needed to tell her about what had happened to them and how they felt they would meet again. He had never kept anything from her, but this story was not his to tell. It was Ed's story, which is why he'd never told her about them. He had spoken to Ed before he married Marguerite, and Ed asked him not to say anything at that time. Chase respected his wishes. They were also the wishes of Lilli, and Chase made that promise to her also.

While he tried to figure out what he should do, the boys and Sarah began calling, almost simultaneously, to say that they were all coming home. It was January, and they had all just been home for the holidays. This took Chase and Marguerite by surprise, and they were thrilled that they would all be coming home again so soon.

Marguerite and Chase went to the grocers where she always shopped, around the corner from their house. It had been taken over by Franco and Anna's son, Joseph, a few years back, when his parents had passed away within a month of each other. Marguerite had been very upset, because they had been like an extended family to her, ever since she first came to London and married Chase. They had been so kind to her and Chase, and they were both upset when they passed away.

They were excited to tell Joseph that their children were all coming home again for a few days, and he could see on their faces how happy they were. They picked up ingredients to make their favorite dishes. Marguerite was thrilled to be able to fuss over them again. With all of them gone, the house felt very empty. Chase's band-mate brothers and sisters, Blake and Abbey, Drew and Cara, and Quinn and Jeanine, all visited often, along with Ed ... but she missed her sons and daughter.

Chase missed his granddaughters as well, all four of them. They loved it when he sang to them and told them stories about their fathers. Sarah did not have any children yet. She and Josh told everyone that they were still trying to decide if they wanted to be parents or not. Marguerite and Chase had their own opinion about it, but knew the decision was theirs and theirs alone.

Chase's phone call to Ed was put on the back burner, because everyone was coming home. The topic stayed on his mind though, and he just couldn't shake worrying about Marguerite's dream and what it meant. Remembering the promise that Lilli made to Ed, Chase thought that maybe the dream meant the worst, and that he wouldn't be with them much longer.

Marguerite was four years older than Chase, and he and Ed were already 64. No one would believe it of course. They still looked quite young, and it was still too young for anything to be wrong with Ed.

10
The Arrival

Marguerite's eldest sons, Zac and Zeke, arrived first, surprising their mother and father. They arrived without their wives, Anna and Ari, or their daughters, Margaret and Mary. Not only did this confuse Chase and Marguerite but it also peaked their curiosity. The boys were not having any marital issues, so they couldn't imagine what was up with them. When asked, all they said was that they needed to see their parents and wanted to wait for the rest of the family to come home.

When they first came in the door, Zac embraced his mother, not wanting to let her go. She found that very odd and they all felt it. Then Zeke did the same thing, making her worry even more. Both boys remained silent. Next they pulled their father into a long embrace. This behavior concerned both parents, and they couldn't tell what was going on.

Sarah was next to arrive, behaving the same way as her brothers did. She'd also come without her spouse. Chase started to really worry that something was going on. He couldn't feel his sons or Sarah at that time, and didn't know what to think about it.

Last to arrive were the middle twins, Mark and Matt, without their spouses, Catherine and Cali, or their daughters, Jess and Amelia. Chase and Marguerite were really worried by then. They didn't know what to make of it, but didn't question it. They figured that, when they were all ready to speak about it, they would.

For the time being, they just enjoyed all their children being home. Marguerite cooked up a storm and fussed over them as much as any mother would, and Chase was grateful to have his family together again. All the aunts and uncles came over the first night, to see everyone, and the homecoming was a great success. Everyone was catching up with each other and it brought a warm feeling to the whole family. Being together, and sharing their love with each one of them, was great.

The old stories were never-ending, from when the Zs first went off to school to Sarah's first date, the memory of which really made everyone laugh. It had been like the end of the world when she'd come home from school and told her father that she had a date. All the boys and uncles remembered that day as if it were yesterday. They remembered Chase stuttering when she told him about it, and how he was walking in circles in the kitchen not knowing how to take it.

The laughter and storytelling went on all night.

Chase called Ed to tell him everyone had come home. Ed was in L.A. at the time, and said that he would come back to London to see them all before they left. He never missed seeing them when they came back home to their mom and dad's in London.

It was late when everyone went to bed. Marguerite stayed up to clean up the kitchen and to have breakfast ready for the next day. Her mind was swimming with emotions. Chase felt that she was troubled and a little distressed. He helped her in the kitchen and then insisted that she come to bed with him, all but dragging her upstairs.

Then he locked the door, which made her laugh. They always locked the door when the kids were little, or back home, if they were going to have sex. He would then unlock the door when they were decent again, in case the boys or Sarah needed them during the night.

"Mam, please tell me what is going on. I feel your distress. I know it's driving you mad right now." Chase opened his arms up to her, and she gladly walked right into his embrace. They had been married for forty-one years and it had been the best forty-one years of their entire lives. They loved each other more than anything.

"I don't know what's going on. I feel something but can't tell what it is. I think the boys and Sarah are feeling just as bad, and I can't make out what they're so upset about. I just know they're upset. Do you feel it too?"

"Yes, now I feel it too. I know the children are upset, and I can't figure out why. We'll have to wait for them to tell us. If they don't discuss it with us tomorrow, we'll have to approach them though. This can't go on. We both know that they're feeling *our* distress too. Tomorrow we'll find out, one way or another."

That calmed her down a little. "Chase, please hold me. I need to feel you next to me."

"You never have to ask me to hold you. I never have and never will let you out of my sight, or out of my arms. I love you. You are the very air I breathe."

Mam smiled and held her husband even tighter. "And you are mine."

Chase opened the door back up, and there they were—sitting on the floor outside their bedroom door, just like they always did when they were little, waiting for their father to open it. They all laughed together, as they ran and jumped onto their bed.

The first thing Matt asked was, "Is Uncle Ed coming over?"

Marguerite and Chase turned pale. They had to know. *Did they dream about Ed?*

11
The Dream

Chase looked at his wife and then glanced around to see his children. He felt the warmth of seeing all of them there on the bed, and said, "Look what we did." It was calming to all of them. They all reached out and held each other's hands like a chain, needing to feel that connection.

Marguerite felt that it was the right time to ask, "When do you want to tell us what's going on?"

They all looked at her, and then Zac said, "We don't know how to start or what to say. We all talked it over and can't make sense of it. We're all confused."

"Well start anywhere," Chase said, "and we can see if we can piece together what's bothering all of you!"

Mark nodded and began. "We had a dream about Uncle Ed. All of us saw the same thing. He was sitting with someone—a woman. He was holding her hand and crying. More than crying, he was completely distraught over her. That's all we saw."

Chase turned so white he thought that he was going to pass out. Then tears started falling down his face and everyone, including Marguerite, just looked at him. He got up immediately and left the room. He couldn't breathe, gasping for air. Marguerite followed him and told the boys and Sarah to stay put, as they all gawked at their father, not knowing why he was so shaken. Chase was in the hall and couldn't look at her. Marguerite was incredibly upset, feeling how much he was hurting but not knowing why.

She did what he would always do for her. She held out her arms and engulfed him in them, until he composed himself ... but he *couldn't* compose himself. Everything that had happened to Ed all of those years ago came flooding back into his thoughts. He let his wife hold him, but his body felt weak and useless.

After he managed to pull himself back together at least a little bit, they went back to their room.

"We need Uncle Ed," Chase said. "He needs to hear this." They were all visibly shaken at this. Luckily, they were expecting Ed the next afternoon. Chase continued. "Ed will explain who she is and why he's so distraught. He's the only one who can. I don't know if he'll share that story or not, but if he refuses, we can't make him. That's all I can say. I made a promise to him back when we were just 23. I can't break it. It's Uncle Ed's story to tell. I am begging you to respect whatever decision he makes. Do you all understand?"

The five of them continued staring at their father. Something bad had happened, and they never knew about it. Uncle Ed was distraught over someone, but they didn't know who or why, although they had just figured out the when: forty-one years ago.

They'd always wondered why Uncle Ed had never gotten married. He had been linked to so many celebrities, but he never brought any of them around.

Marguerite looked at the confusion on her children's faces, "Is there more? Can it wait?"

Realizing the condition their father was in, they decided to wait for tomorrow. They all went over to him, hugging and kissing him. The last time they'd seen him this shaken was when their mother was in the hospital in Italy, fighting for her life after brain surgery. The boys had told Sarah about that when she was about 16 years old. She had seen the scar on her mother's head and her left-hand trembling. Marguerite just brushed it off, not wanting to worry her, but the boys thought she should know, so they told her. It was in Italy, after the surgery, that the boys had first told their parents that they could "feel" them.

Marguerite looked at Chase, but he couldn't look at her. He never in a million years thought the story would come out about Ed and his wife, Lilli. But he still couldn't tell her about it. He had promised, and felt Ed had to be the one to tell her.

She looked at her husband. "I understand what you're going through. I feel your distress. You're hurting for many reasons, but the one that's standing out is that you can't share this with me. I'm telling you, I understand. You're not betraying me in any way! Look at me!" She placed her hands on his face, and turned him towards her. "I understand, and it's all right." Chase looked down, upset again.

"Look at me! It's going to be okay! I love you, Chase." She could tell she wasn't reaching him. "I love you. We can wait for Ed tomorrow. If he doesn't want to talk about it, he doesn't have to. It's okay. I love you Chase! I love you." Tears were falling from her eyes.

He just nodded his head, letting her know that he heard her. With that, she motioned to her kids, who slowly drifted from the room. She led Chase to the bed where she held him tightly, stroking his face and hair, as she always had, trying to get him to calm down. After a while Chase started to relax. She kept him there all night, and did not let go.

Waiting

Everyone just had to wait now for Ed to come home. He was in L.A., and had finally called Chase to let them all know when he would be in.

"Can you please hurry?" Chase asked him. "Everyone is here waiting for you. It's very important. Even urgent."

Ed then got concerned. He thought someone was ill, and they were waiting to tell him. He knew all of his nephews were home, along with his niece, Sarah, whom he adored just as much as the boys, if not just a little bit more. It was no secret that she was the apple of his eye. From the very first time he'd held her as a baby, she had captivated him. He didn't know if his affections were due to her joining the family after four boys, or if it was because Marguerite and Chase finally had a daughter, after they'd lost their firstborn, Margaret, all of those years before. In any case, he glowed around all five of them.

The anxiety of waiting for Uncle Ed, with the seven of them in the house, was too much to handle. Not only were they feeling it themselves but those same emotions were bouncing off of each other through the bond they all shared. It was too much for Chase and Marguerite to cope with. They felt like jumping out of theirs skins. It was dramatic and traumatic.

We have to get out of here or we won't survive the day, Chase thought, as he smiled grimly to himself. He then told all of his children to get ready, and that they were going out for lunch. This would get everyone out of the house and get them thinking about something else.

Marguerite called their favorite restaurant down the street to tell Rocco Jr. (Rocco Sr. had passed away) that they were coming. He was always just as thrilled as his father had been when they all came into their restaurant to eat. He got the private room ready for them, and as usual, they arrived through the kitchen, where he was waiting for them. Rocco Jr. knew them all, because of all the years they'd been eating there. He was always happy to catch up with the family, and enjoyed seeing the joy in Mr. and Mrs. Martin's faces whenever they came in with their children.

Chase dragged out the lunch for two hours, before Marguerite finally said, "It's time to go, or we'll be here for dinner too." Chase chuckled and agreed it was time for them to leave.

They stopped at the grocery store to see Joseph, who also loved seeing them all when they came home. They spoke about Franco and Anna fondly. Joseph was so touched that they mentioned his parents. Matt told him that his favorite part of visiting had been when Anna would give them a present as they left the store. It was normally ice cream or candy, depending what time of year it was. As they were almost out of the door, Joseph's little son, Frank, ran after them and handed them all a candy bar, giggling. It made them all laugh, and they left yelling *"Grazie!"* to Joseph and Frank.

The family had really needed that quality time together. They all felt much more relaxed. Chase and Marguerite had also calmed down. As they stood in the kitchen, Chase took his wife's hand and brought it to his face, kissing her palm while smiling at her from ear to ear. All the children saw him do that, and admired the love their father felt for their mother. They also remembered how lucky they were to be raised by such loving parents. Occasionally, they would forget just how lucky they were.

In that moment, they got together and decided that they would have to come home to visit more often. They had to see their parents more, and be reminded of the good life they all shared with them. Marguerite and Chase saw them huddling together talking about it, arms around each other and smiling.

They were both so proud of their children.

13
Ed Is Back

Ed's plane was on the ground. He was anxious to learn why everyone was waiting for him. His blood pressure was through the roof and his face was all red. He felt like it was on fire. He couldn't wait to get to Chase, to see what was going on. He was hoping it wouldn't be too bad.

He texted Chase that he was on his way, and that's when everyone started to stress out again. Chase told the boys and Sarah that he thought he should warn Ed first about what they wanted to tell him, and they all agreed, so that he wouldn't be blindsided.

As he pulled into the driveway and parked, Chase met him at his car while everyone watched. Ed panicked immediately as Chase's head was down, almost as though he didn't want to look at him. Chase's eyes were filled with tears, and Ed spoke first, with a voice that shook. "Is everything all right. Is it Mam? Is she all right?"

"Everyone is fine, but the boys and Sarah needed to see you," Chase said, trying to sound calm.

Tired from traveling and being alone with his thoughts, trying to get back to London and his family, Ed was confused.

Chase explained. "Sarah and the boys all had the same dream three nights ago. It shook them so much that they all had to come home. They need to see you so badly." Ed's worried expression made Chase realize that he was stalling. "In the dream ... they saw you holding Lilli's hand, and you were crying."

Ed's eyes widened and then he turned pale. He started backing away from Chase, towards his car.

Chase just looked at him. "Please don't go! They're in dire straits and need to speak to you!" He was now pleading with Ed, who stopped because he suddenly felt his legs go weak. He wanted to run away, but his legs weren't accommodating him.

"I didn't tell them who she was," Chase said, "or what they were seeing or anything else. I didn't break my promise to you or your wife!" He was now pleading with him more than ever. "Even Mam doesn't know! I told them this is your story to tell, not mine. If you can't tell it … I begged them to try and understand and respect your wishes." The tears were streaming down Chase's face, bringing all of Ed's heartbreak back to life again.

Ed got nervous and started pacing back and forth in front of his car. He turned finally, as if to leave, when Sarah came running out, unable to control herself. "Uncle Ed! Please don't leave us! We need to see you. Please don't leave us."

Seeing her so distraught, Ed walked toward his niece. He opened his arms and she jumped into them, never wanting to let go.

Sarah looked at him and pleaded with him again, while all of the boys and Marguerite stood at the door to the house waiting for him. The boys were very emotional, and Marguerite was beside herself. They realized then that what they had dreamed about was the worst thing that ever happened to Ed, which is why they knew he couldn't speak about it … and they would try and understand.

They still wanted to tell him what they had seen and felt though. They didn't think they would be able to get over that dream unless they spoke about it with him.

14
The Truth Comes Out

Ed handed Sarah over to Chase, who wrapped his arms around his daughter, almost carrying her into the house while he searched for Marguerite. She was standing with her sons, and as his eyes locked on hers, he was not able to look away. As soon as Ed got closer to Marguerite, she just opened her arms for him, and he went to her.

"I don't know what is going on," she said, "but I truly believe we have to tell you something. My children will never get over this if they don't speak to you. Please help them! Please, Ed! I love you. I'll help you, if you just tell me how! Just hear them out. You don't have to say anything, but the one thing I do know is that they need to tell you something. Something they won't even tell me! They will never get over the turmoil they're in right now, if they can't talk to you."

Ed collapsed into Marguerite's arms, and she slowly ushered him into the house, to the big table in the kitchen, where they always sat and usually talked things out.

That table was where they discussed Sarah, when they'd first found out that she could feel her brothers and their emotions. This was where the boys admitted that they could feel her from the first day they'd met her—the day when someone, who was desperate to give her child a good home with a loving family, had left her at the Martins' front door, for them to adopt. She had known she was dying and wanted to give her daughter a family to love. Chase and Marguerite had promised Sarah's birth-mother just that, when she signed Sarah over to the Martins, right before she passed away.

With everyone sitting, and all eyes looking down at the table, someone had to start. Marguerite took over and spoke first. She was holding Ed's hand and wasn't letting go. "I woke up crying the other night. Chase felt me being upset and woke up as well. I couldn't tell him why I was crying, but I know that I was upset, seeing you in pain."

Chase nodded. "Mam just kept saying your name, over and over. 'Ed... Ed...' I asked her, 'What about Ed? Is he okay? Are you feeling something about him?'"

Marguerite looked at Ed and continued. "I only know that I felt you were upset about something, but I didn't know what it was. I was so shaken, and so was Chase, because he thought that I was maybe feeling you somehow. I still can't explain it."

Zac spoke next, "Uncle Ed, I first want to say that I think you know how much we all love you." He then looked at his sister and three other brothers, who were all nodding in agreement. Sarah then got upset again. She just couldn't control her emotions.

It was paining Ed to see how distressed they all were over him. It was then that he decided he might have to tell them about Lilli, his wife, and where he had been all week.

Zac continued. "We all had the same dream and called each other in the middle of the night to talk about it through the webcam. When we realized that we all had the same dream, it got worse. I called Dad to tell him that we were all coming home. We had to see them and we had to see you! They tried to pry it out of us, but honestly, we didn't know how to even begin telling them what happened. My father looked like he was going to have a heart attack when we started talking about it, so we had to stop."

Ed knew then, what a brother Chase had truly been to him. He always knew how loyal Chase was, but just then he felt so much for him. He got up immediately and went over to hug him. When they calmed down again, they both sat back down.

Zeke asked, "Can we please tell you before we go mad?" Ed nodded, and braced himself for the worst.

Mark began reciting the dream. "We were asleep, and in a dream, we all saw you, sitting at the side of a bed, crying and holding someone's hand. It was a woman's hand. She looked like she was sick ... like she was dying

... and it felt like you were too. Inside I mean. What woke us was how distraught you were. We just can't get that image of you being so upset out of our minds. That's why we had to see you."

Looking at Ed, Matt said, "Zac was right with his statement before Uncle Ed. You know we love you, but I don't think you realize just how much we really do. It's more than we could think." They all then got up and went to Ed. They hugged him like he was a coach in the middle of a huddle, while Chase and Marguerite wiped tears from their eyes. They were so proud of all of their children. They always continued to amaze them!

After they had all settled back down in their chairs, Ed said, "I can't believe you all had the same dream!"

Then Ed looked at them all and just said, "Spooky!" The tension in the house lessened then. They knew that was the word he used whenever they talked about the connection they all had with each other. They finally all smiled and felt a little calmer.

He then continued, "I do know you all love me! I know it's more than you can say, because that's how much I love you all back. More than I can ever say. I had no intentions of repeating this story to anyone. It has been buried for over forty years now. In the end, I guess the truth always comes out, somehow. I have to apologize to *you*, Mam. When Chase told me about you, and that you were getting married, we spoke at length about whether he could or should tell you what happened. He made a promise to my wife and me that he would never talk about it, and he kept his promise." Everyone's eyes just about popped out of their heads, when he said, 'my wife'. None of them knew that he had ever been married.

Ed shook his head in disbelief, and continued. "I hope you don't think he was trying to hide something from you, Mam. To my knowledge, he's never kept anything else from you. I begged him not to tell you, and I watched him struggle with the thought of keeping that from you. Now I see it was a mistake, but honestly, I never thought we would be having this conversation, ever!"

Ed knew he had thrown them, and he looked at Chase, who was nodding, encouraging him to go on.

Marguerite kept hold of Ed's hand, so he would be able to continue. "I know Chase would never keep something from me," she said, "and I understand it was a promise he made to both you and your wife." She then repeated, "Wife?"

He smiled sadly and started to tell the story about where he had been all week.

"I was in L.A. but stopped in Pennsylvania first. My wife, Lilli, was from Pennsylvania. I buried her there, by her wishes, when she passed away. I stop there every year to visit her on the anniversary of her death. It was forty-one years just three days ago. That's when you all had the dream, right? Three days ago?" They all nodded.

"I miss her to this day," Ed said, looking at Chase with tears streaming down his face. He then continued. "We had so little time. I never imagined I could love someone as much as I loved my wife."

Marguerite then wrapped her arms around him again, and held him until he composed himself. Chase, Marguerite, and all the children were beside themselves, listening to Ed talk about the love he had lost.

Once composed, Ed continued, "After Pennsylvania, I had some business to take care of in L.A. Lilli wrote the movie *Waiting for Love*." They all gasped when he mentioned the movie. They all knew it and had seen it multiple times. They knew Ed had written the songs for it, and had won his Oscar and multiple Grammy awards for the music. They just looked at him in dismay as he continued.

"She initially wrote the book, and when they turned it into a movie, she produced it and wrote the screenplay for it. Lilli felt that she would be the only one who could write the screenplay, and produce it, because she had to make sure they found the right actors to play the leads. Lilli had to make sure everyone who ever saw the movie felt how much the characters both loved each other. That was the most important thing to her. She wanted everyone to feel the love."

"Lilli Parker? That's who your wife was?" Sarah asked.

Ed just nodded his head, "We kept telling everyone that we were only best friends. The paparazzi followed us around everywhere trying to catch us, but we never held hands or made it look like we were a couple."

"Why?" Zeke asked.

"She was 35 and I was 23. I was just starting out. She didn't want a scandal. She didn't want people judging us because she was older. I didn't care and told her on multiple occasions. She didn't want me to ruin my career, but there were other reasons." He then put his head down. "She was dying. No one knew. Not even the doctors at the time could tell her how long she had left."

They all felt so sad for their uncle. They were all so happy and secure in their marriages, and for a moment they put themselves in his place. They tried to cope with the idea of their own spouses dying, and they couldn't even fathom it.

Ed continued, "She fought me tooth and nail over our relationship. She kept telling me that she couldn't put me through watching her die right in front of my eyes, but I couldn't let her win. I loved her! What made her finally understand that I wasn't going anywhere was when I told her that I wasn't going to let her die alone. She was only to die in my arms! That's when she couldn't fight me anymore and agreed to marry me. Your dad was the one who made me realize how much I loved her, and he stayed with Lilli and me until the end. He sat at the edge of her bed and held her hand when I had to go out quickly for something, or somewhere for business. If it weren't for him, I could have never survived her death. I knew back then that he was a brother to me. Besides the magistrate who married us, he's the only other person who knew. Lilli made me promise not to tell anyone else. Then she looked at Chase and made him promise her too. She was so worried about it getting out and ruining me, career-wise. She died just as I had promised her ... in my arms ... less than twenty hours after she became my wife. Lilli made me promise to move on and find someone else to marry and have a family. In over forty years, I've never met anyone who turned my head as she did. It's not that I never looked for anyone else. It's just that I didn't *see* anyone else. Can you understand that?"

Everyone nodded their heads. They did understand how he felt.

More Revelations

"I don't know why all of a sudden I was as shaken as I was, visiting her grave in Pennsylvania. I still love her. I still miss her. But this time ... for some reason, it hit me so hard. It was as if she had just left me, even though it's been forty-one years. I just can't describe it," Ed said, trying to explain everything that had happened.

Mark spoke up, saying, "Maybe that's why we were feeling you this time, because we never have before."

That's when it hit Chase, like he was hit on the head with a baseball bat. He remembered something and dropped his head. Everyone noticed, turning to look at him.

Marguerite got concerned. "What is it?"

He didn't know if he could speak or not, he was so shaken. He didn't want to say what he was thinking. The boys felt him, and Matt said, "You have to say it, Dad. Say what's on your mind, or it will drive you crazy."

Chase just looked at Ed, who was also waiting, and then said, "Her promise to you!"

That was all he said, and it was enough to bring back those memories to Ed like it was just yesterday.

How could he forget Lilli's promise to him? She promised that her soul would look for him in the afterlife, and not be born again until he was ready to as well. They were going to be together again.

Ed didn't know what to say. He looked pale and was hesitant to tell everyone the promise they had made to each other.

"Do we need to take a break?" Marguerite asked, noticing how distraught Chase and Ed were.

The children were fine now, because they had spoken about what was bothering them. Now that it was out, all the turmoil they were feeling had been released.

Ed said, "Yes, but I need to speak to Chase first." Chase and Ed headed towards his office, so they could speak in private. On his way out of the kitchen, Ed stopped to talk to Marguerite. "Mam, please don't be upset with me. I really need to speak to Chase right now."

Marguerite went towards Ed and kissed his forehead, before leaving them to their discussion. Ed thanked her and then he and Chase walked into the office and closed the door.

"Is she looking for me? Do you really think that could happen? Is she waiting for my soul so we could both be born again ... together?" Ed was talking so fast, Chase didn't know which question to answer first.

Chase tried to calm him down. "You would have to die first, wouldn't you?" Distress and turmoil were all over Chase's face, saying that out loud. Ed just looked at Chase and didn't know how to respond. They were both pacing, passing each other again and again.

Ed lowered his voice. "Yes, I would have to die first. Maybe she's telling me something, like my time is coming and she's still waiting. I feel her so strongly ... after all of these years. It has to mean something. If my time *is* near, it will mean I'll be closer to seeing her again, feeling her again, and loving her again! Chase! It *has* to mean something! Please, help me sort it out!" Ed sounded very distraught.

"I can't let you go, Ed! I can't see you die before I do! The boys and Sarah wouldn't be able to cope with it, and neither would Mam! I'm counting on you taking care of everyone if I die first!"

Losing Ed was going to be very hard for the Martin family, and there would be nothing that could soothe them if it was going to happen.

Ed sighed. "Chase, you have a good life. I want one too. I understand what you're saying. I know it would break all of your hearts if anything happened to me, but it's my turn. I want what you have. Lord knows, I have waited forty-one years since Lilli first promised me she would wait for me. That she would try and find me. I think she's calling me now. Would you deny me the chance to see her and be with her again! Would you do the same if anything happened to Mam, and if she had made that promise to you?"

Chase began sobbing. "I'm so sorry! I'm being so selfish right now, not wanting you to leave my family and me. Yes, I would do the same ... if Mam were calling to me. I'm so ... so sorry! Please forgive me."

After they had calmed down, they tried to rationalize all that had happened. They truly believed that Lilli was calling to Ed. Maybe his time was coming near, or maybe she was just reminding him that she was still waiting for him. That they did not know.

They also didn't know how to tell this revelation to the boys, Sarah, and Marguerite. Ed suddenly realized something. "Lilli said that we would have a catchword. If two people met and used the same catchword, it would somehow trigger who our souls were in a previous life. That's how we were going to find each other. I know it all sounds far-fetched, but with everything that's happened in the last three days ... maybe that's why they saw and felt her. Maybe so they'd be able to know it's her and be able to help us out, in the future!"

For a split second, Chase thought that Ed was losing his mind. He looked at him that way too. Ed smiled and asked Chase to think about it for a minute. Maybe Lilli was trying to reach out for help.

16
The Connection

"The boys and Sarah felt me and saw Lilli," Ed explained. "They are going to be the ones to help those two people with our souls. Imagine two people, strangers, having such strong emotions or feelings for each other and not knowing why. Maybe they'll even have visions of Lilli and me, which they won't be able to explain. Instead of bringing them together, it could actually make them run away from each other," he said, trying to convince Chase. "Maybe it was Lilli who showed herself to the five of them, so they could help those two people out."

Chase interrupted Ed. "Ed, you are still alive! Your soul can't be reborn again. This is *so* far-fetched."

"I know it sounds that way, but I'm just trying to figure out why all of this is happening now. Can you agree that the boys and Sarah are somehow involved?"

Chase knew what Ed was trying to say and so he agreed, "Yes, I agree, the five of them are somehow involved in this. But I can't tell you *how* they are. I just know they are."

"Do we tell them, or just wait until they can feel something again?" Ed asked, looking at Chase.

"I think they are all calmed down now," Chase said, "and maybe we shouldn't upset them again. We should wait to see if they feel anything again. Maybe they won't until you pass away. Then something might happen to them." Chase began worrying about the thought that had just occurred to him, regarding his children. "One more thing you should know,

Ed. Talking about your death is killing me. It's almost like you're happy about it, when it's only going to bring heartbreak to my family and me. I'm having a very hard time with it right now. I know what it will mean to you, though, and that's the only way I think any of us will survive your passing."

Ed lowered his head, looking at the floor. He couldn't say anything anymore.

Chase hugged his brother. "I really do understand. You've been waiting so long. I will let you go when your time comes, and I will be here for my children if they see anything. I'll help them understand, and they will help your two souls, should you both find each other again. I'll make sure of it. I'll have to leave a note or give them instructions though, if it doesn't happen before Mam or I die, but I won't speak to them about it before then."

Ed agreed, so as not to upset his nephews or niece any more that day. "Don't forget all those plans she made ... and the trigger word I told you about..."

Chase nodded. "I remember. 'Prerogative'"

They both let out a sigh, but really had so many more questions going on in their minds. They hadn't realized how long they'd been talking, trying to figure everything out. Marguerite, the boys, and Sarah were in the family room, still waiting for them.

"Chase, don't keep what we discussed from Mam anymore. I can't do that to her again, and I won't ask you to ever again. But thank you for keeping your word all of those years ago."

With that, Chase hugged Ed one more time, not realizing that it would be the last time he ever hugged his brother.

Ed said goodnight to everyone, and was pleased to see how calm all the children were. It made him happy leaving the house. They hugged him and told him that they loved him very much. Ed reciprocated the feeling and left.

When Ed left Marguerite, he felt calm too, saying goodbye to her.

"Thank you, Ed," she said, "for being the best brother ever. I love you."

Ed kissed her cheek and embraced her one more time, then turned, looking back at all of them. They stood together, smiling and waving goodbye.

17
Ed Is Gone

The next day, Chase got a call from the hospital. It was about Ed. He had passed away at home. His bodyguard had found him there when he failed to show up for a meeting, which had been scheduled in the morning. Chase was his emergency contact person, and first to be called. The boys and Sarah all gathered around their father and mother, who were very upset, not wanting to accept that Ed was gone.

The four boys took Chase to the hospital, while Sarah stayed with her mother. Chase made all of the arrangements for the funeral. It turned out that he had left Chase a letter stating all of his wishes, but Chase already knew, because they had spoken about it, at length, in the past. Chase knew what to do, but there was a second note to be opened in Pennsylvania, after the funeral.

Chase knew Ed wanted to be buried next to Lilli. He had thought that was when they would finally be together again, even if that meant he would only lie next to her grave. He knew it sounded morbid, but that's the way he felt about it.

The boys called their spouses, who already knew what was up. They had all felt the grief their husbands were feeling, and packed to meet them back at the homestead. Sarah called Josh and couldn't control herself when she told him about Uncle Ed. He immediately packed and headed out to join her.

They all made it home by the early evening. Marguerite kept herself busy in the kitchen, cooking and preparing for everyone coming home. Blake, Abbey, Drew, Cara, Quinn, and Jeanine all rushed over as soon as

Mark called them. He had the task of informing everyone, even the cousins in Pennsylvania. Everyone was so distraught over Ed, as he had been so young.

Ed's passing was spread all over the news and social media. Everyone was wondering what had happened, but it was going to take months for the medical review to come back, which would show he had died of natural causes. So far, there had been no disclosure of Ed's cause of death. Truth be told, the Martins already knew the real reason why he had passed on: His heart had just given up on waiting to be reunited with his love ... his Lilli.

18
Pennsylvania

Marguerite, Chase, Blake, Abbey, Drew, Cara, Quinn, and Jeanine, along with the boys, their wives, all of their children, Sarah, and Josh, headed to Pennsylvania for Ed's funeral. The press did not get wind of where they were headed or why. It was kept a secret. They all stayed at the house where Marguerite and Chase lived when they came back home, near Marguerite's family. It had plenty of room for everyone, and there was additional space above a massive garage that had once housed all of their security guards, when they traveled to the States. Marguerite's cousins Donna and Sue had everything ready for them when they arrived. The reunion with Donna and Sue, and their children, Ashley, Marie, and Kristen, was bittersweet. They were just as upset about Ed's passing as everyone else. After all, he was family.

After the service, they all headed back to the house for something to eat, and to read Ed's letter. His instructions were that it should be opened after the service, so the boys, Sarah, and Marguerite gathered in the family room, anticipating what Uncle Ed had to say. With a heavy heart, Chase opened the envelope and started, but didn't know how he would ever get through it.

The envelope contained two letters: One was to be opened and read, and the second was marked with a note telling Chase to hold on to it, and that he would know when it was time to open it. That's all it said. Chase gave that one to Marguerite for safekeeping, without any hesitation.

Chase opened the first letter, inhaled deeply, and started reading it aloud,

To my brother Chase,

How can I ever thank you for being my brother? You saved my life on many occasions. I always knew that we were going to be close. At the time, I didn't know why, but as time flew by for us, I now know. You were supposed to keep me happy and occupied until this day came. You know what I mean, don't you? I have waited many years for this. I will see you again. I just know it. I love you, Chase.

To my sister Mam,

Thank you. Thank you. Thank you. You have been nothing but so loving and kind to me since Chase brought me home to meet you that very first time. By the way, I still remember that nightgown you were wearing! I am smiling writing that down too! You gave me four nephews and one beautiful niece. How rich I feel having them in my life. I promise - I will see you again too! I love you, Mam!

Zac, Zeke, Mark, Matt, and my beautiful Sarah,

Please do not grieve for me. I know, for a fact, I will see you again. I am certain of it. You will eventually see what I mean, and you will know when, at the time it happens. That is all I can say for right now. You all have always treated me like I was so special. Every time we met - I would notice all of your faces lighting up, and I knew that you loved me. We all take those words for granted but I never did. I knew I was special to you and will never forget it.

Please, do not grieve for me, please! I know it will be hard, because it pains me to even write this goodbye to you all - however, know that I am so happy. I leave you all being so happy about it. Someday you will know why. I love you all and thank you for loving me back.

Ed

There was what seemed to be a long silence after the letter was read. They all just clung to each other, trying to get over his passing.

Zac said, "He was happy and we have to remember that. Somehow, I don't think this is over."

Everyone looked at Zac, and his words were soothing. They all started to calm down and then decided to rejoin the rest of the gathering.

Margaret, Mary, Jess, and Amelia all ran to their fathers. For some reason, having them around gave them peace as well. Then they embraced Chase, who they ran to next, engulfing him in their hugs. They knew their papa needed them, and they tried to give him as much support as possible.

Sarah – The New Matriarch

Twenty-two years later

The one problem with living a long life is that you outlive most of your friends, or in Marguerite and Chase's case, your extended family. They watched and grieved when Blake, Drew, and Quinn all passed on, as well as Abbey and Cara. If it weren't for their children and family's support, they didn't think that they could have survived any of it.

Jeanine came and stayed with Chase and Marguerite when Quinn passed away. Marguerite insisted on it, and Chase believed that it really helped Jeanine through it all. During one of the children's visits home, to spend time with their parents, somehow it seemed they were all worried about the same thing.

Sarah asked her brothers, "Have you all been thinking about this along with me? Somehow I feel like you have been." They all felt they knew what she was going to say, because they were thinking the same thing. *Someone needs to move into the house with Mom and Dad.*

"Dad is 86, and Mom's 90!" Matt said. "They're in good shape, and they already have a driver, but Mom has a hard time making it up those steps to go to bed."

Everyone who knew Chase and Marguerite had watched them age gracefully throughout the years. Chase's hair had turned snow white, and still had the same wave to it. He kept it neatly cut, but his curls always showed up, framing his face. Marguerite was still beautiful at 90. She mostly kept her silvery gray hair cut just below her ears, because Chase loved it like that.

"Josh and I have been talking about it," Sarah said. "I don't want to sell the house. They would never want that, and I love it here. I just couldn't part with it."

The brothers were all relieved, because they were all hoping Sarah would want the house. They had not spoken about it to their parents yet. They wanted to have a game plan before they approached them.

Mark spoke up. "Sarah, I think we were all silently hoping that you would want to live here, but it might put a lot of pressure on you. Taking care of Mom and Dad may be hard on you."

"I don't and will never have a problem with that," Sarah said, making sure everyone knew. "After how much they loved me and everything they did for me my whole life, it's no trouble at all. I would be only too happy to return all of that to them. Josh is good with it too. We both agree, if you all do. I can move in as soon as we tell them."

Zeke was worried about something, and they all felt it. "Sarah, will we still be able to come home?" he asked. "Can you still have Thanksgiving and all the holidays? Can we still call this our home?"

Sarah was so moved they all still wanted to come home, to her house now, but quickly responded, "Yes, this is your home too, and always will be. I'll have every holiday we all celebrate together, and I want you to visit here as much as you want to, just like you do now. I will be upset if you don't.

"I've been thinking about this and going over it with Josh," she continued. "I think we should move Mom and Dad's bedroom to where their office is, and build a full bathroom attached to it. There's plenty of room to extend it. They have a hard time making those stairs now. I think we could connect the end of the hall, where Mom's bedroom is currently, and open up the hallway, leading to more bedrooms for the girls when you all come to stay. There's plenty of room over the garage to do that."

They were all stunned. She *had* been giving it a lot of thought, and her ideas were fantastic. They were always so crowded when they visited, and this would give them more room.

"One more thing," Sarah said. "When it's my time, we should determine who should move here next. It doesn't have to be soon, but way in the future. Can we keep the house for generations to come?"

Sarah's brothers were stunned again. They all got up and hugged her, huddling around her like they always did. They had a plan, which was going to take a lot of their worries about their parents away.

When they all approached them about it, Chase and Marguerite couldn't be prouder of them all. Once again, they wanted to take care of them, just like when they'd been children and Chase was on the road touring. He always would say, "Take care of your mother for me." And now they were taking care of both of them. They were so pleased and happy about their plans.

20
Waiting for Something!

Chase and Marguerite were more than thrilled about Sarah moving in. It gave them peace. Everyone would still be using the house as their homestead. They would always come home for the holidays, and it was going to be their main place to get together. There were so many fond memories there—memories none of them would ever forget.

All of the construction changes happened. Marguerite and Chase were hesitant about leaving their bedroom, but they were convinced to move downstairs. The kids had made the office look just like their room, which made them feel better about it.

Then Jeanine started forgetting things ... until she remembered nothing at all. They took her to the doctor, and he confirmed that she had Alzheimer's. Everyone was so upset about it. She just sat there, not knowing who any of them were, and it distressed Chase and Marguerite. She was their last connection to their brothers and sisters, and she didn't even know them anymore. She was moved to a care facility that took care of Alzheimer patients. Chase and Marguerite visited her every other day. They were not going to let her be alone.

Shockingly, during their last visit, Jeanine knew who they were, which took them both by surprise. It was bittersweet, because almost as fast as she recognized them, she slipped back into her own world again. Before she did though, she looked at them both and said, "Quinn said to tell you it's time!"

It floored them both. What did that mean? Time for what? Time for her passing? Was he waiting for her? Or did she mean that it was time for *their* passing, which they did not believe for a moment. They came home and called everyone to speak about it. They thought how strange and cryptic that message was.

Marguerite was 91 now, and Chase was 87. They acted and looked much younger. Marguerite didn't look her age at all! Neither of them did really. Sarah felt that some days they could run circles around her.

To their children, it seemed as though they were waiting for something to happen before they could pass away. They didn't know what it was, but they clearly felt they had to be around for it. No one could figure it out.

Suddenly one night, Sarah woke up and said, "Prerogative." *How strange,* she thought. She froze in bed and nudged Josh, who was sound asleep. He woke up and saw how pale she was, lying there beside him, and panicked.

"Are you not well? Should I call your mom?"

All she could do was nod her head. He ran downstairs to get them and found that they were already up.

"Something's wrong with Sarah. She's shaken about something. Can you please come and see her?"

Chase and Marguerite already knew that she was upset. They felt her and knew it was only a matter of time before the boys all called in as well. If she felt something, so did her brothers. As they walked into her room, they saw her standing and pale. She ran to her mother, who was there waiting with open arms. She sat Sarah down on the big couch in front of the fireplace, where she just held her, rocking her back and forth until she composed herself. Chase just paced in front of them as she told them what happened.

"All I know is I woke up saying, 'Prerogative'! Why would I say that? Why? And why did it make me feel like this? What is that about? I don't understand!" Sarah said, really curious.

Chase now knew what Jeanine's cryptic message meant. *It was time!* They were now just waiting for the boys to call, and no sooner had they thought that then they all called in, one at a time, and appeared on the webcam footage on the TV, like they always did. They were all in their pjs, and for a moment, this made them all smile.

"We have to stop meeting like this," Sarah said to her brothers. "Someday you're going to catch me naked." This made them all laugh.

"No, please," Mark said. "That would be too much."

Zac then cut to the chase, "I woke up saying a word. Anna thought I was losing it. I couldn't even tell her why I said it. It was just one word!"

"Prerogative?" Sarah asked them all. Their jaws dropped. They'd all said the same word, but didn't know what it meant, beyond its obvious definition, or why they'd said it.

Marguerite and Chase just looked at each other. They knew exactly why they had said it. It meant that Uncle Ed's soul had already been born again. He was already on earth, and after twenty-three years, he had found the soul of his wife, Lilli.

Lilli had been right all along. She had said they would find each other again, and they did. Now it was up to the seven of them to help those two people figure out who they were.

21
Mia Addison and David Allen

Mia took a bus from Pennsylvania to meet her best friend Judy in New York. They were meeting each other for the day, and were going to try and catch a play. Judy was taking the train in from New Jersey. Mia and Judy did this all the time. She hated driving into the city and Judy thought that they charged too much for parking, so she always took the train. Mia also did not like driving through the traffic, which was heavy all the time.

They always met at Rockefeller Center. In the winter, they had breakfast watching the ice skaters glide around the rink, and in the summer, they liked looking at all of the flowers decorating the plaza. Judy was late, and Mia started getting concerned about her friend. Then her cell phone went off, and she saw that it was Judy.

"I have to cancel. My water heater broke, and I have a flood in my basement. I have to get a new one and find a plumber to install it today. I'm so sorry, Mia. I know you're already in the city waiting for me. I just lost all track of time, trying to clean up all that water."

Mia understood completely and told Judy not to worry about it. After hanging up with Judy, Mia had the day to walk around or go shopping. The buses left practically every hour, so she had no worries there.

While window shopping, she looked up and saw the biggest, darkest rain cloud she had ever seen coming her way. All she could think of was what store she should run into before she got poured on. She was on a street with small shops and art galleries, nowhere she would normally shop. The storm hit before she even decided where to run. She was caught right in the middle of a downpour, so she had no choice but to run into an art gallery.

As soon as she entered the gallery, she heard someone yell, "Help!"

She looked around to see who was calling. There, standing in the back of the gallery, was a guy trying to hold up a massive picture. She ran to him immediately, because it was clear he was going to drop it. *It's really big!*

She looked at him. His eyes were fixed on the painting, not able to look away, afraid he was going to drop his work. His face was all red from the strain of holding the painting up by himself.

Mia calmly said, "Which side do you want me to hold?"

"Put your palm under the bottom right corner, with your fingers in the back for now … just to get some weight off of me … until I figure out how to hang this or drop it down," he said gratefully.

Once she did that, he began to breathe a little easier and relaxed a bit. Then he asked, "Can you lift this with me, so we can hang it on the hooks?"

"Okay," Mia said. "Tell me when you're ready and we'll lift it together."

"Ready? Lift!" Up the painting went, hugging the wall. "Now slide your fingers around, so you don't get them caught and hurt yourself. Let the painting drop slowly, to see if it catches on the hooks."

They both slowly slid the painting down the wall, and lo and behold, it worked! The painting caught on the hooks, and it was now in place … hung securely.

They both breathed a sigh of relief for saving the painting from falling and getting damaged. Neither of them suffered any injuries doing it either.

The man then held out his hand, which was covered in dried paint, to shake Mia's. "Hello, I'm David. Thank you for saving me and my picture."

"I'm Mia," she said, taking his hand to shake it.

Mia stood back and looked at the picture, and saw that it was just gorgeous. It was full of color, and was light and airy-looking. She really couldn't describe it any other way.

"You painted this?"

"Yes, I did all of them here. I have an opening in two nights, and I'm nervous about it. It's my first one ever. I usually only show a few pieces when someone approaches me for an art show going on, but this time they blew me away and said that they only wanted my work displayed. I'm so honored and grateful that they did that for me."

"Can I look around at your paintings?"

David replied skeptically, "Are you a critic? Is that why you're here? For a sneak peek at my work?"

Mia looked at him and realized that he was serious. She laughed. "No ... you can't be serious. Do I look like a critic? I was just trying to get out of the rain, and your door was open for me to run in here. I don't know a thing about art, and couldn't tell a Picasso from a Van Gogh. So you're safe with me." She began looking around, her eyes not knowing where to settle first. The paintings were all so colorful and beautiful.

David seemed satisfied with her answer. "Well then, you can stay if you help me hang some more paintings." They finally looked at each other then, not having made eye contact as of yet.

Mia had short brown hair and her face was so beautiful that it made David believe she was probably the only person that could pull that look off. She had big brown eyes and was tiny, but strong enough to hold the painting for him.

David looked like he needed to be drenched in a bath of turpentine, he had so much paint all over him. There were stains on his clothes, hands, arms, and in his hair. He even had paint on his face. It made her laugh when she finally looked at him. He knew she was laughing at him, knowing how he probably looked. He joined in the laughter.

"Sorry. I know I don't look presentable, but I was trying to finish and didn't have time to clean myself up." He was smiling from ear to ear. *And what a beautiful smile it is!* she thought. His hair was blond, and he had beautiful blue eyes that were mesmerizing to her.

Mia just blushed, "Don't worry about it. You're an artist, and that's how I always pictured an artist would look!" She then giggled.

"So you have a mental picture of us artists. Do I match up to your imagination?" he asked, flirting with her.

Mia giggled again, and then thought to herself, *Stop giggling like an idiot!*

She just nodded and began helping him display more paintings. After spending hours with him, David commented, "Now that you've been helping me, you'll have to come to the opening. You can be the hostess. I never had one before, but I now think you should be it!"

Mia blushed again, shocked at hearing him say that to her. "I'm only in the city for the day. I have to go back home later. I didn't bring any clothes with me to stay."

"Where do you live?" he asked. He was now intrigued.

"Pennsylvania," she said proudly.

"Can you go home and pack, and come back later? I'll pay you if you decide to help me. I have no problem doing that," he said, hoping she would agree.

"No, I don't want to be paid. I would never expect to be. I would help you gladly, if I were staying in the city."

"Well then don't go back to Pennsylvania. I'll find you somewhere to stay, and we can get you whatever clothes you need, so you won't have to leave."

He seemed to have an answer for everything. Somehow, she started to think about how she could stay ... and where.

After some thought, she came back to reality, and just said, "I really can't. I am sorry."

"How about this ... I will go back to Pennsylvania with you. You can pack, and then we can come back to the city. It's as simple as that. I am asking you to help me. Would you do that for me?" He was now pleading to have her help him. He was not sure why, but he just felt like he didn't want to let her go.

22
Going to Pack

Before she knew it, they were in a car arranged by David, driving back to her house, in Pennsylvania. She couldn't believe that she had just done that—gotten into a car with someone she'd just met, and with a driver she didn't even know. To top it all off, she was leading them right to her home!

Am I out of my mind by doing this? There must be something wrong with me!

David saw the expression on her face change, and wondered if the novel thought of being with a stranger was unsettling her feelings. He didn't want her to be questioning anything about the situation, so he said, "Please don't worry. I won't harm you. This is my driver, Peter. He's also my security guard. Keep your phone on, and if you ever feel uncomfortable or unsafe, have the numbers you need to call ready. I'll make sure you get that call through. You don't know me, but I am asking you to trust me. I'm harmless." He then lowered his head and looked at the floor of the SUV.

"Did you ever mention your last name? I just realized that I have gotten into a car with someone whose last name I don't even know." Concern was clear on her face.

He then took her hand and held it. "My name is David Allen."

David Allen, the artist! Oh my God! Why hadn't she made the connection before! Of course, he had his own driver and bodyguard. She'd read about him. He was the most popular artist on the planet lately. Everyone knew him. He'd come out of nowhere when he was just 18 and made a huge splash on the art scene. People were lining up to commission him for a painting, and he didn't even do that. He would paint when he felt like it, and if people happened to like his paintings, they would buy them. He wasn't the type to paint for anyone in particular. She suspected that was part of the reason he was so successful. *Leave them wanting more,* she thought. Not only could he afford to pay her, but he could also afford to buy her a whole wardrobe if she had taken him up on his offer before.

She looked at him, shocked. "I'm so sorry. I didn't recognize who you are. I do know you and your work. I've read a few articles about you."

She had also read that he was a recluse. He rarely interacted with anyone and kept to himself, which she found untrue. He was wonderful to her, and seemed very forward and friendly.

"Don't believe everything they write about me. I hate giving interviews, and it shows when they write those articles about me. I come off as being snotty and snippy, when I just don't want to tell them my life story, and it never ends. Someone wanting to know what motivates me. Why do I use so much color? What do my paintings mean? I just can't help myself being annoyed about it," he said, trying to give a little of himself to her. "Can you trust me, now that you know my last name?" he asked, as if he were sad to have had to tell her all of that.

"I apologize," she said, mortified. "Please accept my apologies. I had no idea, and hope that you don't feel insulted by my words or actions. Please put yourself in my place for a moment though. What if the tables were turned, and you were me and didn't know who you just got into a car with, while taking them back to your home no less!"

He did understand and finally smiled, "Yes, I see your point. Now it's me who has to apologize to you. I'm so sorry for stressing you out like that. Can we call a truce?" he asked, facing her. She realized then how shy he was, which made the articles make more sense. She was now sure of that. She gave him her biggest smile to let him know she was fine and squeezed his hand to reassure him, because he had not let go of hers yet.

They held hands all the way to her house, talking about everything possible under the sun. It was the quickest ride home from the city she had ever had. For some reason, she felt very comfortable with him, now that they were over all her drama.

As they arrived at her house, he asked, "Do you live with anyone?"

"No. I live alone," she said, not feeling bad or nervous about telling him. "My parents left me some money after they passed away unexpectedly a few years ago, and I bought it. I just wanted something that was mine. It actually belonged to my best friend, Judy. It was her parents' house, and now when she comes home to Pennsylvania, she has somewhere to stay." She smiled, feeling very proud of herself. "With me!"

David could not help but smile back at her. The house was old but nice. As soon as they got inside, he saw that she was very neat. Not a thing was out of place. She went to pack, telling David and Peter to make themselves at home.

Her phone went off as she was packing, and it was Judy, telling her that the plumber had finally arrived to install her new water heater. She was laughing while speaking to her. She told her that she was home and would touch base with her later in the week. She had the biggest smile on her face when she hung up. It was obvious they were close friends.

She returned to where she had left David and Peter, walked up to David, and looked him in the eye. "I know you asked me if I would be your hostess … but did you mean it? I'd let you take it back if you didn't."

She laughed at the notion of everything being a hoax. It wasn't though.

"Yes, I was very serious about you being the hostess for my show. I want you by my side. I feel so calm being around you. I think it will help me."

"I just need to know what to pack. Can you come look, and tell me if I am on the right track please?" Hoping that her request was not too awkward, she waited to see how David was going to react.

He followed her into her dressing room. She had converted a bedroom into a big dressing room with walls of closets and drawers everywhere. There was a chandelier hanging from the middle of the ceiling and the room was a very girly-girl thing. That startled him a little. He just didn't expect it.

Mia showed him some dresses she had, and he told her which ones he thought would be fitting for the shows. "Wait … you just said 'shows'. I thought there was only one show."

"No, the shows are all week."

"As in every day of the week?"

"Yes … I'm sorry I didn't make that clear."

"I have to work on Monday," Mia said, feeling bad about it.

"Can you get any time off? I really want you by my side for the whole week. I don't know if I could do it without you now. You know what a recluse I am." As he said that, they both burst out laughing.

"Let me make a phone call, and see if I can get the time off." Mia made the call, and shortly after, told him that everything was good to go.

Mia owned her own business. She had a gift shop back in Pennsylvania, which she had started with what was left of her inheritance money, and a small business loan. She didn't make a fortune, but it was considered a successful shop, and she had been able to pay the loan off in the first six months. She loved having her own business. She made enough to cover her bills, pay her staff, and take a nice salary. Her friend Phyllis was going to manage the shop while she was away. Phyllis took over whenever Mia had time off, and she trusted her completely.

Mia needed a bigger suitcase if she was going to be in the city for an entire week. She was really planning outfits, talking to herself while David sat on a chair and watched her. He was amused at her, watching her walking in circles and talking to herself. She had forgotten that he was even there, and had not yet even gotten to her makeup drawer.

It had taken Mia an hour to get everything ready, when a thought crossed her mind, "Where am I staying? I want to let Phyllis know, in case she needs me for something."

Looking down again, at the rug this time, David just said, "You can stay with me if you like. I have a lot of room in my condo in the city, and you will have your own bedroom and bathroom."

He was blushing, and just waiting for her to refuse the offer, but she surprised him. "Okay then ... let's go." Mia passed by him, carrying two suitcases and a makeup bag.

His face lit up as he followed her from the dressing room, announcing to Peter that they were ready to go.

23
Back in the City

Time flew by as they drove back, because they spent all that time talking to each other. Every time David spoke to Mia, he looked down. She thought it was so cute, him being so shy like that. They held hands again all the way to his condo, where a doorman met them. He was very formal and dressed in an outfit that made him look like a bellman at a fancy hotel.

Once inside, he introduced her to the guard at the big oak desk in the foyer of the building. The place was lavish and the floors and walls were all marble. *Exquisite,* she thought. David told the guard that she would be there all week, and to expect her when she came in.

"Thank you, Mr. Allen, for letting me know. We will take good care of Miss Addison. Miss Addison, Mr. Allen will tell you how to get in touch with us down here, should you need anything."

Mia just nodded. "Thank you." She was smiling from ear to ear.

The elevator went up twenty-seven floors to their condo. The only way up was by inserting a key to get the elevator to move. It opened right at the condo itself, taking visitors to that floor. The place was huge and so beautiful. While his paintings were incredibly colorful, Mia noticed his condo was not, which intrigued her. It was not what she expected. He saw the questioning look on her face and asked her about it.

"Your paintings are so full of color, and yet your condo is neutral. It just got me thinking," she said, trying not to sound rude.

"Let me show you around. I just got it a few months ago, and have been working on getting paintings ready for my show. I didn't have time to focus on this place yet." He hoped she would like the place.

The kitchen was massive and had windows overlooking the skyline of the city, which was beautiful during the day. Mia couldn't wait to see what it looked like at night, with all the streetlights and building lights on.

There was a dining-room table, which was simple but big, with twelve chairs around it. *He must be expecting to entertain a lot.* She smiled at that thought.

The living room was also large, and again there were windows, overlooking Central Park this time. That in itself was a sight to see. It was like a picture of the park had been painted across the large windows.

The furniture was simple and cozy. Nothing was fancy and the pieces he had picked out seemed to fit him. There was a powder room right off the foyer, when they entered the condo, done in marble to match the foyer decor. Then he took her to her room. It was huge! The walk-in closet alone was the size of her bedroom, and the bathroom was the size of her dressing room *and* bathroom back home.

"I'll leave you to unpack. I have to head back to the gallery to get some things done. I got sidetracked today. I'll call you when I'm coming home, and will pick some food up for us for dinner. Okay?"

She was tired, so it was okay with her. She nodded.

Mia followed him to the door, calling his name, "David?"

He turned, only to notice her walking towards him. She hugged him tightly. He returned the hug and felt the warmness in her embrace. He actually loved the feeling.

"Thank you for today. You had the patience of a saint, waiting for me to pack, and taking me all the way to Pennsylvania and then back here." She then kissed his cheek, which made his face flush red.

I could get used to that, he thought to himself. He smiled widely, and looked down at the floor as he got into the elevator—again, not looking at her.

That made her smile, loving how shy he was.

24 First Night

As Mia puttered around the kitchen, she found that David had food in the refrigerator and started making something for supper. She loved to cook and found the ingredients to make some side dishes. When David called, she told him to just get the main course. She had everything else covered.

She unpacked and set up her room, ironing her clothes and hanging them in the huge closet—lining everything up so she could see them in plain sight.

Next, Mia took a long hot shower to relax her mind a bit, and got ready for David to come home. It was around seven when he finally called, and Mia told him what to get for supper. He was happy she had thought about it and had something made already. When he got home, she had two plates set at the massive table for dinner. She'd found candles in the cabinet while snooping around, and everything was set.

When David saw the trouble she'd gone through, it made him so happy. No one had ever fussed like that over him. He felt close to her, even though he'd just met her that morning, and couldn't explain why. He was comfortable ... like he had known her his whole life. She had been on his mind the whole time he was working at the gallery. He was thinking of her, and wondering why he was feeling the way he did about her.

Mia went to him the minute he got through the door and hugged him again. He just loved the feeling of her arms wrapped around him like that.

What made her do that again? Maybe she was just an affectionate person. Or maybe there was another reason he couldn't think of ... yet!

Mia was so happy to see David. She had been counting the minutes until he got home. She also decided she would go to the gallery the next day with him to help him set up. She didn't want him to leave her again. She didn't know where those feelings were coming from, but she knew that she didn't want to leave him either. Her mind was made up.

They finished dinner and talked again for a while. She told him she would like to go to the gallery with him the next day. He grinned.

"I'm so happy that you want to come with me tomorrow. I could use your help. Maybe you could give me your opinion on some places I want to hang my paintings."

"I'll give you my honest opinion ... whether you like it or not." She started laughing as she said it.

Mia's smile lit up her whole face. In David's eye, she was strikingly beautiful.

"I'll clean up here," she said, still smiling, "while you go get all of that paint off of you. It might never come out of your hair though."

"Yes, I will do as I'm told," David said, as he got up from the table smiling, and kissed her softly on the lips, thanking her for dinner. "I enjoyed sitting at my table, which was a first for me."

Mia was happy she had set that table for dinner, and was thrilled that he liked it.

Before David went to shower, he went into his studio to look at another painting he wanted to take to the gallery with him. Turning on the light revealed a painting that was almost finished, sitting in the scaffold. It was a picture of an English Tudor house. It had a big driveway, a four-car garage attached to it in an L shape, and a big courtyard in front, leading up to the garage. There was a gate in front of the house that had to be opened for a car to be able to enter the property. He had painted that picture from a dream he had. He still didn't know if he might have seen that house or if it was just a dream he'd had. It was on his mind though, and he hadn't been able to stop thinking about it at the time.

David looked at the painting again and just shook his head as if to ask it if it was trying to tell him something.

Then he turned off the light and headed for the shower.

When he was done, he found Mia in the living room, looking very comfortable on his big couch watching TV. She saw that he had gotten most of the paint off, but Mia still dragged him to the kitchen to see if she could get the rest.

"Ouch! Ouch! Ouch!" he yelled like a baby.

"Stop yelling! I am not hurting you," Mia said, smiling and laughing.

David was starting to laugh too. He was just teasing her. She wasn't hurting him at all.

Then she noticed the New York skyline, all lit up, while looking out the window. It looked like a postcard, and it was beautiful. David noticed that she had a look of amazement on her face, like a little child opening up a Christmas present. It brought a big smile to his face.

Automatically, he placed his hands on her waist. She turned to look at him and couldn't resist those beautiful blue eyes. She couldn't look away.

He drew her in for a kiss, and she responded to him. Then she pulled back and kissed him on the cheek.

She felt it couldn't go far. Not yet. This was their first night together. Mia didn't want to rush things, as she had never done anything like the things she had done that day. She had just met someone, took him home, and decided to stay at his house for a week! When she thought about it, she still couldn't believe the day she'd just had.

"This was one heck of a day for me," Mia told David. "I'm really tired. I think I'm just going to my room and sleep. What time do you want to go tomorrow?"

David looked down again. "Is nine okay with you?"

"Nine is great! I thought you were going to say six." She was now laughing.

Then she pulled him in again for another kiss, which surprised him. It was the sweetest kiss he thought he'd ever had.

"Goodnight, David. Thank you for everything today." Mia turned away and headed off to bed.

25
Getting to Know You

David was tired. He had stayed up for only an hour after Mia had gone to bed and felt that it was time for him to head to his room as well.

In the middle of the night, he woke up, dreaming again of that house! It haunted him! Where had he seen it before? *Had* he seen it before? What was it trying to tell him?

He got up and went to the kitchen for some water, and found Mia sitting at the window, just looking at all of the lights of the New York skyline, still mesmerized by them. It made him stop just to watch the look on her face.

He made some noise, so as not to startle her, and she turned to look at him. She had felt him coming. She didn't know how, but she had.

Mia held her arms out to David, and he gladly walked into her embrace, wearing just his sweatpants. She was sitting on a chair at the snack bar in the kitchen, so when David embraced her, Mia's head rested on his bare chest, where his hair tickled her face. They stayed there for a few moments, neither wanting to break away.

"What's bothering you, Mia?"

"I was just going to ask you that," she replied. "I'm trying to figure out why it is that I feel like I know you, when I just met you today. I feel so comfortable around you ... like we were old friends or something more. But it just baffles me. I can't put my finger on it."

"Is it because you read all those wonderful articles on me?" he asked, laughing. "Maybe you feel you know me from reading about me? But we already talked about how wrong most of them were about me, so I'm hoping you don't take any of them too seriously."

"Well, you're right about that. None of them seem a true description of you."

"So, you were able to figure me out already?"

"No, but I did figure out some things." Mia smiled widely as she lifted her head to look at him.

"Is that why you blush most of the time when you talk to me?" he asked. This made her blush again.

"No," she said, but didn't elaborate further. "I've figured out that you're very shy; you look at the floor or just bow your head when you want to say something to me. And your face gets all flushed. I can't help but love that about you."

David was shocked. He didn't even realize he did that. He knew that his face flushed a lot, because he always felt it getting hot, but he didn't realize that he did it every time he spoke to Mia.

"I think it only flushes for you! It really doesn't happen to me a lot, but I did notice it happening a lot today."

Mia's smile reached from ear to ear when he said that, and she could tell that he was sincere. He always was. Perhaps that was why she felt so comfortable around him.

"So, your turn now. Why can't you sleep?" she questioned David.

"I don't want you to think that I'm crazy, and you might if I tell you."

"Come on now. Let me hear it. Then again ... I'll say what I said before; I will give you my honest opinion," Mia said, now totally engaged in finding out what it was.

"I had a dream a while ago. I keep seeing this house in it. I felt so strongly about the house that I had to paint it and tonight ... I had the same dream. I saw the same house again. I just keep thinking ... where did I see this house before? Have I seen this house before? Is it trying to tell me something? For some reason, I think it's trying to tell me something. I'm tired of that dream and want to know what it's about. What am I supposed to do about it? I just don't know, but it gnaws at me. I have to find out!"

Mia reached for his hand to comfort him. She could see the concern on his face. He wasn't distressed over it, but he wanted some relief from the questions that nagged him. "Can I see the picture?" she asked calmly.

David took her by the hand and led her into his studio. The picture was right there, hung center stage in the room.

She went right to it, looking at it. Aside from the painting being beautiful, she saw that he had put a lot of work into it, but she didn't recognize the house. It wasn't a famous person's house; it just looked like an old English house.

When she turned, David was looking down at the floor. She didn't say anything and just took him by the hand and led him to her room.

"Stay with me; I'll help you," Mia said, in a very low-toned voice. "Let me hold you, and maybe neither of us will dream for the rest of the night."

David was never going to refuse that invitation. He was drawn to her, and she was to him, so they both crawled under the covers, where she kept her promise to hold him all night to keep the dreams away.

David and Mia woke the same way they fell asleep, with her holding onto him. *That was the best night's sleep I've had in a long time.*

26 Prerogative

David and Mia headed to the gallery to place more paintings on the walls. They were trying to group them by style, and so far, everything was going really well.

They were getting done sooner than David expected. He was thrilled at the way things were turning out and was very happy with Mia. He was glad that she was right there with him, helping him. He loved being around her.

They gave the place another once over, walking through the aisles, reviewing how the paintings were set up, and were getting ready to leave when he noticed that one was crooked.

As he walked back to fix it, he asked Mia, "Do you think anyone would object to me leaving a part of this wall empty? I was thinking that, if we left it empty, when someone wanted to purchase a painting, we could hang it here so they could view it without being distracted by the other paintings around it."

"That is a great idea!" Mia said. "Let's move these few around and make some room."

"I don't think the gallery would like seeing an empty wall," David said. "They might have an issue with it."

"Well, David, who's show is it?"

"Mine!"

"Right. So ... it's your prerogative!"

When she said that, something, which neither could explain, passed in front of them. That's the only way they could describe it. It was like their lives, but not their current lives, passed right in front of their eyes.

They both froze. Neither one could move. They just stood there, looking at each other but not seeing each other. It was like they were seeing someone else.

They felt something too. They felt love ... love for each other? What was going on? Mia moved away from David, and he did the same ... not knowing what was happening.

Finally, he came around and looked at her, realizing that she had gone pale. His face was all red, and she saw that too.

"What just happened? Something just happened to me, and I know something just happened to you too. You're white as a sheet."

Mia couldn't speak. She just looked at him with her eyes opened so wide that he thought they would pop out of her head at any moment.

"Let's lock up here and try and figure out what just happened. Is that okay with you?" He was so afraid that she might run away from him, and he didn't want to lose her.

Mia just nodded her head as he locked the door to the gallery and set the alarm. He grabbed her hand, which she gladly took, because she was so shaken. Mia had such a tight grip on it that he felt he might never paint again, if he didn't switch hands. He knew she was scared, but so was he and he didn't know why.

27

Back at the Martins'

To calm all of his children down after waking from a dream they couldn't understand, Chase told them that it was time to open the second letter Uncle Ed had written to them before he passed away, twenty-three years before. He had held onto it all of these years.

Ed had told Chase that he would know the right time to open the letter, and now he knew; it was definitively the right time.

The boys wanted to come home to hear what Uncle Ed had said. They all wanted to be together, and they set out first thing in the morning to head for home.

Sarah was thrilled that her brothers were coming home. She loved them, and even though she knew it would be painful hearing from Uncle Ed again, at least they would be together.

This is what mom and dad were waiting for, Sarah thought. She'd always felt they were waiting for something, and she knew this was it. Sarah only had to wait one more day to find out.

Everyone came home and were anxious to know why they'd all had the same dream, saying the same word: "Prerogative." They gathered around the table, where Chase opened the envelope and began to read the letter out loud:

To my beloved family,
If you are reading this letter, it is because you all felt something happening. Something 'spooky'!

Everyone smiled, remembering the word he'd used for their strange bond.

Chase and Mam,
I hope to God you are well and in good health. If you are not with your children anymore, I know they probably miss you to no end. It always amazed me what great parents you were. The five of them are a testament to that. They are all so successful, which is not as important as being happy, and every time I saw them, they were always so happy. That was what is so important in life, I felt!
Now down to why you are reading this.
I am assuming that you all have said the word "Prerogative." Didn't you?

They all gasped when their dad read that to them, and just looked around at each other, amazed. Chase gave everyone a few moments to compose themselves before continuing:

I will tell you why.
When my wife Lilli passed away, she was positive that we would meet again in an afterlife. We both believed our souls would come back to earth after we died, as someone else, and she vowed she would not be born again until I was. She promised to wait for me. She promised to look for me, so we could finally be together again. I wanted to believe her. I loved her so much that she made me believe her. If you heard that word, then you know it is true. We are both looking for each other.
We need all of your help.
We had a catchword, like a trigger word, and that word was "Prerogative." If that word was said between two people, and they were our two souls, then it would trigger something. Maybe it would be memories of how we loved each other, or just any memories tying us together.

I am counting on the bond you share with your parents, and with each other, to find these two people and to help them. I know they will need it. They will be confused about what they are feeling and who they are feeling it about.

I guarantee they will think you are all crazy too, but please find them. Help them! And in doing so, you will be finding me again. I told you we would meet again, and as I write this, I truly believe it. You will finally meet my wife Lilli as well. I have been waiting forever for her, and now we are so close.

I am begging you to help us!

This sounds far-fetched I know, but you said the word! It has to mean something!

I promise you now. We will meet again!

I love you all more than I can say!

Ed

Shaken and Confused

Everyone was so shaken at the table. They had just heard from their uncle, who had been dead over twenty-three years. Memories of how much they loved and missed him had re-surfaced, bringing back all of the emotions they'd felt when they lost him.

Marguerite and Chase felt the pain of his death all over again as well. They had lost someone so precious to them, and they were hurting. All of the children felt the pain of his passing, but because of their bond, they all felt each other's pain as well. In reality, the heartbreak was being multiplied.

Uncle Ed has asked for the impossible, they all thought. *How on earth are we ever supposed to find these two souls looking for each other?*

Zac spoke first. "How impossible does everyone think this is? It will be like looking for a needle in a haystack." Everyone just nodded their heads.

Matt spoke next. "Uncle Ed was confident that we would say the word, and we did, so we have to think about this. We can't let him down."

Mark nodded. "That's why he was always so special to us. Somehow, he knew we would be the ones to help him, not even knowing what or how at the time. He was always the one special person for us, wasn't he?"

Everyone nodded in agreement again.

Zeke continued, "Where do we start? I want to help ... but how do we start?"

"We'll have to wait for another dream or a sign. Don't you think?" Sarah asked.

Marguerite and Chase weren't saying anything. They were still so shaken by Ed's message, holding each other's hands tightly, trying to absorb everything that had happened.

"What do you think, Dad? How can we help? What do we do next?" Zac questioned.

Chase just lowered his head and couldn't say anything. Marguerite pulled him over to her and put her arm around him, kissing his head like she always did to try and soothe him.

They all gave them a few minutes to pull themselves back together.

Then Chase said something that stunned them all. He looked at Marguerite and she looked like she knew what he was going to say. She smiled. They both seemed to come back to life.

"This morning while reading the New York paper, I looked at an article about an artist who was having a showing this coming week in New York. I don't care about artwork, so I would have never read it, normally ... but I ended up reading it over three times. I didn't tell your mother, because I just dismissed it at the time. Then she told me that she couldn't stop thinking about an article she had read this morning, about an artist! Until we read Ed's letter to us, we would not have thought twice about the coincidence."

"Something about that article," Marguerite said, "like it was calling to us ... and until this moment, I didn't know what."

Zac said, "Do you truly feel that strongly about it?"

Marguerite and Chase just nodded in agreement.

Zeke asked, "Do you feel up for a road trip then?" Everyone smiled and nodded at the same time.

"We have to go find out," Matt told everyone. "We have to try, for Uncle Ed ... and all of us."

Marguerite and Sarah called their office, because each family had someone who made their arrangements for them. They told them everything they needed to know, and where in New York they wanted to stay.

In about two hours, all of the arrangements were made. A plane was being made ready to take them, a driver was set up in New York to pick them up at the airport, security (which the office insisted on) was hired, and a condo apartment was booked where they would be staying, right down the street from the art gallery. It even faced Central Park.

Everyone was excited to be traveling to the States again. They rarely got there anymore, and when they did go, they went to Pennsylvania to stay at their house near Marguerite's family.

This trip was more urgent. They were on a mission and hoped they weren't too late. Uncle Ed needed them, and they had to be ready. They just didn't know at the time what they were getting ready for.

Everyone was all packed and ready to go. They phoned their spouses and explained what was happening.

As they boarded the private jet, it brought back memories of how they used to travel with Chase, being on tour all the time. They always felt so lucky to be given that opportunity, and while it sounded like a great life, they were never spoiled. It was, in fact, a very lonely life for them, and they always felt it with their mother. Marguerite missed Chase so much whenever he was gone. Their lives were far from normal, and they cherished every moment they had when they were together.

29
At David's

David and Mia walked hand in hand back to his condo. They had hardly spoken two words to each other on the way back. They were both desperately trying to figure out what had just happened.

The feelings that rushed through them and had almost taken over their whole bodies scared them to the point of confusion and distress. However, they were feelings of tremendous love ... but love for whom? How could this be happening?

It couldn't be love between Mia and David. They just met a day ago!

How could they have feelings so strong about each other?

They both silently admitted that they were drawn to each other, and were definitely attracted, but this went beyond that. It was like they were feeling love for two other people and not for themselves.

Mia went to the window that had her mesmerized from the moment she walked into David's condo, and just stared out ... feeling numb.

David spoke, "Do you want to talk about it or try and process it more first?"

Mia turned facing him. "I don't know how to process it. To process the feelings that seemed to take over my body and mind ... now I said it out loud ... why did I say that out loud?" She felt upset for saying what was on her mind. "You're going to think I'm losing my mind. I'm scared that, at this very moment, you'll run away from me ... when that is the last thing I want." He could see the distress on her face.

"That's the first thing I'm trying to process," she said. "How can I have finally found someone, only to lose them because of what's going on? It's so crazy to even talk about it, and the last two days have been just as crazy!"

David looked down, blushing and not able to look at her, but this time around, Mia couldn't accept that.

"I need you to look at me, David. So I know you are not thinking the worst about me."

David shook his head, and finally looked directly at her. "I am never going to run away from you, so don't even think that. I knew the minute we met, I could never leave your side. I'm going to say it out loud for you now. I've never felt so comfortable around anyone in my whole life ... like I feel when I'm with you. I don't know what it is, but that's what you do for me.

"Let's talk about what we do know," he continued. "We know we're both attracted to each other. We know we're both at ease around each other. We know we don't want to leave each other. We know we don't want to ruin our relationship, and are scared about what happened because of that. We don't understand what happened to us but both feel it has something to do with us. So ... did I make you feel any better ... if only about us?"

Mia had tears falling from her beautiful big brown eyes. David went right to her and held her. She wrapped her arms around him, holding onto him gratefully.

"So, where do we go from here?" he asked. "Do you want to tell me what exactly you felt first?"

"No! You go first," Mia replied.

"Okay ... but again, I am not and will not run away from you. Do you understand that?"

Mia nodded her head. "Yes."

David tried to compose himself and figure out what he felt so that he could tell her. He turned, and walked away, and then turned again and began pacing in front of her, still trying to gather his thoughts so he could tell her what happened.

"When you said 'prerogative,' it meant something. I felt it meant something ... or at least it should have meant something, but not to me. It meant something to someone else. I can't wrap my head around it. I don't understand at all, but I felt something ... like my stomach dropping. It shocked me."

"How confusing is this?" she said, frustrated. "I felt something too, but don't know what."

He nodded. "It shook me, but I don't know why! Prerogative means something, but I don't know to whom."

"That about sums it up for me!"

He stopped pacing and shrugged. "Would you like to take a crack at it now?"

Mia just looked at David, who was now looking down at the floor. Before she said another word, she went to him and grabbed his face with her two hands, forcing him to look at her. She then kissed his lips. At that moment, she felt she needed to kiss him and to feel his lips kissing her back. She wanted to see if she felt any comfort in his kiss.

He looked at her and kissed her again, wondering if she could help him. He placed his hands on her waist as he responded to her kiss, and the feel of his hands on her skin gave Mia her answer.

Yes, he was able to help comfort her, and yes, she could help him.

Mia asked David, "How can we feel this about each other when we just met?"

"Are you worried we're going too fast? Or if these feelings are real?"

She shrugged. "Maybe it's just that I waited so long to find someone I truly connected with ... and finally found that connection with you. Is it supposed to be like this?"

David was silent, trying to gather his thoughts on what had happened that day and how he was feeling. He wanted to make sure that he didn't scare her away and wanted to make sure he was sincere and honest about what he felt he had to tell her.

"We have just asked about fifty questions in the last thirty minutes, and most of those questions, I don't have answers for. The few answers I do have, I'll tell you. These feeling are very real to me. I'm not worried that we're going too fast and I'm not confused. I'm sure about how I feel and what I feel for you. Mia, I have been waiting to meet someone who I feel so connected to, and you're the one. I am so sure of it. I knew when I found someone that I was supposed to be with that it would hit me like a knockout punch, and that's what you did for me."

Waiting, as if to process everything David had just told her, Mia turned away, looking down before responding. She then looked back at him, with an enormous teasing smile on her face. "So, I knocked you out? Hmm! I like that!"

David couldn't control himself anymore. He took her in his arms and planted the biggest, most passionate kiss on her, and Mia responded with sighs of approval and happiness.

He finally released her from his arms. "Let's sleep on it. Maybe something else will happen, or maybe our thoughts will be clearer tomorrow. Please ... let me love you tonight. Will you accept me as I am? Right now, standing before you? All painted up and scruffy looking? Will you take me as I am?"

Mia just took him by the hand and led him up to her room, where she showed him that she did accept him as he was, paint and all.

30. The Arrival

The Martins all arrived at the New York airport, where their driver and security team were waiting to pick them up. The driver and guard sat in front, while the seven of them sat in the back seats of the massive SUV. They wanted to travel together in the same car, and did not want to split up. There was a second driver in another car, which carried another guard and all their luggage.

During the forty-minute trip from the airport, they were all anxious to get to their condo, and felt it through their bond. They tried to defuse their anxiety by watching where they were going and trying to take in all the sites in the city, passing by landmarks and commenting whenever one noticed something odd or entertaining.

Finally, they arrived at the building and entered, acknowledging the doorman who was dressed in a uniform like a bellman at a lavish hotel. Building security was waiting for them at the big entrance desk. Everyone had been alerted and was aware of their impending arrival. Even after many years, Chase and his family were still well-known and popular. Their fans had remained loyal to him, and all loved him.

To say that the staff were excited that they would now be tenants in their building was an understatement. Everyone was waiting by the desk for them to arrive. The security-team manager introduced himself and went over some routine protocols and safety measures, making sure that the Martins were fully aware of everything around them. The London office had selected that particular building because it was one of the safest in

New York. The Martins were used to this. It was how they'd lived their whole lives. Chase and Marguerite were always worried about their children and made sure they were safe, just like Marguerite's adoptive parents, Joe and Mary, always worried about her and Chase when she was on the road with him. Joe and Mary were concerned when the children were born all the same.

They got into the elevator, where the guard showed them how to use the key and up they went to the penthouse! It had a garden terrace, which had beautiful flowers planted in pots everywhere and big outdoor furniture. That's where Marguerite went first. As soon as the door opened, she saw all the colors and the flowers and went right to them. Chase just smiled, knowing she would head there first. She loved eating outside in the summer, and loved planting her flowers all around the patio at their home.

They all followed her to the terrace, mesmerized at the view of the city, and just around the terrace, they noticed a spectacular view of Central Park. It seemed to bring them all peace. With the beautiful views, they knew that they were going to spend a lot of time sitting outside.

Once they came back into the penthouse, they finally noticed how beautiful and massive the place was! The office had informed them of finding a suitable place, and that it would accommodate all of their needs, and all of them, but they had outdone themselves. There was even a separate area off the foyer where security could settle in.

The furniture was, for the most part, comfortable. There were TVs hanging on the walls in every room. The kitchen was large, with a massive snack bar, and the dining-room table could seat at least sixteen people. Massive was a word they all used a lot, when they were trying to take it all in.

Everyone picked what bedroom they wanted to stay in, and once unpacked, they ventured out to grab dinner somewhere. They wanted to walk a little, because it was so nice out and there were restaurants everywhere on their street. They took a walk and looked around. They finally found a suitable place to eat, as security followed behind them. They didn't think they would have an issue. Chase's popularity was at its peak over fifty years ago. They felt that no one would even know who they were anymore.

Those thoughts didn't last long, as a photographer happened to notice them all walking around and knew immediately who they were. He started snapping pictures of them, and Chase began to get upset. The security guard went and asked him to kindly stop taking the pictures, when Chase intervened. "You can take them, but please don't publish them until we leave the city. We will even let you take more if you could just wait."

Marguerite felt really touched by what Chase had just done. When they were young and out to dinner with their brothers and sisters, no matter how many times they were interrupted, they were always so gracious to whoever wanted to meet them. It was the one thing she loved about all of the brothers and sisters. They were always so grateful and gracious to everyone. It brought back so many memories.

Zac took over and said to the photographer, "Do you want to give us your card, so we can call you for more photos? We *will* call you. If my father told you he would let you take more, he means it, and will never go back on his word."

The sincerity of Zac and Chase made the man feel like they *would* call him, so he gave them his card and Zac took it immediately, shaking the man's hand, securing the deal.

Then they all smiled at him, and said thank you one at a time, which impressed the photographer. "My name is Jim," he yelled, as they all walked by. They looked back, waving, while Sarah said, "We'll be seeing you again, Jim!"

31 Happiness

Mia woke up in bed smiling. She felt so happy, and when she opened her eyes, she saw David lying next to her, just staring at her, "Why are you staring at me?"

"I can't seem to take my eyes off of you. I'm feeling very happy right now!" He smiled back at her.

Mia fully understood what David was saying. She snuggled next to him. He then wrapped her in his arms. "I'm going to get all of this paint off of you one way or another!" Mia told him while laughing, which made David laugh too.

"There you go. Trying to change me already," he said, while they both smiled, hugging each other tightly. "How did you sleep?"

She took his face in her hands, and kissed him. That was her answer, and he was pleased that she had slept well.

"Do you want to get up now?" she asked. "I'll make you something to eat before we go back to the gallery."

He shook his head and kissed Mia passionately. She knew they wouldn't be getting up just yet.

They stayed in bed for a little longer and then got up. They knew there was plenty of work to be done, and Mia made something for breakfast before they headed out.

She was standing in the kitchen, just staring out the window and looking at the skyline, when David came up behind her and wrapped his arms around her waist, kissing her neck. They were both so happy at that moment.

"We have to go, or we'll never have time to fool around later," he said, smiling from ear to ear. He then closed his eyes and buried his head in her shoulder.

32

I Know You – Or Do I?

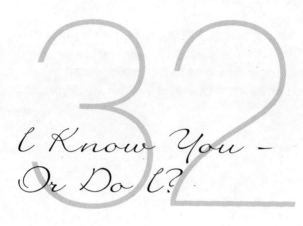

Walking through the foyer of their complex, Mia and David saw a couple entering and approaching the guard at the desk, with bagels and pastry. The woman handed some wrapped treat to the guard, who was clearly pleased at her thoughtfulness.

David and Mia didn't pay much attention to either one of them as they walked by, but just then ... something happened again, just like the day before. This time they didn't see anything though. They just felt something when that couple had walked by. They looked back and saw that the couple were looking at them as well. It was obvious that they had felt something too. They looked at each other, clearly thrown by the sensation.

David finally broke the awkward silence and asked, "Do I know you from somewhere?" He reached out his hand to introduce himself.

Zac and Sarah were so shaken that they could hardly speak, and knew that all of their brothers and parents had just felt something too ... through the bond they all shared.

Zac finally replied, "Not that I know of. We only just arrived last night from London." When he said London, David felt something.

"You came in from London? Are you here on business?" David asked.

"No, we came to see an art show down the street. We haven't been to New York in years, so we thought we would just take a few days to enjoy the city. I'm so sorry. I'm Zac Martin, and this is my sister, Sarah."

At that moment, David thought he was going to pass out. Mia saw the look on his face, and knew he was feeling something again, but this time she didn't feel anything.

"I told you you would see me again!" David told them.

Just then, his face turned all red. "What made me say that? I don't know why I said that to you. I don't know you!" He looked incredibly flustered. "Please, I apologize to the both of you. I have to go!" He took Mia's hand and walked away so fast that it was almost like he was running out of the building.

Sarah and Zac knew exactly what had just happened, and they couldn't move a muscle. All of a sudden, the elevator doors opened and Zeke, Matt, and Mark came running towards them.

"What happened? We felt you! Mom and Dad said to come down and get you.

"Let's go to Mom and Dad, *right now!*" Sarah said quickly. "We need to see them!"

Chase and Marguerite were waiting by the elevator door. As soon as it opened, Sarah ran to her father and Zac walked into his mother's embrace.

Marguerite immediately said, "Let's all calm down and figure out what happened. We all felt you, but we couldn't tell what you were feeling. Come sit down." She then dragged Zac by the hand to the seating area, just like she used to when he was a child and would have a bad dream.

Zac said, "We just met someone and his girlfriend. I think it was the artist whose work we're going to see. When we passed them by in the lobby, I felt something and so did Sarah. We both froze and just looked at each other. Then the couple stopped and turned back to look at us. We knew they felt something when we passed them by too. He asked if I knew him from somewhere, and I just told him no, we came to see an art show and were from London. Then I introduced Sarah and myself to him. He looked point blank at me and said, 'I told you you would see me again!' We couldn't believe what we'd just heard."

As soon as Marguerite and Chase heard that, they both began feeling distraught. They were rattled, and so were the kids. They were all upset.

"There's more," Sarah continued. "After he said that to Zac, he got upset and added, 'What made me say that?' He didn't know why he even said that to us. He said that he didn't even know us and apologized."

"He was so upset, he all but ran out of the building," Zac said. "Then the guys came to get us and found us just standing there, flustered."

Marguerite and Chase just sat with their heads down. Matt finally said, "What is it? Tell us."

Chase reminded them of the letter their uncle had written, with his request to have it opened when they all heard the word 'prerogative.'

"In that letter, he mentioned a few times that he would see us all again," Chase said. "He said he was positive of it. He was trying to let you know! It was him. I never thought in a million years this would happen. I hoped for his sake, and went along, but thought it was so far-fetched ... the whole idea that he and Lilli would somehow meet again. I hoped it would happen for him. He waited for so many years. He deserves to be happy and to have love in his life again."

"What's our plan?" Zeke asked. "Where do we go from here? Do we stay on plan and attend the show? Do we all go at once? It might not be a good idea to bombard them like that. It will scare them as much as it's scaring all of us right now."

Chase and Marguerite nodded their heads, admitting it would scare them. Chase looked at his children. "Maybe we should reach out to them and arrange for a dinner or something to try and talk it out. We can convince them that we know what's happening, and might be able to help them out ... if they will agree to it."

Mark added, "Mom, Dad, we could introduce you both to them, and see if they get a reaction out of your presence."

"I think that, once they see you two, it will be unbearable to them," Sarah agreed, "so we will have to help them out and try and explain all that's happening."

So that was the plan. The couple had already met Zac and Sarah, so it was agreed that Mark and Matt would go to the second showing. They thought that they would let him at least enjoy the opening night before startling him again.

33
At the Gallery

Mia took David's hands and held them to her body. "What just happened? Something just happened to you in particular. I felt like I knew those two people. I know you felt like you knew them too, but how?"

"I don't know, and I don't know why I told them that I was going to see them again. Why did I even say that?" He continued, rambling and asking questions. "How more confusing could this get for us? What's going on? Am I going crazy? Am I losing my mind?"

"You are not crazy. That would mean that I am too, and the two of us can't be going through the same thing at the same time. Now *that* would be crazy!"

"Did you hear them say that they were from London, and in town for an art show down the street? That would be *my* art show they are planning to see. Why would they come from London for *my* art show?" he continued with amazement.

Mia tried to compose herself. "I am certain that this all means something. In time, it will reveal itself to us, but for now, I believe we just have to keep going on with our lives as much as we can. We'll talk out every experience that happens to us and try to make sense out of it all. We'll find out what's happening to us here and why. We'll do it together and get through this together!"

David needed to hear something logical at that moment, and by looking at Mia, he realized that she was trying to help him. She wanted to fix it and it made him feel love for her.

"What you just said makes more sense to me than anything that has happened to us in the last few days. Thank you, Mia. Thank you for agreeing to be the hostess at my show. Thank you for staying with me. Thank you for helping me," David said, making sure she knew how grateful he was. "Most importantly," he added, while looking down at the floor like he always did when speaking to her, "thank you for loving me. I know you do, because I love you!" He then lifted his head so their eyes could meet.

Mia could only smile and nod her head at his statement, declaring their love for each other.

David smiled. "I know we will figure this out, and I knew all along you would help me. You're keeping me calm. I'm happy because of you. Remember when I first asked you to be the hostess for my show, and I told you that I didn't think I could do it without you by my side? I meant it then, and now I mean it more than ever."

Mia dropped her gaze from his eyes, because she didn't want him to see tears forming. He then lifted her head back up, placing his finger under her chin, and said, "I will let you see me cry and when you do, it will be because I'm so happy, and I want to see your tears because you're so happy. Don't turn away from me. Let me see them! Let me see everything about you. Let me be the one you can show yourself to!"

With those words, they both let go of their tears, which ran down their cheeks. They were happy tears, as they both now knew how they felt about each other. They had a plan, and it was to go on as normally as possible. They were going to talk to each other, if they felt anything odd happening, and no matter how scary it was ... they were going to love each other regardless.

First Showing

The first showing of David's artwork was a huge success. People were waiting in line just to get into the gallery, and he was glowing all night. The gallery looked exquisite that evening too, with everyone walking around enjoying glasses of wine and admiring David's work. He had a very big following, with many people just waiting for the exhibit to open. He kept Mia close by his side, because after all, she was his girlfriend. When she wasn't holding his hand, she was walking the room and speaking to everyone there, listening to people commenting on his paintings. She helped out as much as she could. David watched her from the corner of his eyes the whole night. If he wasn't standing by her, he kept a close eye out for her. He couldn't stop looking for her, always wanting to know how far away she was. He knew he was right when he thought he couldn't have done this without her. The press was also there, taking pictures of everyone. It was very exciting.

They both semi-enjoyed all of the attention, because of how shy David was, but most of all they both felt proud.

Mia felt proud of David and his work. Every time their eyes met, she flashed him the biggest smiles he had ever seen, and it was more special to her because ... well ... she felt David was hers now. Mia even managed to get most of the paint out of his blond curly hair and helped him pick out the tan summer suit he had on that night. She couldn't stop thinking about how hot he looked, and she smiled every time she saw him.

David felt so proud of Mia, and how she handled herself with all that was going on. She seemed to take right over and had no trouble interacting with so many people. He did need her by his side. She completed him somehow. He was glad that he'd asked her to bring that turquoise summer eyelet dress that left her shoulders bare when she was packing back in Pennsylvania. He knew she would look beautiful in it, with her short hair and the long earrings she paired them with to match. Her eyes seemed to sparkle every time they met his.

They sold so many paintings that night. After the gallery had closed, they got more paintings they had stored there and hung them on all of the open spaces left on the walls. They were at the gallery until midnight, setting up and getting ready for the second night.

They didn't expect the second night to be as busy though. Usually, the opening nights were the busiest. They felt they might be able to enjoy the show more in the nights to come. Once they were finished, they headed back to the condo, hand in hand.

They had been stressed, even though the show was very successful. They were tired from all the work it took setting up, worrying about the show being a success, and socializing with all of the people there.

It had to be more stressful to David, Mia thought. He was very shy and she felt it probably freaked him out having to talk to so many people that night.

Mia was right. When they got home, she asked him if he wanted a drink before heading to bed. He nodded his head, and she opened a bottle of wine, pouring two glasses for them. She sat at her favorite spot, looking over the skyline of the city. That somehow calmed her down.

She held her arms open for David, and he gladly walked right into them. He loved it when she would wrap her arms around him. They went over everything that happened during the show and laughed at some of the comments people were making.

Mia was worried that he wouldn't have enough paintings for the whole week, if they had another night like the one they just had. David wasn't worried. He had a barrage of paintings waiting in the wings to bring out when they needed more.

Mia was just staring at David.

David saw the expression on her face. "What is it? What are you thinking?"

"I was wondering how someone can be as talented as you are. How does that happen? You never really told me how you started painting. All those articles you mentioned annoyed you, because they wanted to know what inspired you to paint like that. Well, why do you paint with such color? What inspires you? Does it just come to you while you're looking at a canvas? Or do you already have an idea?"

David smiled. "Those are a lot of questions for this time of night. I will tell you right now that you inspire me. I already have tons of ideas for more paintings as soon as this show is over, and I started thinking about them the moment I met you. So, who knows? Maybe my next show will be dedicated to you, my wife!"

Mia's face just dropped, and she stared at David. *Did he just say, my wife?*

David realized what he'd just said, and he looked at her. "Why did I just say that? I called you my wife! Why? I wasn't thinking of you in that context, at least not yet." He saw her face fall a bit. "Oh … I'm sorry. Please accept my apology. I didn't mean to insult you. I just meant that I felt something strange again. I think that's why I called you my wife. I wish we could figure out what's happening here!"

Mia realized that David was becoming distressed over what just happened, so she took him by the hand and said, "Tell me what you felt at the time. Let's try and see what triggered you saying that."

"I was just feeling warmly towards you, at that moment. Then I felt like I drifted off … I heard myself speaking, but they weren't my words. I came back around when I said, 'my wife.'"

He was still looking at her, trying to search her face to see if he was scaring her.

Mia noticed. "I'm not going to run away, David. I did say that we were going to talk it out every time something like this happens. We will figure it out and we will do it together, okay?"

David was relieved and remembered her promise that they would find out what was happening to them and why. Mia then took him by the hand, and they headed off to bed, where she just held him, trying to get him to relax. They didn't talk more about it that night. She felt that he just needed to calm down, and left it for another time. Something strange was happening though, and they needed to find out what, and why it was happening to them.

35
Second Night – Second Showing

Matt and Mark were ready to attend David's second show. They were anxious all day and everyone was feeling it. The whole family walked through Central Park, and shopped in most of the boutiques around their building. The boys bought gifts for their children and spouses. They felt that they had to keep busy or else they were going to lose it.

They sat on the benches in Central Park, taking in the beautiful sunny day. People passed by them and they spent some time just watching the crowd until it was almost time to go. They found an Italian restaurant and Marguerite and Chase met with the manager to order some food for their dinner that night. They didn't want anything too heavy, because of how late the dinner would be, so she ordered a big Caesar salad and some chicken Française, with fresh green beans sautéed in butter and lemon. They had plenty to drink at the condo, and stopped at the bakery near the hotel to pick out a cake for dessert. The boys wanted chocolate and Marguerite wanted a white cake, so they compromised with a chocolate and vanilla checkerboard cake, with rich chocolate buttercream frosting. Then they all suddenly realized that the only reason their mother had argued over the cake was to keep their minds off of what they had to do. Just like that, dinner was settled and it was almost time for Mark and Matt to go.

Mark and Matt waited until almost the end of the showing, not wanting to create a commotion if anything happened when the artist possibly recognized them. With much anticipation, they finally headed out. Everyone back at home was just waiting for them to come back, and kept open minds to see if they could feel anything. If it got bad or if the artist felt something towards them, their instructions were to invite him back to dinner at their penthouse.

"Reassure them both that we can help them," Chase had told his sons.

As they stood at the elevator door, waiting to leave, Chase and Marguerite experienced a warm moment between them. At that moment, they looked around at all of their children and felt happy to have them all together. It was almost like their lives were passing right in front of them. Chase smiled warmly at Marguerite and told her how much he loved her, and she did the same, saying, "You are still the very air I breathe."

Chase then looked around at each of them, and turned directly to his wife, "Look what we did!" The children got worried when he said that. Chase and Marguerite felt it, but just looked at them all and said, "Don't worry. It isn't our time yet. We are not done. You will know ... just like we will."

The siblings felt sad because they didn't know how they were ever going to let go of their parents, and they all felt it at the same time ... even their mother and father. Automatically, they all moved in to hug their parents, surrounding them and demonstrating the love they had for one another.

The elevator door opened and it was time for the M&Ms to leave. Mark and Matt didn't want to go; they wanted to stay with their family. Chase told his sons, "Go. You have to help these people. We promised Uncle Ed we would." They nodded, released their hold on their family, and off they went.

Matt and Mark walked down the street to the gallery, pausing before they opened the door to go in. To say they were anxious and nervous about going into the show was an understatement. They were hoping to see their uncle, whom they had loved all of their lives, and possibly meet his wife. Even after all these years, they were still shocked by the revelation that he was even married.

Matt and Mark took a deep breath, opened the door, and walked in.

The show was busy. There were a lot of people walking around looking at all of the paintings. They copied the crowd, trying to act normal. They noticed how colorful his paintings were and came across one that was very familiar. Not the painting itself, but the colors he used were enticing. There were blues and yellows in an abstract form on the canvas. They looked at each other and wondered why the painting spoke to them.

The boys talked about it, and both agreed that it reminded them of something, but at the moment, they couldn't think of what. They just left it and kept walking, looking at the other paintings.

As they were looking around, Mia came over and introduced herself to them. She noticed that they were identical twins and extremely good-looking, making her almost stare at them. Their light brown hair was wavy but neatly combed, laying just above their ears. They each wore dress pants and a polo shirt under a summer suit coat—Mark's was navy and Matt's was tan. She shook their hands and they introduced themselves.

"I'm Matt Martin, and this is my brother Mark."

Mark chimed right in, and said to his brother, "Thank you! I think I can introduce myself! We're not 5 again!" The three laughed. "Just because he's a few minutes older than me, he thinks he's my spokesperson and protector," Mark said, smiling at his brother. "In all honesty though, it never gets old and I'm only kidding with him."

Mia asked, "Have you met David yet?" They both shook their heads. "Come and let me introduce you to him."

Matt and Mark got very nervous at that moment. They didn't know what would happen, and they knew everyone was waiting for a report. They looked around and saw that almost everyone had left the show, as it was close to closing time.

Mia made small talk, as she escorted them over to David. "Are you in the market for a painting? Did any of them catch your eye?"

They couldn't even reply; they were too anxious to meet David. As they got closer, they noticed that he was standing and talking to someone else. They waited for a while and that increased their anxiety.

Mark leaned into Matt, and said, "Deep breaths, brother. Deep breaths."

Finally, David became free, and Mia called him over.

36 Reminiscing

"David, do you have time to meet some new people?" Mia asked.

David walked right over and kissed her, smiling at her. She returned the smile. Matt and Mark could see how happy they were.

Matt held his hand out to shake David's, and said, "It's a pleasure to meet you. I'm Matt Martin." This time he let Mark introduce himself.

Mark held out his hand. "Hello, I am Mark Martin."

David looked at the both of them and couldn't believe how alike they were. Then something hit him, and they all saw it. When he looked back at them, he could see they were rattled too.

"The M&Ms. I am so happy to see you again!" He hugged them both enthusiastically.

Mia was stunned. She knew something was happening but didn't know just what.

Matt and Mark had tears streaming down their faces. They returned David's hug. At that moment, they saw and felt like they were hugging their uncle Ed, not David.

When David released them, they both noticed the color had drained from his face. He was speechless. He wanted to pass out, and they all knew it. He backed away from Matt and Mark, and just stared at them. He saw the tears running down their faces, and it confused him. Then he looked at Mia. She was holding onto him, as he looked like he was going to faint.

107

In the meantime, back at the penthouse, everyone knew something was going on but didn't know exactly what. Chase, as usual, just paced back and forth until Sarah said, "Dad, if you don't stop, we are going to have to tie you down!" That relieved some of the tension in the room, and they all laughed. Marguerite opened her arms and he immediately walked into her embrace.

"After all of these years, I will never get tired of you holding me," Chase said to his wife.

"After all of these years, I am just so happy we still need each other," she told Chase, as she shared a warm kiss with him.

"I wish I wasn't so old," he said to her quietly. "I want to make love to you the way we used to. I always wanted to show you just how much I loved you."

She replied, "I always knew you loved me, and it wasn't only because we could make love to each other."

"I am so sorry, Mam!" Tears began forming in Chase's eyes.

"Sorry?" she paused, looking surprised at his apology. "For what?" she asked, smiling and trying not to upset him as she stroked his face and hair.

"Sorry for leaving you all of that time when I was touring. I left you with five children all alone."

"Chase, you have nothing to be sorry for. I loved our life together, with you being gone and all. I had lots of help and we spoke a million times a day when you were gone. It was like you were still with us at home." He couldn't even meet her eye.

"Look at me," Marguerite said, as his head was down, kissing her both hands.

When their eyes met, it felt like they were young again. All of those feelings and emotions surfaced just like it was yesterday.

"I think we are both feeling sentimental being here with our children the past few days," she said. "Memories of when they were young and just so sweet. We haven't had this happen for so long and our feelings for Ed have been brought to the surface again too."

Chase could only nod his head in agreement. Zac, Zeke, and Sarah could do nothing but look at their parents with great affection. They always said the boys and Sarah amazed them, but at that moment, their mom and dad were the ones who amazed *them*.

They all felt the love their father had for their mother, and were worried about how they could ever let them go. They were looking over at the two of them, watching their father kiss their mother's hands, so gently. It was as if she were the most precious thing on earth for him. The warmth they all felt made them smile and feel so happy about their lives with their parents. They had supported their father by taking care of their mother when he was away. This was from the time they were young, going to the studio with their father to 'work,' traveling with him on tour... How lucky they felt at that moment.

37
Still in Shock

David just stared at Matt and Mark, still in shock and visibly upset!

Finally, he was able to speak, "Do you know why I just called you the M&Ms? Please tell me if you do."

Matt and Mark were trying to compose themselves before they could even speak. They felt like they were just embraced by the uncle they loved so much and had missed for the past twenty-three years.

Mark nodded. "Not only do we know what that was about, but we know what's happening to you." He looked at Mia. "And to you also."

Matt said, "Would you please join our family and us tonight for dinner? We can help you. I know we can. We have been waiting for this for twenty-three years now. You already met my brother Zac and sister, Sarah. Please come and join us and we can help you. This is very important to so many people. We will explain once we're all gathered together."

Mark added, "We know this is upsetting you both, because you can't understand what's happening. You don't know us, but in reality, you *do* know us. Please dig deep within your souls, and see if you can trust us. We would have no reason to want to hurt or upset you. I think you can feel that much, at least."

David looked at Mia who was still holding him up, "I think we should go with them. Someone has to know what's happening and maybe they can help us out."

Mia agreed and spoke to Matt and Mark, "We will come to dinner, to talk about this. We know you're in our building. Tell us where and what time, and we'll come over."

Matt and Mark both shook David's hand and left with the plan in place. Matt turned as he was going out the door, "Thank you for trusting us. We know how concerned you are. I'm trying not to say 'scared', but I guess that would be the right word to use."

Everyone waiting at the penthouse knew they were on their way back. When the elevator door opened, they saw their two brothers, sister, and parents standing and waiting for them. Matt and Mark just had the most amazing experience they could ever think of, and that is how they started the conversation.

"Their names are David and Mia, and they agreed to come to dinner!" Matt said. "We spoke to Mia first. She came over to us when we were looking at some of the paintings, and she introduced herself. We didn't feel like we knew her and that would be correct, right? We didn't know Uncle Ed's wife, so we didn't have that connection to her," Matt said.

Then Mark continued. "She brought us over to meet David, and we shook his hand, and then he just blurted out 'The M&Ms. I am so happy to see you!' He came right over to us and hugged us. We all but lost it, because at that moment we felt like we were hugging Uncle Ed ... not David!"

Everyone's mouths were hanging open, not knowing what to say or how to react to what they were just told. How could this happen? How could two souls wait for each other and look for each other to be together again?

The worse part was figuring out how they were ever going to be able to tell these two people about Ed and Lilli.

All of those questions had to be answered soon, because in less than an hour, they were having two guests, whom they had promised to help.

38
Meeting Everyone

Mia and David hardly spoke at the end of the show. Mia didn't know how she could help David. She was thankful that they were both busy enough, placing more paintings on the walls, to not think about it. David, however, was eager to leave and just couldn't wait to find out what was happening to them both. As the time approached, she said, "Do you want to bring some wine or something else to dinner?"

He smiled at her and that calmed her down a little. "Yes, good idea. I have a case of some Pinot here somewhere."

They grabbed four bottles and headed out, locking up the gallery. They both felt anxious and yet somehow excited to meet everyone. They had no idea what to expect, and it kept them on edge. When they arrived, David took Mia's hand, and after being cleared by the front-desk guard, they went up the elevator to the penthouse for dinner.

Everyone was waiting for them except Marguerite and Chase. They were going to come out later, because they truly thought that, once Ed saw his brother and sister, it would trigger something even greater than what they had experienced so far. They did not want to startle David and Mia that badly.

Matt and Mark decided that they would greet them initially, being that they were the ones who had invited them in the first place. They waited in the foyer for the door to open, and once it did, it seemed to calm them down. They shook David and Mia's hands again, and told them that they were very happy to see them.

They took the wine and thanked them for bringing it, then invited them into the living room to meet Zeke, Zac, and Sarah. Mia was stunned when she saw them. There was another set of twins in front of her! They were introduced and she couldn't help staring. Everyone saw her and just smiled.

"We get that all the time," Zeke said. "What are the odds that our parents would have two sets of twins?" They laughed about it, and they all seemed to calm down.

"Are you all brothers then? Because Matt and Mark don't look anything like Zac and Zeke!" Mia asked.

Matt said, "It was a common joke with our aunts and uncles, about how Zac and Zeke looked exactly like our father, and then when we were born, they said my mother got him back ... and that's why we look just like her." They were smiling.

Sarah was shaking and almost hiding behind her brothers. She had a hold on Zac's shirt, and he coaxed her out from behind him, taking her hand reassuringly and motioning her towards them.

Everyone noticed that. "Hello again," she said. "I'm Sarah Martin-Foster." She shook their hands and regrouped, taking over. "Why don't we all sit down for a few minutes, and then we can open that wine. I think we need it!"

David, however, seemed off. He was staring at Sarah and shaking subtly. No one had noticed it, because they were all too busy with Mia. He could not move much and he looked suddenly pale.

Mia took him gently by the hand, knowing something else had just happened. "Let's sit down and talk about it."

The boys and Sarah were looking at him, silently hoping that he knew who they were.

"The Zs, M&Ms, and my Sarah," David said, in a hushed voice. He was remembering.

Sarah couldn't help getting emotional. Her eyes filled with tears as she went and knelt down in front of David, knowing it really wasn't David. She was kneeling down in front of Uncle Ed. She took both his hands, and said, "You remember ... don't you?"

He nodded his head, looking over at Mia.

Zac went over and practically picked Sarah up. "Let's give him some room to breathe." Sarah retreated with her brother, sitting down—not wanting to overwhelm him.

They knew it was then time to bring their parents out. Chase and Marguerite felt it was time too, having felt what was going on. They couldn't wait to see them. The boys and Sarah all stood as they heard them coming out from their room.

They looked at Mia and David, and Zac said, "We'd like you to meet our parents. They have been waiting to see you both."

Chase and Marguerite walked into the living room and everyone turned back to see David and Mia's reaction.

All of a sudden, Mia looked at Chase and ran to him "Chase! I have been waiting to see you. I need to thank you for taking care of Ed all of those years!"

Chase knew at that moment that he was holding Lilli, and everyone else knew it too. David, however, was stunned. Then all eyes went towards Marguerite. David's eyes filled with tears. "Mam!" He almost shouted as he rushed into her arms.

There were tears running down his face as well as Marguerite's. She was holding her brother Ed, and he was holding his sister Mam. They felt comfort for some reason, and couldn't explain why, as David and Mia came back around to being David and Mia again.

Chase nodded to them. "I'm Chase Martin, and this is my wife, Marguerite. Why don't we all sit down and talk about this? We have much to tell you. In fact, we might not be able to tell you all about what's happening in one night, but it would be a start."

Mia said to David, "You just called her 'Mam'. Mr. Martin ... you just introduced your wife as Marguerite."

Chase nodded. "That was my name for her. It represents her initials. Marguerite Angeli-Martin. Mam! When we were getting married, we were thinking about her new name. I suggested Mam, and I asked her if she would mind. She didn't mind at all. Only I call her that now ... but so did my best friend, Ed Mehan. He was a brother to me, and Mam was a sister to him."

Having said all of that, Chase took Marguerite's hand, just like he always did when he was feeling warmly towards her, and brought it to his lips to kiss. Then he placed her hand on his cheek to feel her.

He looked back at both Mia and David, "I know something is happening to you both, and you can't understand it, but we can explain. You might want to run away from us screaming though. It will be one heck of a story to tell your children. My children are living it now. We need you both to try and keep an open mind, which will be very hard to do, once you know what is happening. You will not believe it. It is so far-fetched and I told my brother that ... when we talked about it over twenty-three years ago.

"Mam and I both know this will scare you ... supernaturally. But we want you to know that we are always here for you ... if you have anything you would like to talk about, no matter what time, no matter what day ... and even if we are no longer around, my sons and daughter will be here for you too. They will help you and make that commitment to you also." Chase said looking around at his family.

They all were nodding their heads, simultaneously feeling the sorrow of knowing their parents were in the twilight of their lives. They knew it was only a matter of time, especially now that Lilli and Ed had found each other. Sarah knew this was the 'something' that had kept them alive for so long. They had been waiting for something to happen and it was happening now.

Sarah stood and said, "I am going to open that wine now. "

Marguerite agreed. "Good idea, my love. Thank you."

From the Beginning

Who they all were suddenly hit Mia. "I know who you are now!" They knew she wasn't speaking on behalf of Lilli. "You're Chase Martin! *The* Chase Martin ... of The Band 4."

Chase smiled at her and nodded his head in agreement.

Mia sat back in her chair, amazed at who she had just met. David looked at her, shocked that they were going to have dinner with Chase Martin of The Band 4, his beloved wife Marguerite, and their five children.

"You are legendary!" Mia continued. "Your music is still played everywhere, and the song you wrote for Mrs. Martin, 'It's the Little Things', has probably been played at every wedding for the past sixty years."

Chase again looked at his wife, and leaned towards her so that she could plant a kiss on his head. Mia thought they were the cutest couple in history, and the love they felt for each other was adorable. You could just feel it. Everyone was smiling and seemed to relax as Sarah arrived with wine for everyone.

Then Mia looked at Matt and Mark. "You are correct, by the way. You look just like your mother and Zac and Zeke look just like your father. Sarah, you look just like your mother too."

Everyone smiled and waited for Sarah to say something, which she did.

"I am adopted, actually," Sarah said out loud. This shocked both David and Mia, and it showed on their faces. "My birth mother was dying and she wanted me to have a good home, so she left me on their doorstep, somehow knowing they would keep me." Mia and David couldn't believe how much Sarah looked just like Mrs. Martin.

"Somehow she knew I belonged to them. They found her in a hospital and talked to her before she died. She happily signed the proper documents, turning me over to them and she held me one last time before she passed away. I have always felt like their daughter though, and always felt like a sister to my brothers. I knew in my heart they belonged to me ... all of them ... and that I belonged to them." Sarah was still emotional about it.

With that, the boys all went to Sarah and kissed her. They all told her they loved her, as did her mother and father. When they sat back down, they all reached for each other, forming a chain, just wanting to feel one another.

The warmth and love between them all amazed both David and Mia. At that point, with what they were seeing, they felt they had no reason to doubt anything they were about to hear from them.

As they all had their wine in hand, Chase stood and said, "To love, family, happiness, and to finding each other again." They all held their glasses in the air for the toast. They all drank, and then he sat down, took a deep breath, and tried to figure out where and how to begin. Finally, he just did.

"I am going to start at the beginning," he said, "and I am going to tell you a story filled with love, sorrow, and hope for a future.

"My best friend was Ed Mehan, who was like a brother to me, and over sixty-five years ago, when he was just starting out in the music industry, a producer named Lilli Parker called and asked him if he would write songs for a movie she wrote the screenplay for."

Mia interrupted Chase. "Wait a moment. Do you mean the Ed Mehan who won six Grammys and an Oscar? The same Ed Mehan who wrote some of the most beautiful love songs on the planet?"

Chase smiled. "Yes, *that* Ed Mehan. My brother."

He paused for a long moment, waiting for that to settle in. Then he picked up the story where he had left off.

"He and Lilli fell in love, but she didn't want that to happen because she was very ill and knew she was dying. She didn't want him to have that heartbreak so early in his life. He was 23 and Lilli was 35, which was another reason she did not want him to love her. Before she died, she agreed to marry him. He promised her, knowing she was going to die, that she would die in his arms. He promised never to leave her, and that is how she passed away ... with my brother holding her until she took her last breath.

Right before that, she made a promise to him that she would wait for him in heaven.

"She felt that God did not mean for their love to be cut so short. She felt that her soul would be able to wait for him, so they could be born again at the same time and somehow find each other again in the future. That plan was so far out there ... none of us believed it could happen. Ed wanted to hope that he would see her again and tried to believe her. After she passed away, he never found that kind of love again. It was a true, deep love ... binding them together forever.

"Ed passed away twenty-three years ago. Until this week, we never thought this could ever happen. None of us did."

David spoke, "Are you suggesting ... that we have the souls of Lilli Parker and Ed Mehan?"

They knew Mia and David couldn't believe what they'd just heard, which was expected, so Chase was prepared. He knew what to say to earn their trust. "Did either of you say the word 'prerogative' this week?"

Mia and David looked like they were going to pass out. They both took another big gulp out of their wine.

Chase continued. "That is how we knew you found each other. Lilli told Ed that they should have a catchword, a trigger. When the two people said that word ... if they truly had *their* souls ... it would trigger something within them. Maybe they would have some kind of feelings for each other or maybe they would finally recognize each other ... to let them know they were finally together again."

David and Mia both got up, not wanting to believe what they had just been told ... but believing it anyway. It explained all they had been feeling and seeing lately. They both remembered, when Mia had first said the word, feeling like they saw two other people when looking at each other.

"How could this be happening?" David asked. "I've never heard of anything like this before."

"Ed knew my entire family would find you, and be the ones to help you," Chase said, sounding much more convincing. "He was the most special person to my five children, as they were to him. If Mam and I weren't still around, instructions would be left for them, which would tell them somehow how to find you both. Before I get to that, I want to tell you this first.

"We have had similar things happen in our lives ... and we asked those same sorts of questions." David and Mia looked doubtful, but he continued,

"When I met my wife, I was thinking of leaving the band and my mates. They were also brothers to me. I cannot even describe the distress I was in. I wasn't sleeping or eating. I didn't want to tour anymore or write songs. I just felt lost. The night before I was going to go to the studio to quit, I met Marguerite. I was in a coffee shop, and she walked over to me, and her first words to me were, 'I can feel your anxiety six tables away. You should stay away from caffeine.'" He gave Marguerite a look and smiled.

She smiled back and shook her head. "When I went back to my table, I just slumped in my chair and couldn't even believe I'd just done that. I wanted to hide."

Chase continued, "What you are both missing, I think, is that Mam could *feel* my anxiety. She *felt* me. When I met her, she was only on holiday in London. She was from Pennsylvania and had to leave soon. So a few days later, when she was distressed about leaving, I *felt* her distress also. I knew what she meant then. She had felt me, and I finally felt her. We can feel each other all the time, to this day. I always knew when she was upset, and she always knew what was wrong with me. No matter how far away I was touring, we always knew. I felt her morning sickness when she was pregnant with the boys. I felt her when she was very sick, and I almost lost her. We always feel each other's love for one another. Now, you may say any couple would feel that, but it's not the same ... because what we feel is multiplied."

Chase took a sip of his drink and then continued. "Even when she was in labor, I felt only a small part of the pain she was going through, but it almost dropped me to my knees. I was forever grateful for everything she went through to give birth to my sons, all four of them. When she dreams, I feel her and I wake up immediately with her. I could go on and on, but there is more. Mam was very ill in the hospital in Italy. She almost lost her life. She was in surgery for sixteen hours. The doctor told us to send for her parents and our sons, because they did not know if she was going make it." Chase stopped and looked down at the hands he was holding, not knowing if he could continue retelling the past.

Zac took over, "We knew our mother was in trouble. We were all home in London. We *felt* our father's distress. Our grandparents were staying with us. We knew they were getting a plane ready to take us to them. We all packed our suitcases and just waited in my room for them to get us and tell us we were going to Italy. We don't know how we knew, but we did.

When they did come in, they were shocked to see us already prepared. We had been feeling our parents for years, but had never told them. We could feel our mother's happiness whenever she was with our father. We knew we had to get to him, because he needed us, and we were determined to take care of them both until my mother was well again. We were 5 and 9 at the time."

At this point, Mia and David were mesmerized by what they were hearing.

Chase continued, "When they got to the hospital, I felt them arriving before they ever got to the room. I looked at my brothers and sisters and said, 'The boys are here'. I just felt them. Until then, I'd only felt Mam. Not them too. We had no idea they could feel us until that time. I asked them if it scared them, and they all said, no, it didn't. I asked if they could feel each other. And they said that, yes, they could. That was the first time we found out we could all feel each other.

"Can you imagine feeling someone's distress? Now multiply that by the number of people you are connected to. The feeling is multiplied by the seven of us."

David frowned, confused. "But there are really only six of you connected. Sarah is adopted."

Chase nodded his head. "When Sarah was 16, she told us that she was able to feel us all. She also knew when any of us were upset or happy about something. Being that Sarah was not our biological child, we had never given it a second thought. We assumed that she couldn't. That was when we realized Sarah was supposed to be ours, right from the beginning." Everyone was now smiling at Sarah.

Chase continued. "My brother Quinn always told us that what we had was a gift from God, and that is how we always took it. When the boys all got married, they found out that they were connected the same way with their wives. We realized that them finding each other was another gift from God. That is what their mother and I always took it to mean."

Chase took a breath, hoping he wasn't giving them too much information too fast. He then continued, "My brother Ed took Mam to the hospital when she went into labor with Zac and Zeke. I was in the States with the band. Ed took her to his concert at Wembley Stadium, and when he was taking her home, she went into labor. I felt her. I closed my eyes, and said, "I am coming, Mam."

Marguerite repeated the line, "'I'm coming home, Mam.' I heard it. I looked at Ed and told him that Chase was coming. He was shocked and asked how I could even know that. I told him that it was because I could feel him."

David shook his head. "Spooky." They all looked at him. "I don't know why I just said that. It wasn't what I was thinking."

"Ed just said that, not you," Marguerite replied. "That was his term for the connection we all had to each other, and we used that word all the time. Spooky!"

Chase then took over again. "We could never understand how this all could be possible. Who could we tell? We were afraid." He paused, not knowing how he was going to continue. "Someone might think we were delusional and take our children away from us."

"That would have killed us!" Marguerite said, tearing up.

Chase continued. "Only immediate family knew about our bond, and now you both do as well. When Ed passed away, he left letters for us all. His trigger word, as I mentioned before, was 'prerogative'. My children did not know that. Only Mam and I knew the word. Then a few nights ago, my daughter woke from a dream and her husband came to get us immediately, because she was so shaken. At the same time, in the middle of the night, the webcam came on in her bedroom, on the big screen TV. All of her brothers were trying to reach each other. They all had woken up at the same time, saying the same word, 'prerogative'! They were all upset, and that's when I had to give them the letter from their uncle Ed, explaining what it meant. I knew then that Ed and Lilli's souls had finally found each other."

Mia and David were amazed. They just looked at all of them. They believed every word, but found it hard to grasp everything that was said. They had all woken up saying the same word!

"How did you know who we were?" Mia asked.

"Mam and I were reading the New York paper, and there was an article on your art show. Art never really interested me—no offense David—but for some reason, I read that article over three times. Then later, Mam said to me that she had read an article that morning about an art show that she just couldn't stop thinking about. That is when we all realized that we had to come and see if you were the ones, and if this was really happening to you both. Now we see we were right coming here."

The boys and Sarah all felt their parents getting weary, remembering things from the past, and it had upset them thinking about someone possibly taking them away from them when they were young.

Zeke said, "Mom and Dad, I think we should take a break. We all feel you getting weary, and we need to get some dinner before we all drop."

Everyone was relieved. They did need a break. As everyone was getting up to move towards the dining room, Sarah asked David and Mia, "How are you feeling?"

Mia spoke up, looking at David. "I can't believe I am saying this, but better ... now that I know about the whole situation." David agreed, nodding his head.

After dinner, it was late. David and Mia thought that they'd had enough for one day, and everyone else felt it as well.

"Let's call it a night," Sarah said. "I don't think my parents should continue anymore today." She was worried about them and they all agreed.

"Do you want to come for dinner again tomorrow, and we could continue?" Matt asked.

Both Mia and David agreed. They knew there was much more to say, and they had to find out the whole story.

Mia said, "How about you all come over to David's place tomorrow, and we can have dinner there."

They hugged and kissed them both when they left, which shocked them, but somehow ... they welcomed the affection.

40 Concerned

Mia and David were unusually quiet coming back into the condo. They had been given quite a lot of information, and to find out that they were carrying two souls that were in love somehow changed things between them.

Mia asked David, "Are you looking for Lilli or me?"

David asked, "Are you looking for Ed or me?" They both just smiled.

"They were right ... the Martins," Mia told him. "This is far-fetched, but they believe everything they just told us to be true, and they are so sincere ... you could just feel it. They want to help us and I believe them." She stepped in closer to him. "Are you scared, David?"

"I don't think scared quite sums it up. I'm confused, concerned, and trying to make sense out of what has been happening." David then took a moment to collect his thoughts.

"Why us?" he asked. "Mr. Martin knew we wouldn't believe them, but he had that ace in his back pocket. When he asked, 'Did you say the word prerogative this week?' I thought I was going to pass out. That is how all of this happened, and all of his children having the same dream with only one word in it? That confirms this is really happening. Do you feel that way about it too, Mia? Because at this point I believe it. I believe that Ed and Lilli are somehow inside of us ... and I can't believe I'm admitting it out loud."

Mia let out a sigh. "I agree. I feel something so strong. I just can't explain it. I have so many questions right now, and don't know which ones to ask first. Is it just that I'm afraid to ask some questions first?"

David looked at Mia, and appeared to answer what he thought was on her mind. He took her hand and held it to his heart. He then said, "This is the most important question on both of our minds. Is what we feel real, or is it just Ed and Lilli causing this attraction towards each other?"

David hit the nail right on the head. That's what Mia was so afraid to ask.

"What do you think, David? Tell me the truth."

David smiled, as he was aware that she kept turning the question back to him. "Let's think about it. When we first met, you had not said the word, so the feelings I had towards you were all David. I am the one who felt that attraction to you, not Ed. I am positive of this! Our feelings grew quickly towards each other, and maybe it was because Ed and Lilli wanted us to feel something on our own, before they showed themselves to us. More importantly, until I met you, no one had ever moved me as you did and currently do. It is not Ed saying this. It is all me. I want us to see this through, Mia. I want us to see our relationship through, and we will try and help Ed and Lilli out. I don't know how or what to do about them, but I am counting on the entire Martin family to help us. I'm only beginning to imagine how they must have felt, having their love cut short on them and Ed missing out on it for all of those years ... *just waiting to die* so he could somehow find his wife again. What a story to tell our children!"

Mia was in tears. She couldn't hold them back. He had repeated all the words she was hoping he would, and she believed every single one of them.

David took her face in his hands and kissed Mia very tenderly, so much so that she wanted to melt right into him. She responded to his kisses to let him know she felt the same.

After she had composed herself, she looked at David. "I was thinking about when we first met and how attracted I was to you. I thought maybe it was just because there was no one in my life until I met you. It isn't as though I never dated. It was just that ... I never had strong feelings about anyone before. Then you happened! How happy you made me and make me now, I just can't explain, but I want you to know that you do make me happy. More than I can say. You told me that you knew I loved you. Could it be love, so early in our relationship? That's the question that concerns me. Well, I am saying yes. It is. Yes, I do love you. I know I do, because I never felt it before and I know this is how it should feel. This is how *I* feel. When we met, we were David and Mia, not Ed and Lilli. Our feelings were our own. No one else urged us on. It was us! Simply us!"

David interrupted her and said, "I love you, Mia! I know I do, because right up until I met you, I never felt like this before either, so I know it is love and I feel it for you. We will get through this. The love between us can only grow stronger by the day. We're now carrying Ed and Lilli's love with us too." David was now shaking his head, still amazed.

Mia smiled. "That pot has been boiling a long time. I just hope we can keep up with them." She smiled and then laughed.

David picked her up and threw her over his shoulder. "Well, we better start practicing so we can!"

Mia began screaming, laughing, and asking David to put her down, but David was having none of it, and continued to their bedroom where neither emerged until the next morning.

41
Encountering Ed and Lilli

Chase was talking to Zac about how they shouldn't forget to call Jim Post, the photographer they met their first night in New York. He was thinking of possibly telling him the day they were going to be at the gallery, and ask if he would like to take some pictures there. "That's the reason we're here, so we wouldn't be lying to him, and it would also provide David with more publicity for his art show."

Zac replied, "David is so well-known for his work and he's already so popular. We would have to check with him first to make sure he is good with the idea. We wouldn't want to offend him in any way."

Chase agreed that they could discuss it at dinner. He thought that it would be best to call Jim once they had settled on the day they were going to be at the art show.

∞

When David finally woke the next morning, he found he was still in the same position as when he had fallen asleep, with Mia wrapped in his arms. He leaned into her and kissed her forehead, and she stirred when she felt him.

At that moment, all of a sudden, she looked and saw Ed in front of her, and David looked and saw Lilli in front of him. They both jumped up out of bed, and backed away from each other.

David said to Mia, "I know you're going to think I'm crazy, but let's see if we can get them to speak to each other. They have been waiting for decades."

"I don't think you're crazy. I think that's what they're waiting for. We have to let them, or we might never have any peace between us and our relationship."

David and Mia stood in their bedroom, and Mia spoke to Ed softly and affectionately, "Ed and Lilli. We know who you are, and we know you were waiting forever to find each other again. How can we help you?"

"Do you want to speak to each other?" David asked. "We will let you. We want to help you find peace."

With that, David looked at Mia, and finally ... Ed began looking at Lilli.

The tears streamed down both of their faces, as Ed spoke first, amazed at the whole situation. "I can't believe this has happened. I can't believe you were right in saying that God would not have wanted our love to be cut so short. As clear as I am looking at you right now ... I am thanking him for this second chance. I have waited sixty-four years to see you again. Sixty-four years to be able to touch you again. Can you still feel how much I love you, and how much I have missed you?"

"I always felt it, Ed," Lilli said, not being able to control the tears falling from her eyes. "Even though I was not with you, your love always stayed with me. I hope you always felt mine, because I never stopped loving you!"

They walked slowly towards each other, and Ed reached for her hand and took it with his, bringing it up to his face.

"We cannot upset this couple," he said. "We have already scared them half to death, not knowing what was going on." He just looked at her for a long moment.

"Chase and Mam will continue the story and help them," he said. "They promised me they would continue to help them until everything is figured out. I left the letters for them, trying to explain, and other surprises for them as well. Chase will handle everything."

"It was so good seeing him again, Ed," Lilli said. "He was truly a brother to you, as you were to him. I also wanted to tell Mam that I took care of baby Margaret for her all these years. I just felt like I wanted to, because they both took very good care of you, for all the years we were apart."

Ed was smiling, especially when Lilli told him about baby Margaret. "We should let these two have their thoughts back now. Maybe, down the line, they'll let me love you before we turn ourselves over to them completely. Never forget how much I love you, Lilli."

Lilli replied, "I never did or will. It's as much as I love you, Ed." Then he kissed her softly, after waiting for what seemed like forever to touch her lips again.

Mia and David were suddenly back to being Mia and David. They, of course, had heard everything said ... or were they the ones saying it?

"Were you able to feel the emotions between them?" Mia asked, smiling and pleased about what had just happened.

David nodded his head. "I did. They were so strong. Can you imagine two people carrying that torch for each other for sixty-four years? I'm trying to wrap my head around it and this whole situation. But again, why us? What made us so special that these two souls chose us?"

Mia countered, "Maybe they didn't choose us," she said, glancing upwards. "Maybe a higher power chose us. Did you ever think of that?"

"I'm not very religious. Oh, I believe in God, but I'm not a church-going man. I try and live a good life, because I *do* want to get to heaven someday. But I wouldn't think I was a candidate for God to pick *me* for this kind of a task."

Mia tried to grasp everything she had heard. "I think we've had enough heavy talk for this morning. Let's think about it some more and talk about it tonight." She then walked towards David and wrapped her arms around him, wanting to feel his embrace. When he welcomed her, holding her so tightly it was almost alarming, she just stayed there until he was ready to let her go.

Checking History

While there were getting ready to go to the gallery that afternoon, Mia asked, "Are you nervous about visiting with the Martins tonight?"

"No. If anything, I felt better speaking to them. I was kind of star-struck the whole evening though. Even with all of the drama going on, I felt almost honored to be in their company."

"I know what you mean. I still listen to his music ... or The Band 4's music anyway. I don't think anyone can replicate what they accomplished. They managed to stay together as a band for a very long time, performing, and they helped many people in the music industry as well."

"Did you hear what Mr. Martin said about Mrs. Martin being very ill in Italy?" Mia asked. "Do you know what happened?"

"He was shaken speaking about it ... even to this day."

"David, I'm going to look it up. I want to pull a history on them, just to see them all. Do you think that's a terrible thing to do? I feel like I'm snooping on them."

"No, I don't think it's terrible. Their lives are public knowledge, so I don't think they would even mind. Let's look and follow their history. It will help us to get to know them better also."

Mia pulled out her computer, and they both sat down and searched for Chase Martin. There was a tremendous amount of history about him online. Many pictures of Chase with The Band 4 were available. There were pictures of Chase and Marguerite's wedding, and all the children too. There were also pictures of Marguerite with all the wives of the band, with her parents, and with Ed too.

"It seems that they're all very close ... and always together! You can just tell from the pictures," Mia said smiling at David.

Mia started reading. "The internet and social media crashed when it was announced that Chase had gotten married! Oh, my goodness!" Mia couldn't believe it. She had never heard of that happening before.

"The announcement when they were pregnant with their first child ... a girl?" They were confused. The article went on to explain that she had miscarried at almost eight months. "Oh, David!" Mia said, as her voice was shaking.

The picture of thousands of fans lining the streets around the hospital when she miscarried was overwhelming. The image showed fans with their flashlights in the air.

"It must have been where they stayed," Mia said. "Here it says the fans organized a silent march, so as not to disturb anyone, and sang "It's the little Things" in a whisper to help them cope. The four band members, standing in the window of the hospital room, turned on their flashes to let them know that they saw the crowd's reaction. The four of them were together. There again... look they are together again!"

They both then came across a link titled, "Valentine's Day Concert."

David read it out loud: "Marguerite Martin, wife of Chase Martin, along with the girlfriends of Blake Thomas, Drew Bishop, and Quinn Howard, surprised them at their concert in Verona Italy on Valentine's Day, by singing three of their love songs on stage to them. Click to view."

They clicked and watched the video.

"Oh my goodness! I don't know if I would have had the nerve to do that. Look at all of those people, and they sound so good. Look, David! Mrs. Martin was pregnant. It was probably with their baby girl." They were so amazed.

David continued reading out loud. "Over a year after she lost her baby girl, they announced they were pregnant with twin boys. They then had the birth and left the hospital." Again, everyone was there, in sight.

"Look who's there," Mia said. "It's Ed. He's there with them."

"The announcement said that Ed took her to the hospital and stayed with her until Chase could get there. He was in the States when she went into labor prematurely. He must have been out of his mind waiting to get there, because of what happened the first time with the baby girl!" She continued reading.

"Yes, I see him," David said. "Mr. Martin said he was with them all the time. He was a brother to him."

"Okay, there isn't much in between then and four years later. There's another announcement here ... pregnant again with twin boys! Can you imagine?" Mia said in amazement.

"Here they are leaving the hospital again. Ed is with them here as well."

"Okay, I see them touring in Italy. Oh, my goodness, David, here it is. Remember when Mr. Martin said that he almost lost his wife. She was rushed to the hospital just after landing due to bleeding in her brain."

As they read it, they both stopped dead. Both of their faces turned pale. They couldn't help but stare at the screen, at a picture of Chase walking down the hall at the hospital, holding onto the hands of Matt and Mark, who were holding their brothers' hands, connected like a chain.

"Do you see the look on Mr. Martin's face?" Mia asked. "He looks so distraught ... as if he just wants to die. Look at the boys all holding onto him and to each other."

At that moment, they felt like they could almost feel the pain he was in ... wondering if he would lose his wife, with his four young sons there, and then they both started to cry. They couldn't control themselves.

"I can't read anymore. I was so fond of them before, but now seeing everything they went through, I feel closer to them. I guess it wasn't perfect. You would never know, being with them," Mia said.

David agreed and closed the computer to shut it down. Then he pulled Mia into the biggest embrace.

"You asked me this morning if I was nervous about visiting them tonight. I said no before, and now I'm saying I cannot wait to see them. For some reason, I just can't wait to be with them all tonight."

Mia said, "I know what you mean. I feel the same way. I'm going to set the table so we can be ready for tonight without rushing around."

"Okay, I'll help you."

43 Another Session

The Martins were counting down the hours before they could head out to David and Mia's place for dinner. When the hour finally arrived, they headed in the elevator to the twenty-seventh floor, where David's condo was.

David and Mia were anxiously awaiting their arrival and met them in the foyer when the door opened.

Instead of shaking everyone's hand this time, they went right over and hugged each one of them. The boys and Sarah were so pleased to see that, but when they got to Chase and Marguerite, they pulled them into the biggest embrace they could give them. They felt much warmer towards them, and felt so badly for all the pain they had gone through in their lives. Chase and Marguerite were also pleased and felt that David and Mia trusted them. They knew what was said was true and that they were going to help.

Mia poured wine for everyone, and David helped pass it out while they all made themselves comfortable.

Chase spoke. "David, the first night when we were in town, walking down the street, we didn't think anyone would recognize us, being that it was all such a long time ago. However, a photographer did notice us and started snapping pictures. Our bodyguard went to him immediately and asked him to stop, but I told him he could take pictures, as long as he didn't publish them until we left for home. I also told him we would grant him more, if he would just leave us alone at the time. We hadn't even met you yet, and I didn't want any pictures of us to surface that might trigger something with Ed before we could help you."

David didn't know where he was going with this, so he remained quiet.

Zac saw his confusion and continued, "My father promised the man more pictures, and he never goes back on his word. He is wondering if you would mind us calling the photographer and having him take pictures of us at the gallery. We know your work is known worldwide, but thought it would be free publicity for you, because you *were* the reason we were in New York."

David and Mia looked at each other and thought how kind they were to think of them. David said, "That would be great. I would love it! What day would you like to tell him to come? I need to know so I can get more of this paint off of me!" He smiled and laughed, looking at Mia.

Mia started to laugh too. "When I met him, he looked like he needed a bath in turpentine."

With that everyone started laughing, and it settled them all down. Mark excused himself, made the phone call to Jim, and spoke to him. "Is tomorrow too soon? He can be there around five." David nodded. It was settled. They had a day and a time.

Now David could not wait to tell everyone what had happened that morning.

"Mr. Martin," David said, but Chase stopped him.

"Please call me Chase, and my wife, Marguerite. We're grateful for the respect you both have shown us, with the way you address us, but I don't think there is anything formal about our relationship now. Would you agree?"

David and Mia both nodded their heads in agreement, smiling at each other.

"Okay, sorry that I stopped you, please go on," Chase said.

"Mia and I woke up this morning, and when I looked at her, I saw Lilli, and when she looked at me, she saw Ed. I asked her if we could just see if Ed and Lilli wanted to speak to each other, because they kept popping up. I thought, let's just let them talk to each other, as they have been waiting sixty-four years!"

Everyone was amazed. Chase asked, "That was brilliant. I didn't even think of that. What happened next?"

"When I looked at Mia, I saw Lilli standing there, and she saw Ed." Mia was nodding her head.

"They spoke to each other, Ed and Lilli. They were so happy. Ed took hold of her hand, and they spoke with so much love and affection in their voices, and they both started crying."

Everyone was shocked and amazed, sitting there with eyes wide and mouths hung open in surprise.

"Ed told Lilli he couldn't believe what she hoped for was happening and that they were able to find each other. They didn't say much more, because they didn't want to upset us. But they reconfirmed their love for each other, and were so happy. Ed said that you and Mam would continue to help us. Those were his exact words. One more thing, he said that he hoped Mia and I would let them make love to each other before they turned themselves over to us completely!"

Everyone started crying. No one could help it. It was so overwhelming. They were all reaching out to hold onto one another, when Mia remembered one more thing. She struggled with giving this message but felt they should hear it.

"Wait, I have a message from Lilli to give Chase and Marguerite. It may be hard to hear."

"What is it, Mia?" Marguerite asked.

Now they were both standing, looking concerned.

In a low shaking voice, Mia said, "She asked me to tell you both that she has been taking care of Baby Margaret all of these years, in return for you taking care of Ed for her."

44 Shaken

With the revelation that Lilli was taking care of their first-born daughter for them, Chase turned white, but Marguerite was in worse shape. She suddenly passed out cold.

Chase caught her and started crying, while he was shaking her. "Mam! Mam, please come back to me. Mam!" he shouted, as he held her in his arms.

The boys and Sarah were in a panic, when Matt yelled, "Can someone get a cold washcloth, quickly please!" Mia rushed off to get one.

Zac and Zeke had quickly taken their mother and laid her down on one of the sofas, and were trying to wake her up.

Mark said, "I'll call the front desk and see how quickly we can get a doctor here. If we can't, then we'll go to the hospital."

Matt pushed his brothers away so he could take a look at his mother, and try and help her. Neither he nor his twin brother, who were doctors, had brought their medical bags.

In the meantime, David and Mia felt terrible. Mia especially felt upset, and it was almost as if the boys could tell what they were thinking.

Matt looked at them, "This is not your fault. Please don't feel bad. You did nothing wrong so don't worry. She'll be upset to know that she worried us all when she wakes up and will most likely be apologizing to the high heavens."

Matt was holding the cold cloth to the back of his mother's neck, and after a few more minutes, which seemed like hours to Chase, she started coming around.

She looked and saw Chase with tears coming down his face and smiled. He leaned his head into hers, and as their foreheads touched, she started crying too. She then stroked his face and hair to try and calm him down, as everyone else watched the exchange between them. It was like no one else was even there. She was worried about him, and he was worried about her. No one said anything until they acknowledged them first. They let them go until they felt they were ready.

Once Marguerite felt Chase calming down, she smiled. "All better?"

He smiled and kissed her lips. "Yes, now that you're with me again."

"Do you feel better knowing someone was taking care of Margaret all of these years?" Marguerite asked. Chase just nodded his head, and she continued. "It makes me feel so much better. She wasn't alone, and now I know our brothers and sisters are taking care of her too." Chase again just nodded his head and kissed her forehead, while smiling at her angelic face.

They then looked at their children who were now kneeling in front of them. David and Mia were standing with their arms around each other. Marguerite immediately did what Matt said she would do and began apologizing to everyone for upsetting them.

Mark said the doctor was on the way, and of course, their mother said that no one was needed, but they insisted. He was on the way and was going to check her out anyway.

"Mam, I want you to let him take a look at you. Do you hear me? Just to be safe," Chase said worriedly.

"Chase, my sons are doctors, if they can see I am well, then I won't need to see anyone else," she said stubbornly.

Mark stepped in and said, "Mom, we didn't bring our medical bags with us, and we can't risk your health just because you are conscious and seem fine."

As Marguerite looked around at everyone, and saw the concern on all of their faces, she agreed, but she didn't like the idea one bit.

The doctor arrived and Mia helped her to her bedroom so he could check her out. Chase followed and would not let her out of his sight. Something else amazed David and Mia. The boys and Sarah all followed them or paced outside of the bedroom door, as the doctor was examining their mother.

Half an hour went by before the door opened and everyone smiled when their father saw them. Mark said, "If you had not opened the door in the next ten minutes, we were going to start pounding on it." Everyone smiled.

They walked in the room to see their mother and to find out what the doctor said. David and Mia were right behind them.

Chase said, "You better tell them before they all pass out, or else you will have more patients to contend with."

The doctor just laughed. "Your mother is in good health. She just had a scare, and at her age, she couldn't process it, so her body tried to protect her—to keep her calm until she could cope with what was said to her."

It made perfect sense to all of them and they relaxed immediately.

"Doctor, while you are here, can you take a look at my father as well?" Sarah asked. "We want to make sure he's fine too."

"I already did, at the request of your mother, and he's in good health also. His blood pressure is normal and his heartbeat is strong."

They all walked out to the living room, and Mia invited the doctor to stay for dinner, but he had to go. Then something hit him when he was writing out his information on the call.

He looked up at Chase, and then back at name on his sheet. "You're not Chase Martin from The Band 4, are you?"

Everyone started laughing. Chase thought no one would know him anymore, but everyone they met knew exactly who he was and who they all were.

Chase smiled, shaking his head. "Yes, that would be me."

The doctor looked at all of them. "Two sets of twins, of course. I didn't put it together until just now."

They all began laughing again.

45
Dinner Is Served

Mam went straight to Mia and took her hand. She then pulled her to the side saying, "Please don't feel bad about what happened. I appreciated the message from Lilli and now feel comforted by it. Losing a child is the worst possible experience for any parent, and we can never seem to get over losing Margaret. She was our first-born, and Chase and I wanted children so badly. You do see how blessed we have been, though, even with that hole in both our hearts."

Mia nodded her head. She understood what Mam was trying to say. Just then Chase came to get his wife, not wanting to leave her side for even a few minutes.

Everyone settled down and they decided to eat before any more conversations took place. They all enjoyed being together, and it showed on all of their faces. The dinner was excellent that Mia had prepared. Being that they'd had chicken the night before, she and David had decided on salmon with a dill cream sauce and roasted rosemary potatoes. They chose ice cream for dessert, with a warm cherry sauce to go over it. The conversations were pleasant, with the boys telling Mia and David about their daughters and how they were forbidden to date. They then had to admit that they had lost that war, which made everyone laugh.

They even shared the story about when Sarah was getting married, and how their father stole the shears from her purse so that her husband would not be able to get her out of her wedding gown. The dress had one hundred and twenty satin buttons, and that made everyone laugh even harder.

Chase was still proud of himself for doing that, and the fact that he still felt that way made it even funnier.

Sarah got up and went to her father, who had his arms open for her. Chase kissed her, telling her that he loved her. It made everyone smile. David and Mia felt the love they all shared with each other, and hoped they would have the same kind when they had a family.

David asked, "Why are you all so close? I may find it hard to understand, because I have no family, but what makes you all feel the way you do about each other?"

They didn't know how to answer that.

Matt said, "We see how you are with Mia. How do you feel about her? Not to put you on the spot, but we would all have to be blind not to see how much affection you both have for each other."

Mia and David looked at each other surprised. They were embarrassed that their feelings were so apparent to everyone else.

Matt insisted, "What makes you feel love towards her?"

David thought about it. "From the moment I met her, I felt drawn towards her. There was just something about her. It was a feeling I guess. It made me want more. I am not talking about sex either. I wanted more of her. I had to find out about her. I wanted to learn more, and the more time I spent with her, the deeper my feelings grew towards her. Lastly, I think it's because she is so warm and sincere. You could see it on her face and in her mannerisms. I know she would never hurt me. I knew somehow she was supposed to be with me. I can't explain it better than that."

David looked at everyone who was smiling at him.

Matt said, "That's how we're all so close. We have always been like this. I don't think there's an explanation for why. You're right David. They are feelings ... things that draw you in and hold you captive. How sad I feel for people who don't embrace the feelings they have towards someone! To let it slip away from you would be so ungrateful and ... sinful almost. Ignoring what God was giving you, sometimes practically looking you right in the eye."

Zeke said, "Who's to say that we'd be this close if we didn't have the parents we do. First of all, the love they feel towards each other drips off of them. We all feel it, and not just trough the bond we all share. You can see it in their faces and hear it in their voices. In the kindness they show everyone. They have been grateful to everyone they have ever met and included in our lives. Making them family and feeling the love they have for them. They are amazing."

At that point, the conversation stalled a bit, with the siblings all looking down at the table, wondering how they were ever going to let them go.

Marguerite looked at Chase. "Let's go and leave them to it tonight. I think David and Mia will be in good hands." They looked at their children and knew everything was going to be okay.

Chase was on the same page. "I was just going to suggest that." They both got up and went to leave. They were hugged and kissed by their four sons and one daughter, all telling them that they loved them, and saying goodnight.

Then they went to David and Mia. "I hope you know that you're family now," Chase said. "I'm happy my sons and daughter feel that way about you too. Without family, we have nothing. They will need you as much as you need them; remember what I just told you." David and Mia both nodded but didn't know what he was referring to.

The boys and Sarah stayed up late, not wanting to leave Mia and David. The hosts felt the same way, and didn't want them to leave either. They made them feel like they were part of their family now, and were very happy about it.

At that moment, everyone felt so lucky and so blessed about everything that was happening.

Josh and His Dream

With Sarah gone, the house felt so empty. Josh was feeling lonely and very sentimental as he was heading to bed.

He was missing Sarah very much. He loved her and knew her father would have never let him marry her unless he was sure he would take good care of her. That also meant loving her with all of his mind, body, and soul.

Josh took over his family's business, which was operating a lumber yard and tool center. Marguerite thought that was ironic, being that Chase barely knew what a hammer even was! Chase was pleased Josh had his own business, because he knew Josh would be able to provide for Sarah, and he always saw how hard he worked. He was well-respected in the community and Sarah worked for him in the office, taking care of his books.

When Chase walked Sarah down the aisle, he looked up at Josh and saw that he had tears running down his face. That was the moment when he knew Josh was right for Sarah. Later Chase admitted to him that he knew he would take care of his daughter until the day one of them died.

Josh was so happy Chase felt that way. He knew he didn't have the connection that all of the others had to each other, and sometimes he felt left out, even though they always tried to include him.

In the end, they all hoped somehow something would just snap with him and he would eventually start feeling them.

Sarah, on the other hand, was attracted to Josh the minute she saw him. He had blond hair and the faintest, shining blue eyes. Maybe she felt attracted to him because there wasn't all of the drama surrounding him that there was with all of the feelings everyone else was sharing. She felt peaceful around Josh, and in herself, when she was with him and loved him with all of her heart.

While Sarah was in New York with her brothers and parents, Josh woke in the middle of the night from a dream he was having. He couldn't make out why it startled him, because the dream was not upsetting.

He was dreaming about someone painting a picture of their house. The house in question was the one Sarah grew up in, the Martins' house, which now belonged to him and Sarah. He saw the man as plain as day, standing in front of the picture and asking it, "What are you trying to tell me?"

He got up and called Sarah immediately. It was still early in the States, so he knew he could reach her.

"I just had the strangest dream, my love!"

Sarah got concerned and felt bad, because she wasn't there to comfort him.

"Mr. Foster, are you dreaming without me being there? Tell me about it, and we can see what triggered that for you."

Josh smiled and said, "Well Mrs. Foster, in my dream, I saw a guy standing in front of a painting, which I think he painted himself, of our house here. How strange is that? I'm not upset about it but just thought it was odd, because it startled me and I don't know why."

Sarah thought about it for a moment. "Maybe you had it because in the back of your mind you knew we were coming to New York to the Gallery, to view an art show?"

"Maybe," he said, considering. "Oh, and one more thing, Sarah! When he was looking at the house in the painting, I heard him say, 'What are you trying to tell me?'"

That's when Sarah got concerned, but she made light of it, so as not to worry Josh. She didn't know what it meant, but for some reason, she felt it meant something.

"I am so sorry I'm not there to help you. I'm so sorry I left you for a week. I am so homesick and miss you so much." Sarah was upset that she was not there when he needed her.

"No, my love! I'm fine. I just needed to hear your voice. A week is nothing compared to how long your father was gone when he was touring. I'm fine and can't wait to see you this weekend. Now go back to what you were doing. I'm fine."

"I love you, Josh, and I miss you!"

"I love you too, Sarah, and I'm counting the days until you come back to me."

When she hung up, Sarah stared out the big windows overlooking the New York skyline.

Sarah was upset, and they all felt her. They all knew why too. She was missing Josh and something else had surfaced in her thoughts. Something they hadn't felt from her in years. In truth, they all loved Josh like a brother. They saw how he treated Sarah. He behaved like she was the most precious thing on the planet, and they were grateful to him for loving her like that.

They envied the fact that his emotions were free of all the drama they experienced on a daily basis, feeling their wives and other brothers, parents, and sister. Even though they knew it was a gift they all had, now and then, they would have just liked to have a clear thought without everyone else knowing too.

They all huddled and looked at their parents, as if to ask which one of them would be going to her.

"Sarah is holding something back. She has been for years, and I think maybe she would like to tell me now," Marguerite said. "I know we all felt the same thing, and maybe now she can say it out loud and free herself from this pain she's been carrying around. She needs her mother now, so I am going to go to her. Please give us room!"

Chase just kissed his wife, knowing the conversation was going to be painful for them both.

47
Sarah's Heartbreak

Marguerite took Sarah by the hand, and they headed out towards the terrace for a talk about what was bothering her.

"Sarah, I love you so much. You have been so wonderful your whole life. You always amaze me and even now you surprise me. I have been waiting for years for you to tell me what is hurting you so much. Will you finally speak to me about it? Let me help you! Maybe if you say it out loud, it will free you somehow!"

Sarah collapsed into her mother's arms, crying, and Marguerite just held her until she could compose herself. Time passed, and she was still upset, with her mother just rocking her back and forth trying to sooth her. Chase and her brothers were a mess, feeling her pain. They all wanted to go to her, but knew she needed to talk to her mother. Somehow, they knew it was a woman thing.

After a long while, she was composed enough to start talking. "Mom, I should have told you years ago about this, but I just couldn't talk about it. I want to say that I'm sorry for not coming to you first. I hope I didn't cause you, Dad, or my brothers any pain."

"You could never cause us pain, my love. You are and will always be the sun shining for us. Don't you know that? Don't you see how your brothers' faces light up, to this day, when your name is just said? And you know that you're your father's girl ... even now, you still are ... and will always be."

Sarah cried some more, but they were happy tears this time. Not the tears of sorrow she was shedding before.

"Now, tell me what is wrong?" Marguerite asked, gently but firmly.

Sarah tried to compose herself, as she began to speak. "I know you always thought we didn't want children, because that's what we have been telling you all this time, but the fact is that I can't have children. I've been to every doctor I can find, and it just isn't going to happen for us. I wondered if it had something to do with my birth mother, since we didn't have any information about her medical history for us to check. I was pregnant once, twenty-three years ago, but I miscarried after only five weeks, and that's when I found out. I'm so sorry I kept that from you. I begged Josh not to tell you or anyone. I didn't want to worry you all. I am so sorry!"

Sarah was now sobbing uncontrollably. Marguerite thought it would be best just to let her cry it out. The men all felt her pain, and were in horrible turmoil over it. Marguerite didn't know how she could control her emotions either, and they betrayed her. She started crying, and everyone felt her as well.

The boys had to practically hold their father back from going out to the terrace to help his wife and daughter. The boys were feeling the same way. They just wanted to take care of their sister, who at that moment, was more distraught than they had ever felt her.

"Let's give them more time," Zac said. "We have to. They won't be able to talk to us in the state they're in right now anyway." Everyone nodded and just paced back and forth ... but out of sight, so their mother and Sarah would not see them hovering.

After a while, Sarah was able to pull herself together. She felt the calmness her mother was sending her, lying in her arms, and she started feeling better.

"My sweet child. You have kept this bottled up for twenty-three years. God love you, Sarah! Why did you choose not to let us help you? What you have done is noble, but that's what families are all about. We share in everyone's joy and everyone's sorrow. For you and Josh to carry this by yourselves had to eat away at you both, for all of this time. Please don't ever do that again, my love. I do understand your reasoning. I know the bond we all share is sometimes taxing on us all. To tell you honestly, we all knew you were holding something back all of these years, but could never imagine it was this!"

"I should have guessed you would all know," Sarah said, "but I just couldn't tell you, and I can't explain why. I can't explain why Josh or I decided not to try to adopt a child or children either, especially since you took me in. I should have been happy to take a child into my home, but we both felt we didn't want to adopt. Is that terrible of us? Especially since you adopted me?" She got upset again.

Marguerite knew that was the other part of Sarah's pain. She felt guilty for not wanting to adopt a child, because she was adopted.

"Sarah, it is not terrible of you to not want to adopt. Your father and I did not go and seek out adoption. You were given to us! You were a gift from your mother! And what a gift you have been. Every day of your life, you bring joy to us all. I know you feel and sense us all loving you!"

Somehow those words reached Sarah the way nothing else ever did. She was able to compose herself and her brothers and father all felt her calm right down. They all looked at each other and knew it was time to see her, so they all went to the terrace where Sarah was. She ran to her father, who had his arms open for her, and he just held her. Zac and Zeke went straight to their mother, while Matt and Mark grabbed hold of everyone, and they all stood there in a circle, arms wrapped around each other.

Marguerite filled everyone in on why Sarah was so upset, and they felt so badly about it, realizing how hard it must have been for her and Josh. The shock and sorrow on all of their faces confirmed how badly they felt about it.

Mark said, "Sarah, just when we didn't think we could love you more, you surprised us."

Everyone had the biggest smiles on their faces, looking around at each other. Marguerite and Chase couldn't feel any prouder of their sons and daughter then they did at that moment.

Matt asked Sarah, "What triggered this all tonight, Sarah?"

"Josh called because he had a dream and it woke him up. He said he saw someone painting a picture of our house in London. The dream didn't upset him, so he didn't know why it woke him. He saw a man standing in front of the picture asking, 'What are you trying to tell me?' Like the picture was supposed to mean something. That's what he wondered about. I felt bad, because I was not there to be with him, and it just all snowballed after that, with my emotions taking control of me."

Everyone smiled, and they all reached out to hug each other again, wanting to feel their connection and to calm her down.

48. All Aboard

The next morning, David and Mia woke up with smiles. They were happy about the place they were in, regarding Ed and Lilli, and happy about their new family. In fact, they were thrilled with their new family.

David said to Mia, "How could anyone not like those people?"

"I know. You can't help but fall in love with them all. They're so kind and loving."

"Are you okay with them being in our lives?"

"Yes, absolutely. I wouldn't have it any other way, and now I believe we are very lucky to be included in their family."

David said, "I agree, and I think that's why I'm so happy today. What a great night we had yesterday, and they will all come to the gallery today for photos, but I know Marguerite and Chase are coming to see my paintings as well. I'm almost anxious for them to see them, like a child bringing home his report card and just waiting for their parents to see it. Does that sound … I don't know, corny?"

"No, not at all. Maybe because you have no family, it's hitting you harder. Being accepted into one and now belonging to one must feel great. I feel we now belong to their family and them. You're right; I feel so happy about it too."

They just looked at each other and David drew Mia in for an enormous kiss. His emotions took over, and they made love like they never had before, filled with feelings of affection and contentment. When they were done, they lay happily in each other's arms, taking notice of how good life was.

David said, "You know the painting I did of the English Tudor in my studio?"

Mia replied, "Yes, the one you said was almost like it was trying to tell you something."

"Yes, that one. I was thinking of giving it to Chase and Marguerite as a gift, for befriending us and helping us."

"That's a great idea. I think they would love it too!"

Mia kissed David, "I think they're rubbing off on us already." She then rolled over on the bed, making fun of David. "Maybe they could rub off some of that paint all over you." He grabbed her again and made her pay for it, which she did happily.

It was time for Chase and his family to show up at the gallery. They all looked for David and Mia first, to let them know that they were there, and they immediately came over to greet them.

Chase said, "We don't want to hold you up. We just want to see your work. Matt and Mark have been telling us how much they liked your paintings. We couldn't wait to get here." Chase was smiling.

David said, "Just call if you need me. Mia will stay with you."

"No," Chase said. "We don't want to monopolize your time. Let us look, and we'll motion for you if we have any questions."

They both agreed, and watched them start walking around. Chase had ahold of Marguerite's hand and off they went.

Mia said to David, "When we are in our eighties and nineties, I hope you still want to hold *my* hand."

David said, "We will be doing more than that." He smiled and planted a kiss on her cheek.

While going from aisle to aisle, Zac noticed an interesting painting in front of him. It was blue and yellow in an abstract pattern, and it grabbed his attention, so he called his siblings over to see it. They all agreed that it reminded them of something but didn't know what. David saw them all looking at that painting and went to see what they were talking about.

Chase and Marguerite came right over as well, and as soon as she saw the painting, she stopped in her tracks. "Oh … my …God!"

Chase and Marguerite started laughing. Everyone began staring at them, not getting the joke.

Finally, Chase said to David, "Can you remember what you were thinking about when you painted this?"

"Yes. I was thinking about food, and for the life of me, I didn't know why I thought of food when painting this. None of those colors represent any food that I know of, so how strange is that?"

Chase grinned. "Oh, it's going to get stranger, David, because Mam and I know exactly why you thought of food, and who was urging you along to paint this." Now everyone was intrigued. "This is the pattern of our first set of dishes when we first got married."

Marguerite laughed even louder. "So now you know who influenced you on this, right?"

They all broke out in fits of laughter and couldn't stop.

Zac shook his head. "I knew it reminded me of something, and all the others agreed." It was their china pattern.

Mia looked at David. "Ed made you do this?"

"Did you have any other paintings that were weird like that?" Sarah asked.

"One more, but I was saving it for last. I'm saving it for last for sure now." They all laughed again, as they broke up the congestion in that aisle so others could pass by and went their separate ways to keep looking at the exhibit.

Jim, the photographer, came in right on time. Chase and Zac went right to meet him and shook his hand, thanking him for not publishing those photos he had taken the other day. He still couldn't quite believe it. *Mr. Martin kept his word ... he called me.* He said he would, and he did.

"Mr. Martin. I want to tell you that it's an honor meeting you and a privilege being able to take your pictures," Jim said.

Chase was pleased with him, and they spoke about how he wanted to take them and where. Chase told him to make sure they included David and Mia, because it was his show after all.

"What made you come all the way to New York to see an art show?" he asked Chase.

"My wife and I needed to get out a bit, and my sons and daughter wanted to come along, so we rented a condo for a month and here we are. It was just as simple as that!"

At that point, everyone came over to see Jim. The boys and Sarah formally introduced themselves to him. He saw the two sets of twins, knowing about them from all the articles he read on the Martins, and even knew about Sarah being adopted.

Jim thought that he landed the biggest photo shoot of the century.

Chase said to him, "Do you think people will be interested in us even being here? I didn't think so, but everywhere we go it seems that they remember my family and me."

Jim was shocked to hear Chase's humble thoughts. He remembered reading that the whole band was always very unpretentious, even when they were extremely popular.

"Sir, you are still big news, and I have a feeling you *will* be until the end of time."

Chase did not know how to react to that statement and just put his head down and shook it, like he couldn't believe it.

"Mrs. Martin, you're so popular too. Everyone always loved you so. I would like you to know that my mother was in the street at the hospital that night, singing 'It's the Little Things' to you ... along with about four thousand other people."

Marguerite and Chase were shocked to hear that, and were amazed by what a small world it was.

"Imagine that!" Marguerite said. "Can you just imagine that?" She went to Jim and kissed his cheek. "Thank you so much for that. Can I still thank her?" He knew what she was asking, and he said, "Yes, she's well, and was thrilled when I told her that I was going to meet you."

"Can you call her, so I could say hello?"

Jim was practically jumping out of his skin. "Are you sure? You don't have to do that. I just appreciate you letting me take your picture."

Chase said, "Jim, we are honored that your mother came to the hospital that night. Please get her on the phone, if you could, so we could thank her. What is her name?"

"Angela," Jim replied.

Jim did what he was told. "Mom, Chase and Marguerite Martin are here and want to say hello to you. No Mom, I am not kidding. Can you speak to them?" With that, he handed the phone over to Chase.

"Hello, Angela. This is Chase. Your son is a good man. I just wanted to let you know we're enjoying his company and are happy that he's the one taking our pictures tonight... No, I am not kidding!" He then broke into laughter. "My wife would like to speak to you. Would you be up for a conversation with her?"

Marguerite took the phone while everyone listened, including David and Mia. They even knew what Jim was talking about when he mentioned that his mother was in the street singing, 'It's the Little Things', because they'd had just read about it online.

"Hello, Angela. This is Marguerite. I hope you are well. I just wanted to thank you for coming to the hospital that night so many years ago. This is a belated thank you. We appreciated everything that you all did for us that night, and to this day, we have not forgotten how special you all treated us. I also want you to know how much it helped us... You are very welcome. Please take care of yourself... Thank you, bye!"

She then drifted off and everyone knew she needed a moment.

Chase followed her, and after a moment, asked, "Are you thinking of that night?" He was holding both of her hands and keeping them next to his heart.

She nodded her head. "I was trying so hard to get back to you, but my heart was so broken. Then I remembered how much I loved you, and *that* is what brought me back to life again."

They touched foreheads, after he softly kissed hers ... and all the while David and Mia watched from a distance. With that, Chase handed Jim his phone back and said, "Do you want to get started?"

Jim took as many pictures as he could. He took them from everywhere, every way, alone, all together, with Mia, and just with David. Chase put the icing on the cake for Jim by asking if he wanted to do an interview with him and Marguerite. Jim was over-the-moon excited. They went and sat down in the office at the gallery, and he had so many questions that Chase got tired just talking to him. Chase then asked Jim if he would like to interview David. "Yes, I would love that."

Marguerite went to get him, and realized that David was reluctant. "What is it, David? You don't like giving interviews?"

"No, they always make me out to be weird in the articles. They paint me, no pun intended, as standoffish, and tell people that I'm a recluse. I'm just uncomfortable speaking about my paintings."

"Chase will stay with you. Would that make you feel better?"

"For some reason, it does feel better, knowing that Chase would be with me." He took a deep breath and let it out. "Okay, let's give it a try." David went to the office to meet with Jim and Chase.

Jim once again had many questions, and David was a chatterbox with his replies. He couldn't even believe it himself, that he was talking so much, but with Chase there ... he felt calmer.

Jim knew he had just landed two of the biggest interviews in decades, and the smile on his face said just how happy he was. He even had the pictures to back them up.

As he left, he shook Chase's hand and thanked him to high heavens about everything he had done for him that night. Everyone shook Jim's hand, and thanked him for keeping his word by holding on to those pictures like they originally asked.

Chase still had his card. "We might need you for an article later on. We will call you when the time comes. Is that all right with you?"

"Yes, whatever you need from me, please just call. I'll do whatever I can. Thank you again for everything."

The crowd died down, and it was easier now getting through the aisles, so they continued looking at David's paintings. Chase wanted to buy the one with the china pattern. It made them laugh every time they looked at it, so they told Mia to mark it as sold.

They made plans to go out to dinner when the gallery closed that night. They were just going to walk down the street, and Mia had made the reservation, when Zac got a call from his wife, Anna. It was bad news. Aunt Jeanine had passed away earlier that day.

Zac decided to hold that information from everyone until after dinner. He felt his parents needed to get something to eat first, and didn't want to spoil David and Mia's night. Everything was going so well. He had to keep his emotions in check though, because he knew they would feel that something was wrong. He just kept thinking about his daughter Margaret, and that brought joy to his heart, hiding his pain.

Anna told Zac to call her later that night, no matter what time it was, so she could speak to him about Aunt Jeanine. Zac just thought it was going to be about her funeral arrangements, so he didn't give it a second thought. Later, he came to find out that it was something even more unexpected. It was going to shock everyone even more than they already were.

Getting the News

Dinner went great. They all sat around the table provided for them and spoke of everything and anything they could set their minds to. Eventually, everyone saw that Chase and Marguerite were getting tired and asked them if they wanted to go back to the penthouse.

They agreed, but they wanted everyone else to stay and enjoy themselves. They insisted on it, and when they insisted on something, you just did what they wanted you to do.

David, Mia, and Sarah were deep in conversation all night. Zac had noticed how they'd kept looking for her at the gallery. He'd even noticed at dinner the night before. They seemed so interested in her, David especially, and he didn't know why. He wasn't upset about it, but he felt something, and couldn't explain what it was.

When they felt that they had overstayed their welcome, David and Mia invited them over for a nightcap, and they all happily accepted. They went up to the twenty-seventh floor and sat around the living room, making themselves comfortable.

"What's happening, Zac? I know something is bothering you," Sarah asked.

"I was trying to mask my feelings. How did you get through them?" Zac asked, feeling defeated.

"I don't know. I just felt you were hiding something."

Her brothers all looked at the two of them and said, "We didn't feel anything. How did you?"

David and Mia just watched the exchange, mesmerized by the connection they all had to each other.

"I can't explain it. I feel you thinking of Margaret, trying to hide something painful." By hearing that, all the brothers got up immediately.

"What is it? Mom or Dad? Anna?" Before everyone went into a panic, he said, "Anna did call earlier. Aunt Jeanine passed away. I'm supposed to call her now. She said it didn't matter what time; she had more to tell me. I am assuming it's about the funeral."

Sarah became annoyed. "Really Zac? What's wrong with men? If it were just about the funeral, then she would have said to call her back tomorrow. She wouldn't have asked you to call her back no matter what time tonight. Not if it wasn't important. Where did that one hundred and eighty-nine IQ go? Out which window so I could go catch it and give it back to you?" Everyone was shocked at what Sarah had said and just looked at her.

Mark went to her immediately, and wrapped his arms around her. "What's wrong, Sarah? Tell us. What's happening? Are you all right?"

"Nothing is wrong, and yes, I'm fine," she said, as she took deep breaths to calm herself. She didn't know where that had come from.

"I'm sorry, Zac, that I got so annoyed with you. I was just thinking about how Anna has been waiting all night for your call." She went right to her oldest brother, and he embraced her immediately, realizing she was right.

"I deserved it my love. Please forgive me. I'll call Anna right now and apologize. I'll see what she wanted to talk to me about." He bent down to kiss her head.

Sarah thought her behavior might have been due to being upset over losing Aunt Jeanine. They all were upset, because she was the last one of the original group left besides their parents. They all loved her too, and were upset by the news.

Zac excused himself and went to the dining room to make the call.

Zeke explained, "Aunt Jeanine was Uncle Quinn Howard's wife, and the only other family member from the band, aside from my parents, left."

Zeke said, "He really did deserve that, Sarah." He knew she felt bad blowing up at him like that. Twenty minutes later, they were still waiting for his call to come to an end so they could find out more information. Finally, he was finished and came back in.

"First, let me say, I decided not to tell everyone about her death, especially our parents, until after dinner. I felt we should get them to eat first, because they probably wouldn't eat after hearing she had passed away. They're going to be very upset, because they weren't there with her when she died. That's the first thing that's going to happen. Anna, Ari, Catherine, and Cali were all with her until the end though. Knowing this will be the only thing that will be able to soothe them."

They all breathed a sigh of relief, because they knew Zac was right. As the brothers realized that their wives had been there, it made them feel incredibly proud and homesick.

Zac was looking down, and Zeke said, "Just say it, brother. Please!"

Zac nodded. "David, this may shake you." Everyone looked at him, and then stared back at Zac, waiting. He was shaken, and they all could see it.

"Before she died, Aunt Jeanine said that Uncle Quinn told her ... that David is Sarah and Josh's!"

Sarah looked at David, and David looked back at her. Silence settled over the room. Then everyone began talking at the same time.

"What? What does that mean?" Sarah said, crying and not understanding what was going on. "David is Josh's and mine? Why would she say that? I have to talk to Josh! I have to talk to Josh!"

Then they all looked at David, who was pale and staring blankly ahead. It was obvious that he wasn't looking at anybody in particular. Mia shook him to get him to come around, and he finally did. He looked at Sarah and said, "Somehow I know this." Hearing that threw them all into turmoil.

Sarah asked, "Do you know something? Do you feel something? Can you explain it?"

"No. I can't explain anything that's happened to me this week. I was just feeling good about everything, and now I feel like there's another iron in the fire."

He was so upset. He looked at Mia and said, "I wouldn't blame you if you wanted to run away from me screaming. I've turned your life upside down this week. I am so sorry!" This time it was him with tears running down his face.

Mia did not know how to react to what was going on. She knew she had to say something but didn't know what or how to help him. She was confused herself, so she took a deep breath and took him in her arms, holding him until they both could compose their thoughts.

Sarah said, "I swear to you I do not know what that meant. I am so sorry this has all happened to you both. This week has to have been right out of a horror film for you two. Everything you've had to process is beyond comprehension. Nothing we've said can even be taken seriously." She couldn't even speak anymore. Sarah was so upset, and they all knew their parents were up waiting for them. They got up and said they would talk it over again and see if they could make sense out of it, and all but carried Sarah up to their penthouse, to try and see if their parents could help them out.

Mark said to David and Mia, "Will you be all right this evening? Matt and I will stay here with you, in case you need us."

David and Mia were so touched, and remembered that they were family to them now and felt that they really did want to help them, but they said no. They were going to talk it over also, and see if they could make sense out of it.

50
Mom and Dad are waiting

Marguerite and Chase were waiting at the elevator door. "What happened? When we left, everything was going so well. What is going on?"

"We better go sit down," Zac said. They all went to the living room, so that he could explain things better.

Marguerite and Chase looked at Sarah, and again saw how shaken she was. They felt it, and quite frankly, they were so weary from all the drama that week that it was taking a toll on them.

"Aunt Jeanine passed away this morning," Zac said.

Marguerite and Chase became very upset. "Oh no, no … no…we weren't there!"

Just then the front guard called and asked if they would allow David and Mia up to see them. Matt said, "Yes, grant them access whenever they want to come up."

When David and Mia entered the room, they noticed how distraught Marguerite was. She was still overcome. "Chase … we weren't there. How could we have left her alone? She died alone!"

Zac stepped right in. "Mom, that is not true. Anna, Ari, Catherine, and Cali were all there with her. She did *not* die alone. They stayed with her until the end. *She did not die alone!*" He was trying to get that through to them both.

Chase let out a sigh of relief after hearing that. They were still upset, but it made them feel better that family was there with her at the end.

Zac sighed. "There is more." Marguerite and Chase raised their heads to look and see what else there was to be said. "Before she died, Aunt Jeanine said Uncle Quinn wanted Sarah and Josh to know that David was theirs." Now both their jaws dropped. They both got up and just started pacing. "What? What does that mean? What *could* that mean?"

David spoke up. "I feel it's true, but I don't know how. It's just a feeling I have had, and I can't explain it."

Chase asked, "David, are you feeling Sarah? The way we do, I mean?"

"No!"

"How do you feel it's true then?"

"I have a ... a feeling. It's a feeling of peacefulness when I think of it. It's leading me to believe it's true."

"Do you know what it means then?" Chase asked.

"No. I have no idea."

"Do you want to tell us about your family? Maybe something about them will help us figure this out."

"My grandmother raised me. She died when I was 18, and I have been on my own since. Both my parents were in the army, and both were killed in Afghanistan when I was 12. Other than those three people, I've had no family."

Mia hadn't known those details about David and put her arms around him. His grandmother had raised him, which was why he was so thankful for all that he had. She was the one who put the manners on him too. She knew that to be true.

"Sarah, how are you feeling my love?" her mother asked. "This has most likely shaken you, and I can see it on your face ... and we all feel it too."

"What does it mean?" That is all Sarah could get out.

"I don't know, but we will find out for you both."

Marguerite took over and started shouting out instructions to everyone. "Mark, make arrangements for the plane to come get us tomorrow. Then call Josh and have him come here to be with Sarah. We have to get back to London, and he needs to be here. Sarah, are you okay with that? Shall we get Josh here for you?"

All she could do was nod her head. She knew she needed her husband. "Thank you," Sarah said, looking at her mother now.

"David, will you come back to London with us? I know you have your show. It's open until Friday correct?" He nodded. "Then we will send the plane back to get you both on Friday night."

They had broken into smaller groups, talking things out, when Marguerite went to Mia and took both of her hands. "Mia, this is so hard for you both, but women are stronger than men when it comes to emotional things. David needs you. I know you have a shop to run, but please don't abandon him now. He's been abandoned enough in his lifetime."

It wasn't until Marguerite finished saying this that something clicked deep within Mia's heart.

"I could never leave him. I love him and will never leave him ... no matter what comes up, spooky or not." Now tears were falling from her eyes.

"Please go tell him before his heart breaks again!" she whispered to her. Mia walked to David and wrapped her arms around him.

"You told me earlier that you wouldn't blame me for running far away from you. I am telling you now; I will never run away from you. I want to be with you until the day I die, if you will let me and have me! I love you David, and promise to help you however way I can." Her voice was fading to a whisper. "I will never leave you, never."

David couldn't control the tears forming in his eyes, and as he looked at Mia in amazement, he believed that she would not leave him.

He kissed her softly. "Thank you. Thank you for loving me. Thank you for not abandoning me."

Mia was stunned. He had used the same word as Marguerite: Abandoned. That is how he felt when his parents died and when his grandmother died. It explained a lot. When he kept asking her to stay by his side at the gallery, or to stay with him at his condo, it was all because of that. He had told her multiple times. It stunned her and all made sense now.

"Mia and David, you are staying here with us tonight," Marguerite said. "Please get your things and come back. Don't even think of refusing. I will give you twenty minutes to complete what I just told you to do."

They both looked at her and knew she meant it. Off they went to get their things, and once that elevator door closed, they all started talking over each other and it was just crazy.

"Enough!" Chase yelled.

They all just stopped. Chase had never raised his voice.

"I'm sorry," he said, taking a deep calming breath. "Can we just blame the crankiness on the events of this week? Please? I am so sorry."

"Let's make some coffee and something to eat, and try to relax for what is left of this evening. As tired as your mother and I are, I don't think we can close an eye yet."

Sarah and Mark went to the kitchen and started the coffee, and made something to snack on.

Mam and Chase went to the terrace and just stared out at the skyline, trying to clear their minds and find some peace while silently grieving for their sister Jeanine.

David and Mia were back within fifteen minutes. There was plenty of room for everyone in the penthouse.

51
Taking control

The boys were shocked and stunned that their mother had turned into a drill sergeant. Of course, she was always in control, but this time, it was different. She was barking out instructions left and right. Even David and Mia were doing as they were told.

Everyone settled down. The coffee was made, and Sarah also made some sandwiches. Everything was at the snack bar so the family could help themselves.

They left their mom and dad alone on the terrace, so they could regroup. For some reason, it felt like they were kids again and had just been scolded for something. They had been surrounded by drama and they just needed a break from it all. Sarah delivered two cups of coffee to them, and practically ran back to the condo. Everyone was quiet. No stories were being told, as they were all trying to regroup.

After about an hour, Marguerite and Chase came back in to say goodnight. Everyone got up and went to hug them. As Chase followed Marguerite to their room, he closed and locked the door. Marguerite couldn't help but laugh when he did that.

She just looked at him as he undressed, walking over to her. She giggled like she was young again. "What are you up to?"

All he could do is smile back at her. She was 91, and he was 87, and he looked like he was ready to chase her around the bed. Her eyes got wide and she couldn't believe what he was thinking. They hadn't had sex in a while. They'd lost track of how long it had been, but for some reason, he was all stirred up and ready to go.

She was 91!

Marguerite crawled under the covers and held her arms out for him, and he gladly went to her. Then he kissed her, as strongly and passionately as he could for an old man, and began to try some old moves on her. All she could do was laugh like they were in their twenties again. Everyone in the living room could hear them laughing, and it made them all smile and laugh too.

David said, "You don't think they're ... you know ... having sex?"

As soon as they heard David say that, they all burst into laughter. Mia, Sarah, and the rest couldn't even think about it.

Mark said, "Please change the subject. Please!" They had needed that laughter though and everyone calmed right down soon after.

Matt said, "It's quiet in there. I hope they just fell asleep!"

"Should we go knock or let them be?" Mark asked.

Zac said, "I'm not knocking."

Zeke said, "No way, not me."

Sarah said, "I am not getting in trouble with them again today."

Mia and David were laughing so hard listening to them all.

Everyone was very tired, so they all headed to their rooms and went to bed smiling. David's hug with Sarah lingered a little longer than the others. For some reason, they couldn't let go of each other. They knew that, sooner or later; they were going to find out what Aunt Jeanine's message from Uncle Quinn had meant.

Leaving for London

Marguerite and Chase got up early in the morning. They went out to the bakery and got pastry and bagels for breakfast before anyone else was even up. When they woke up, the coffee was on and that delicious smell was spread throughout the penthouse. The table was all set and they found them on the terrace having coffee and reading the paper.

No one said a word to them about what they heard or didn't hear the previous night. They were all trying not to think about it, or look directly at them, because both of them had red chapped lips.

They went to them and kissed them good morning after getting coffee and joined them on the terrace. The morning was beautiful. The sun was up and shining brightly; it was already warm. It was a good day to be outside, and it was a good day for flying home.

Security called and asked if they could let Josh up, and Mark told them it was quite all right.

Sarah couldn't wait to see Josh after everything that had happened in the past few days. Josh had brought a bigger surprise with him: Anna, Ari, Catherine, and Cali all came with him to the States to retrieve their spouses.

When the elevator door opened, revealing them all, the joy was overwhelming. Hearing all the commotion, Marguerite and Chase came in to see what was going on. All her daughters-in-law ran to Marguerite and hugged her, and then did the same to their father-in-law, Chase.

One by one, they were introduced to Mia and David, and they were so happy to meet them. They'd heard all about them from their husbands, and were hoping for a private viewing of David's show before they boarded the plane to go back to London. David was shocked and thrilled that they wanted to see the gallery.

Sarah introduced Josh to Mia first, and he shook her hand. Then David stepped forward.

"Josh, this is David Allen."

Josh suddenly turned pale, and everyone saw it. When they looked at David, he was pale too.

"I know you from somewhere," Josh said, "but I just can't place you."

David said, "I feel the same about you, but I *know* I've never met you before."

Not to start any more drama so early, Marguerite said, "Let's have some breakfast. We have a lot to do before we leave today for home."

They all went to the dining room, where the table was already set for fourteen people. That's when they figured out their mom had made the arrangements for all the wives to arrive with Josh. All the boys were surprised at their mother for arranging that, and not even giving it away. Once again, she seemed to fix everything, just like when they were children. She cured whatever ailment they had, and took the pain away from every bump and scratch they got.

After breakfast, David set a time for everyone to meet at the gallery. He wanted to open it up for them before they had to go.

53 The House

David and Mia went back to their condo to get ready for the show that night. They were also excited about opening the gallery early, so that all of the Martins could see his paintings before they headed back to London.

"I'm going to bring the painting I was going to give Chase and Marguerite as a gift, and give it to them when they come to the gallery this afternoon. What do you think? Do you still think it's a good idea?" David asked.

"Yes, I think it's a great idea. We could pack it up with the other painting they purchased." They both laughed, remembering how funny it was that everyone knew what those colors and pattern meant. They headed towards the gallery to make everything ready for the influx of their new family.

Back at the penthouse, everyone was packed and ready to go. They all walked down the street to the gallery and all the girls were excited to see David's work. David and Mia were waiting at the door for them, and greeted everyone with hugs and kisses, thanking them for wanting to see his work. Mia locked the door behind them, because after all, this was a private viewing. They were with their family and did not want to be disturbed.

Everyone walked up and down the aisles, amazed at David's work. They loved all of the colors he used. The paintings were light, airy, and happy looking. Mia and David were watching them and were happy to see smiles on everyone's faces. They knew they were all pleased with what they were seeing. All the wives picked out a painting they wanted to purchase, and all the husbands happily agreed.

Sarah and Josh got to the end of the showing and suddenly stopped. Up on the wall was a painting of their house in London, and it took their breath away. They just stared at it, amazed.

"David!" Sarah almost yelled. Everyone became concerned and followed her voice to find her.

Chase and Marguerite were first to find her, and followed Josh's eyes right up to the painting. They couldn't believe what they were seeing either. Then everyone else arrived, and they all just stood there gawking at a painting of their parents' house.

David said, "I'm so glad you like this, because it's a gift from me to you, Marguerite and Chase."

They looked at him, and Chase asked, "When did you paint this?" He sounded amazed.

"I have been painting it for months now. I see it in my dreams all the time, and I just had to paint it. I still dream about it, and can't figure out why it's always so vivid in my mind. I dreamed about it again just the other night. I always look at it and say the same thing."

Then, at the same time, Josh and David both said, "What are you trying to tell me?"

Everyone realized that this was in the dream Josh had the other night—the one he'd called Sarah about. Josh and David just looked at each other, shaken.

"I know why you look familiar, David. I had a dream the other night that woke me up. I dreamed of you painting this picture, and then I saw you standing in front of it, asking, 'What are you trying to tell me?'"

Sarah remembered him telling her that as well. She had told the family about it. At the time it didn't mean anything, so they'd all dismissed it.

Chase asked David, "Do you know whose house this is?"

"No, I thought it was just an English house. I never saw it before. I'm sure it's just something I dreamed."

Chase shook his head, looking at David. "David, this is our house in London! You have captured it exquisitely. There isn't anything missing. From the front gates to the courtyard, the garages, and the color of the house ... everything is there. This is our home."

David thought he was going to pass out. He had been feeling like that a lot since meeting the Martins. Once again, Mia had him around his waist, so he wouldn't fall over.

Chase said, "Tell us more about your dreams."

"The dreams were not upsetting, which is why they confused me. I just kept seeing this house and felt like I had to paint it. Then after we met, Mia and I discussed it, and decided I was going to present it to you as a gift for helping me all week, and for making us part of your family."

At that moment, Josh and Sarah went to David and embraced him while everyone watched.

"I don't know why I felt like doing that," Josh said. "Do you, Sarah?"

"We just feel drawn to you, David, and felt we needed to go to you." She then looked at Josh, "Did you feel that way?" Josh just nodded his head yes.

"I didn't mind at all," David said. "It made me feel better. I hate even to term it this way, but I felt like your child ... and you had come to help me when I was distressed."

Anna looked at the four of them. "Aunt Jeanine's message from Uncle Quinn meant the same thing. She said, 'Tell Josh and Sarah ... David is theirs.'"

"What could that mean though? David *had* parents. Josh and I never had any children." Sarah's voice broke when she said that.

Mia said, "David, you feel drawn to Sarah, don't you?"

"Yes, but I can't explain how or why."

"And Josh, in your dream, you saw David. Was it David for sure?"

"Yes, I'm sure it was David."

"The four of us are all tied together. Now we just have to find out why. I have a feeling we will, but not right at this moment. Would you all agree?"

Everyone nodded. They all agreed.

Mia continued, "I think we're trying too hard right now to figure out and make sense out of everything that's happened to us. This isn't over. Do we all agree on that also?"

Again, everyone nodded in agreement.

Marguerite said to David, "We will gladly accept this gift from you. It is so beautiful, and we all love it." The smile on David's face revealed how happy he was that they loved it and accepted his gift.

They took it down and went to pack it up. They also went to retrieve the other painting Chase and Marguerite had purchased, and when the girls saw it, they all started laughing.

"Mom, isn't this your old china pattern?" Anna asked. Everyone started laughing over that painting all over again. They knew they were going to laugh every time they saw it hanging.

Marguerite said, "This is a good story to tell when we are on the plane. You'll all love finding out what possessed David to paint it."

It was time to go. The cars were waiting outside the gallery to take them to the airport. They were sad for a few reasons, and told David and Mia how they felt.

Marguerite took one of each of their hands, and said, "We're sad leaving you. I don't think you know just how much you mean to us all now. We're sad too because we're going home to a funeral of someone who was a sister to Chase and me. She was our last connection to our past, and we wish we weren't so old right now."

Chase sensed Sarah's distress, leaving David and Mia, so he said, "Sarah, do you and Josh want to stay here with David and Mia? You can come home with them on Friday."

Josh spoke right up, "Would you mind if we stayed? I feel like we should for some reason, and come home with them." Sarah's face lit up when he said that, because that was exactly what she was feeling as well. It was killing her to leave them, and she didn't know why. They all said their goodbyes, but knew they would be seeing each other in two days.

Chase and Marguerite were the last to say goodbye. Marguerite grabbed Mia's face and kissed her. "Call me for any reason at all, but most of all, call to check in with us. You are family now, and this is one of our rules." She ended her talk, smiling at Mia.

Mia was so happy, and the smile on her face confirmed it. Then Marguerite kissed David and told him the same. Chase kissed Mia, and said, "Take care of David and yourself. Call if you need anything."

Then, as they are both in the doorway, holding hands, Chase looked back and said, "I think the only way we can leave you now is knowing we will see you in two days."

Chase's last statement blew David and Mia right out of the water. Josh and Sarah went right to them and engulfed them in their comforting arms.

54. Arrangements

It seemed like Chase always had the daunting task of arranging all the funerals for his brothers and sisters, including Ed. Arranging Jeanine's was even worse, because she was the last of their extended family. She had already discussed the arrangements with both Chase and Marguerite, regarding what she wanted when it was her time.

After everything was arranged, Chase called Jim, their new photographer friend, and asked if he would like to do a short article on Jeanine and her passing. Jim was amazed that he'd even called him, but then dismissed the feeling. *He said he would and he did.* Just like with the pictures, he had given his word that he would call for more pictures, and he kept it. Chase threw in a bonus this time.

"Would you like to come to London, so you can write the article after the funeral is over?"

Jim practically jumped out of his skin, "I would be honored to cover Mrs. Howard's funeral for you Mr. Martin."

"Can you be ready on Friday night? We have a plane ready to pick up my daughter and her husband, Josh Foster. David Allen and Mia Addison will be joining us too."

Again, Jim said yes immediately, and told his paper where he was going and the reason for his travel. They were thrilled with him and his new connections. All the arrangements were made, and they were all set.

Jeanine did not want a viewing, but she did want a mass, celebrating her life. Only family were allowed—no one else—so the service was not publicized. Many papers and TV stations tried to reach Chase for a statement, and to find out what was happening with the funeral, but he didn't return any calls. Their office issued a statement that simply read:

Jeanine Mercer Howard—the wife of Quinn Howard of the Band 4— passed away peacefully on the 29th of August. Mrs. Howard was surrounded by family when she passed away. The funeral arrangements are private at the request of Mrs. Howard and her family.

The papers went wild, wanting to talk to Chase and Marguerite. Chase was the only living member of The Band 4 left, and it grieved him to no end. He was missing all of his brothers so much more with Jeanine's passing. You could just see it on his face. Marguerite didn't know how to help him when he got like that. She knew he wanted to be alone, so she let him go so he could mourn the loss of all of his family in his own way.

After hours of being locked up in their room, Marguerite finally thought, *I have to get him out of there*. She went in and found him just lying down, staring at nothing. She remembered that he'd looked the same way when she first met him.

"Come back to me, Chase," she said. "I can't feel you, and it frightens me." Once she said that, he snapped right out of the state he was in.

"I'm so sorry. I didn't mean to frighten you. I would never want you to feel that way." He took both of her hands, kissed them softly, and held them to his cheeks. "You can't feel me?"

"No, I don't know why but ... right now, I can't feel you."

When he thought about it, he realized that he couldn't feel her either, and it alarmed him. If he had been able to, he would have felt her fear. This made them both upset and scared. They couldn't feel each other. Was their time coming now too?

"Lay here with me, Mam. I want to feel you in my arms, and maybe our feelings will return to us."

Mam climbed under the covers, and he wrapped her in his arms. They both sighed with relief.

"I'm not ready to go yet, Mam. I feel like it just isn't time for us yet. Do you feel that way too? Something isn't right yet. That much I do feel ... and now with Jeanine's death ... maybe that's why I feel it's not our time yet."

"I feel that way too," Marguerite said. "I thought that once Ed and Lilli found each other it would be time ... but now I feel like that's not what we've been waiting for."

"Yes, exactly. That is *exactly* what I feel, so maybe we *are* going to be around a little bit longer. Mam, are you tired? Do you feel like you *want* it to be our time? Do you want it to be over?"

"No." She looked into his eyes. "I will never want us to be done. We are so lucky! We both feel good. We have no health issues. The only issue we have is old age! I cannot even think of not being with you. How lucky have we been? There is so much love we still share between us. I can only thank God every day I wake up for allowing me to keep living my dream for another day."

With that, he kissed her. "Thank you. I feel better already ... and surprising enough, there it is. I feel you again. I feel your happiness, and I feel your love for me."

They both smiled as she snuggled closer to Chase, and he held her tighter.

55
Heading to London

David and Mia were all packed and ready to go. They were so excited to be going to London to be with the rest of their new family. They couldn't wait.

Mia checked in with Phyllis, who was managing her shop back in Pennsylvania. Everything was going fine, so she told her what her plans were. Phyllis was surprised to hear that Mia was heading to London, not realizing all that had been happening in Mia's life that week. Mia also checked in with her best friend, Judy, to let her know what was happening. Judy was shocked. She told Phyllis and Judy both that she would explain more once she got back, and they both said they couldn't wait to hear *that* story. They knew it was going to be a good one!

Sarah and Josh were also excited to bring David and Mia home with them. Even though they were headed home to a somber occasion, they were still happy to have David and Mia with them. They were pleased Jim would be making the trip with them as well. He was very nice, and they took to him immediately.

The pictures he took and articles he had written were plastered across two full pages of the New York Paper. When Chase picked up the paper and opened it up, it shocked him and Marguerite. He couldn't believe they had dedicated two full pages to David's show, Chase, and his family.

THE MARTINS INVADE NEW YORK

This was the headline at the top of the page, with all of their pictures and the article. He was so stunned. Chase and Marguerite looked at all of the photos and read the article three times, because it was so good. He was wonderful to them all, throughout the whole article. No one could believe how great Jim's article was about David, and even Mia ... calling her his girlfriend. Jim had credited her with helping David with the show, and helping him emotionally get ready to receive the public.

In the end, it all had turned out very well.

The gallery was all locked down and Jim was already there along with Josh and Sarah. The cars arrived right on time to pick them up, and take them to the plane.

David and Mia were shocked when they got on the plane along with Jim. The pilot and flight attendant were there to welcome them on board. They followed Josh's lead, shaking both their hands and thanking them for coming back to get them. The pilot just replied, "It's a privilege to fly you again, Mr. and Mrs. Foster." He then turned and introduced the rest to them, and they did the same, shaking their hands in amazement.

Once they settled in, the pilot announced that they were second in line for take-off, and before they knew it, they were up in the air. David and Mia just looked around the plane, trying to take everything in. They noticed Jim doing the same thing, and they all smiled at each other.

Once they hit cruising altitude, Josh got up immediately to see if they were doing okay. The attendant came over as well, and offered everyone something to drink, to which Josh said, "Yes, we'll all have something, I think. How about some white wine? Is everyone okay with that?" Mia and Jim nodded. They loved it!

Sarah also came over after Josh motioned for her to come see everyone. It was a fun trip home. David had a million questions about the plane, and Josh was able to answer all of them. They were bonding. Sarah and Mia noticed this, and smiled at the two of them deep in conversation.

Jim just sat back and enjoyed every minute of the flight. Mia said, "We are all going to be in a chapter of Jim's autobiography, I just know it. I see his wheels turning as we speak." They both laughed and got a kick out of him.

Next, it was time for dinner. Some took naps, after Josh encouraged them to, because the time difference was going to be a killer. They left at eight in the east, which was two in the morning for London, and it was a seven-hour trip, arriving at nine o'clock in the morning.

A car picked them up at the hanger in the airport. Marguerite and Chase were at the house, waiting for them. The boys and families were going to be in later that day.

Marguerite made room in the den for David and Mia, and they had a room over the garage for Jim. Even with all the bedrooms, space was still tight, but everyone was comfortable enough.

When David and Mia arrived at the Martins', they just stood in the courtyard looking at the house. Again, David was shocked. How could he have painted this house when he had never seen it in real life before? The building looked just like he had painted it.

All at once Josh felt something. He didn't know what to make of it. He thought he was feeling David and his emotions, when he looked at the house. David looked at Josh and felt like he was feeling him too! Neither said anything, because they couldn't explain it, but it was on both of their minds.

This must be what Sarah feels all the time with her family, Josh thought. *Amazing.*

56 · The Funeral

Everyone had arrived home, and the house was full. David and Mia had already met Anna, Ari, Catherine, and Cali. They felt very comfortable around them, especially after they'd immediately hugged the two of them when they arrived. After that, the daughters arrived, which included Margaret with her boyfriend, Henry, Mary with her fiancé, Ben, Jess with her boyfriend, Will, and Amelia with her fiancé, Stefan.

The Martin men immediately got tense when the boyfriends arrived with their daughters. Chase was feeling them all. He just smiled and shook his head, thinking it was funny because that was the reaction he'd had when Sarah brought Josh home. You could tell all the fathers were trying to at least tolerate the boyfriends.

David and Mia saw it and also laughed, because they remembered talking about it at dinner one night. They thought that, if they could, the Martin men would kidnap their daughters and hide them until they said they hated men and didn't want to ever date or get married.

Marguerite showed David the old China pattern she had, and held it up to the painting, which now hung in the kitchen. She wanted him to see how it matched exactly, and they all got a kick out of that.

"Mom told us the story of how you painted this," Anna said, "and we couldn't stop laughing on the plane home. Now every time I see this painting, I'll laugh about it."

Jim piped up. "What *is* the story behind it?"

Everyone just got quiet.

"Let's save it for another time," Chase said, trying to dismiss the question quickly. They had to remember to keep those conversations in check in front of Jim. They didn't want to explain about how they could feel each other. What an article that would have turned out to be!

THE MARTINS LIVE IN A DELUSIONAL WORLD.

Not so flattering a headline.

Everyone settled down and headed to bed that night, as they set a time for leaving the next day. The service would be at nine, so they had to be there at 8:30.

Chase delivered an ultimatum speech to all: "Be ready by eight or we're leaving without you. Breakfast is at seven." Everyone knew he meant what he said. The siblings knew that both of their parents were going to be emotional that day, and they didn't want to upset them any further.

The next morning the coffee was on early. There were scones and pastries on the table, along with eggs and toast, and everyone was in the kitchen by seven for breakfast. There were a total of twenty-two people in the house, but it always had many visitors, so Chase and Marguerite knew they could fit everyone. Sarah and her mother got mostly everything ready the night before, of course, with the help of the other Martin women.

By eight o'clock in the morning, everyone was ready, waiting for all the cars with security guards to take them to the church where Jeanine's service was being held. They got more and more subdued as the time neared.

Chase said to Jim, "Please don't take any pictures of the church service. I think once we get to the yard, you'll know what to take and when."

They all arrived at the church, and the press was already there, having gotten wind of the service. They were all lined up, snapping photos left and right. Most of them expressed their condolences.

"We are so sorry for your loss, Mr. and Mrs. Martin." Chase nodded to everyone, acknowledging that he'd heard them. Then they were all ushered into the building by their bodyguards.

The service was so moving, and Father Holland did a fantastic job of recapping Quinn and Jeanine's life. His mentor had been Father Cummings, who was the spiritual adviser to all of the band members and their families, so he knew about all of them, and was able to personalize the service, which made them happy.

ED - FOR LOVE AND HOPE

Jeanine's body was not at the church. It was already waiting at the chapel yard, where they were going to say their final goodbyes to her before following her to the crypt.

The bodyguards and police kindly asked the press to leave, and they complied out of respect for the family. No one followed them. The fans, on the other hand, knew where she would be, and the streets were lined five deep up to the chapel. The family was amazed by how many had come out. It was very overwhelming for Marguerite and Chase, who just closed their eyes, hanging onto each other.

The fans stopped right at the opening of the yard, out of respect for Jeanine and the Martins.

Chase had told Jim, "You will know when to take pictures," and at that moment he knew. He took pictures of all of the people in the streets, waiting to see the family. Chase was the only one left of a legendary group that had shaped history with their music.

Emotions were kept in check until they reached the crypt—a massive marble building that held the remains of all Chase's brothers and sisters, baby Margaret, and Sarah's birth mother, Sarah. There were also spaces for all of those who had not yet passed away, and more.

On the front of the crypt was labeled simply the #: 4. That is all Chase and his brothers had wanted, when they got together to design it before any of them had died. They knew they wanted to be together, even in death.

Chase and Marguerite became distraught. Everyone felt it coming and were trying to control their emotions so as not to add to their distress, but they couldn't control their feelings for much longer. They were all in bad shape. Mia and David became upset as well. They now felt like they were family, and seeing how overwhelmed everyone was also upset them.

They walked into the building, and Marguerite stopped with Chase to put a single rose on baby Margaret's marker. Then they both kissed her and just hung on to each other, remembering holding her when she was born and saying goodbye because she hadn't made it. The siblings paid their respects and kissed their sister too. While Chase and Marguerite had five other children, they never seemed to get over losing baby Margaret.

They did the same for Sarah's birth mother, forever grateful to her for giving them a daughter, and for that, they placed a rose on her marker as well.

It wasn't over yet though. They both went to each of their brothers and sisters and laid a hand on each of their markers, while hanging onto each other. Then they lowered their heads and let their foreheads lean against the cool marble where each one of them was laid to rest. Everyone felt their hearts break, and just lost it, when Marguerite and Chase kissed every single one of them, before they left.

The children knew this was killing them, missing them so much. They knew how much their parents still loved them, and could feel how unbearable it was to them. They tried to control their own emotions, knowing their parents could feel them, but lost that battle when their grief took control of both their hearts and minds.

Everyone knew there was nothing any one of them could say or do to help them at that moment. Although they had all known it would be bad, it was worse than any of them could ever have imagined it would be.

57 Something New

Mam and Chase went to their room after the funeral and did not come out, even for dinner. They were just spent from trying to cope with what had just happened that day, and missing all of their brothers and sisters.

"David and I were looking online and noticed that, in almost every picture, they were always together. Your aunts, uncles, and even Ed!" Mia commented.

Matt nodded. "Yes, we were all family. They went everywhere with us, and we went everywhere with them. They came along even when we went to Pennsylvania to see my mom's family. No one could separate them."

Mark smiled. "My dad always said that they were one-quarter of each other, and not one-quarter of the band. They went to every ultrasound appointment when my mom was pregnant with us. They also went with them when they were checking out schools for us to attend, and they all had to agree on everything, which they usually did. They were their own little democracy."

Talking about the past and the family made everyone in the room feel better somehow. After the trying day, everyone went to bed early, and all the hugging and kissing started again. Mia and David just loved all of the warm feelings they received from their new family.

The next day, Chase and Marguerite were up early again. The table was all set, and they were just waiting for everyone to come down for breakfast. Jim said that he had to get back to New York, and made arrangements for a return flight. Chase offered to have the plane take him back, but he refused and said that the paper was picking up the return flight home.

He was getting ready to leave, and thanked Chase and Marguerite for all they had done for him. He wished them well, and said, "If there is anything you ever need from me, please just call. You have my number."

Marguerite said, "Please send our warmest regards to your mother."

Jim was pleased to hear that.

Chase said to his wife, "Let's get out of here this afternoon."

"Okay ... where to?"

"Let's go to lunch. Just the two of us."

They made arrangements to go to lunch at Rocco Jr.'s, where he was always so happy to see them. He sat them in the private dining room and they stayed talking for hours, enjoying the calm after the week they'd just had.

"Chase, do you think anyone got upset that we left them?"

"No, I think they knew just to let us go."

"You're probably right."

Back at the house, Sarah asked David and Mia how long they had been together.

Mia said, "Only seven days." The response shocked them all.

"That's it?" Anna said. "Seven days? You two look like you've been together for years!"

Mia told them the story of how they met, and all that had happened between them. She explained how drawn they were to each other. They knew, somehow, that they were meant to be together.

"It sounds like how my parents met," Mark chimed in.

David and Mia just looked at him. "Tell us about it. We kind of know how they met, because they told us that first night we came over for dinner."

Zeke continued, "They met on a Friday, he asked her to marry him on Monday, and in eight days they were married. This was sixty-four years ago."

"When Dad told Uncle Ed that he was getting married, the first thing he asked him was 'Are you going to be a dad?' He thought my mom was pregnant, and that's why they were getting married in such a hurry, but Dad just said no. They hadn't even had sex yet, which threw Uncle Ed off. This was until he met my mom and saw the connection they had to each other."

David and Mia were shocked, "We didn't know that. Is that why the Internet froze up when everyone heard he got married so quickly?"

Matt said, "Maybe. Everyone was used to seeing all of my uncles with my aunts, so if one of them had gotten married, they would have expected it. My dad was never with anyone. He hardly dated and never had a steady girlfriend, so when the news broke that he had gotten married, everyone went crazy and flooded the internet to find out about my mother."

"Did the fans hate her when they found out?" Mia asked.

"No, because once they got back from their honeymoon, my dad had a concert at the O2 Arena. He introduced my mom to everyone at the concert. He brought her right out on stage. She thought she was going to have a coronary when he did that, but she asked the fans if they would take care of my dad for her when he was on the road, and she couldn't be with him. With that statement, she won them over, and they loved her from that moment on. Then she thanked them for being so kind to her that night. That did it! They made it their mission to love her right back. That's why everyone loves her so much. Every time something tragic happened to us, they supported her and my father more than they could have ever imagined."

"I think that's why they're always so kind and grateful to everyone around them," Matt said.

58. The Proposal and Revelations

All of a sudden David looked at Mia and said, "You told me you wanted to be with me until the day you died, if I would have you or want you. The truth is, I do want you. I do want to be with you until the day one of us dies. I know I love you. I know you love me. I told you I wanted you by my side at the gallery, but in all honesty, I want you by my side forever and everywhere, not just at the gallery. I feel it in my heart that we were meant to be together. I know it's right somehow. Do you feel it too?"

Mia had tears running down her face, as she was looking directly at David. She noticed that he didn't look down when he spoke to her. He had the courage to look right at her, and it warmed her heart.

"Yes, I feel it too. I feel your love for me, David. I somehow know we should be together. I'm sure of it."

Marguerite and Chase arrived just in time to hear David and Mia's declaration of love to each other, and were so happy for them. As they stood there with arms wrapped around each other, they heard the rest.

"Mia, I love you. We can figure out where to live and all the little things later. Please marry me. Please let me be your husband. I have never wanted or needed anything more in my entire life than the way I want and need you. Will you marry me?"

Mia was so overwhelmed at that point, she could barely get out the words of her answer. "Yes ... I will marry you. I love you too, David, and I know I want to be your wife!"

Everyone erupted at the same time, with best wishes, hugs, and kisses. It was amazing what was going on. Everyone needed some happy news, and this just did it.

David and Mia went over to Josh and Sarah, and said, "Will you give us your blessing? Will you love us as if we were your children? Somehow, I feel like you are our parents, and I wish with all my heart that I could explain why I feel that way towards you."

At that moment, Josh looked at Sarah and said, "I feel David!"

Everyone was shocked when he said that. David replied, "I can feel you too, Josh."

Sarah asked David, "What are you feeling?"

"I feel Josh thinking I was a son to him, and I feel the love he has for me already. I feel the love he has for you, Sarah. All of these feelings are so strong, and I feel them!"

Josh said, "I feel the love you want to send us, but you're holding back, because you don't want to be hurt if we don't return the sentiment."

Sarah and Josh pulled David and Mia into the biggest hug. They both wrapped their arms around the two of them and didn't let go. "Of course, you have our blessing, and we are so honored that you want it from us," Josh told them.

All this was happening right in front of everyone. The shock on all of their faces was amazing. Josh couldn't feel Sarah, but he could feel David.

Anna said, "Uncle Quinn told Aunt Jeanine that David was theirs, and to tell them. Now I think we all know what that means."

Now David and Mia were bound to Josh and Sarah, and they knew it would be a strong bond.

Marguerite and Chase were the last to congratulate them. Mia and David walked right over to them and saw that they too had tears streaming down their cheeks.

Chase said, "We are so happy for you both. Finding love is hard enough, but you did find each other and are making a wise choice ... committing to each other. Don't ever let love slip by you. You will always regret it if you do." Marguerite just stood there, nodding her head in agreement.

Then Chase spoke to Josh and Sarah. "I don't think you fully realize what has happened. In New York, you finally told your mother and I about losing your child twenty-three years ago ... how hard it hit you then and how that loss still affects you now. Do you not think it is odd that it hit you like a brick on the head right when you were about to meet David? Sarah, David is 23!"

"Uncle Quinn's message to you and Josh meant this exact thing." He kissed Sarah on the cheek. "You, my love, were led right to us when you were a baby. Your mother and I believed at the time that you were *supposed* to be ours. Especially since you had the same bond to us all that we had with each other. How odd was that?"

"Now your husband, who was never able to feel you or any of us the way we feel each other, has a bond with David. We were all led to David. We were on a mission for Uncle Ed, and now not only did he find his wife, whom he had been pining for almost sixty-five years, but he also just gave you a gift from God. That gift is David."

Everyone just stood there, shocked by Chase's revelation. It all started to make sense.

Zac said, "Sarah ... David was meant to be yours, just like you were meant to be ours all of those years ago. Josh didn't have that bond with you, because his bond was supposed to be with David. Not us! Does anyone else see it as I do?"

Everyone agreed that they all felt it too.

"David," Chase said, "is there any way we could speak to Ed?"

No sooner did he say that than Ed appeared.

"Chase and Mam," Ed said, and walked right to them. They embraced. Everyone began crying.

"Ed, are we on the right track with what is happening with David, Sarah, and Josh? Could this be happening to them, the way it happened when we got Sarah?"

"Yes brother, you are exactly right." Ed nodded, smiling gratefully. "We are so happy you all helped Lilli and I find each other. We wanted to give you a gift back. David is that gift, for Josh and my Sarah. Spooky?"

They all laughed, which released a lot of tension in the room. Ed looked around at all of them, seeing that they all had their arms wrapped around each other.

"I know you buried Jeanine yesterday. I am so sorry. I know how you're all feeling. She was the last. But before I give my thoughts back to David, I want to tell you this." He looked at the boys and Sarah. "I know you're worried about losing your parents, but they still have time left. Heaven's not ready for them yet, but please know that that is truly where they will be going. That's my final gift to all of you. It's not time for your parents to leave this earth yet." Looking back at Chase, Ed said, "One more thing brother, it's time to give David and Mia the letters I gave you. You remember what to do right?"

"Yes, I know, and will carry out your instructions as you wished them."

"I love you, Chase. I love you, Mam."

Before they could even reply, David was back.

Oh my God! All of the brothers were looking at each other, and the wives and the grandchildren were amazed. They couldn't believe what just happened.

Marguerite said, "Let's sit and try to process."

They all nodded their heads, because none of them could put two sentences together right at that moment.

Settling Down

They sat and talked for hours about what had just happened. They felt a peacefulness surround them, because now they had so many answers to so many questions they had been wondering about.

Cali said, "Why don't we all let David and Mia talk now. I'm sure they want to talk more to Sarah and Josh without all of us around." They got up and hugged Sarah, Josh, David, and Mia, and then left.

When Marguerite and Chase got up to leave, David said, "Can you stay? Please?" So they sat back down to hear the rest of the conversation.

David looked at Sarah and Josh. "Is it too early to ask you if we could call you Mom and Dad. I feel like that's the way it should be between us."

Josh and Sarah started crying. They could barely get the words out.

"You really want to call us that?" asked Josh.

"Are you offended? That we want to address you as our parents?"

"No ... not at all. We are so honored you want us to be your parents. We could just not be any happier at this moment in our lives," Josh told them, looking at Sarah, who was nodding her head.

Sarah reached out to take David and Mia's hands. "We love you so much already."

"I can feel the love you have for us through Josh," David said. "He's sending it to me now, so I know this is how it's supposed to be."

Then they all looked at Chase and Marguerite, who were smiling and so happy for the four of them.

"What can we call you?"

Chase smiled. "My granddaughters call me Papa, and they call my wife Nana."

"Would you be offended if we called you that too?"

"No. We would be honored." They both got up and hugged David first, and then Mia. "Now you both really *are* family."

Chase and Marguerite decided to head off to bed to let the four of them continue their conversation. Marguerite hugged Sarah and told her, "I am so happy for you, and I can feel how happy you are. That hole in your heart was just filled up, and I think it will overflow for all the days of your life."

Chase hugged his daughter, and told her he loved her. Then they both went to Josh again, and told him they loved him and were very happy for him as well. As they went to bed, Chase and Marguerite just looked at each other, remembering what Ed had told them.

"Maybe we should stop trying to look for a reason to leave this earth," Chase told her.

"I think you're right about that. All the while we were looking for signs telling us our time was nearly up, and today we find out we have a ways to go yet!"

"Spooky!"

They both laughed when she said that word, and at the same time, were relieved they had more time left on earth.

"Do you have the letters for David and Mia from Ed and Lilli?"

"Yes, we can go tomorrow and set everything up for them. I think they'll be shocked and surprised at what's been planned for them for sixty-four years!" With that, Marguerite went and locked the door. All Chase could do was laugh as she turned down the lights and started undressing him.

The giggling started all over again between them, until they finally fell asleep as they always did, with their arms and legs wrapped around each other.

New Beginnings

Chase called for a driver first thing in the morning.

"Where are you going?" Sarah asked. "One of us can take you."

"No. Your mother and I have business to attend to. Don't hold lunch for us. We'll call you if we can't be back for dinner either."

Well, that got them all going. When Sarah relayed the message to everyone else, confusion reigned.

Zac said, "Where did they go?"

Josh replied, "They just said they had business they had to attend to and nothing more."

Zeke asked, "Sarah, how did they look? Were they upset about anything?"

"No, they looked normal. Mom's outfit was pressed to a T, and she had Dad looking the same. Nothing out of the ordinary."

David and Mia just watched the exchange.

"Just let them go!" Matt told everyone, annoyed. "They are old, not stupid. They went out. Let them go somewhere where they don't have to report to us every time they have to take a wee!"

"It's amazing how we worry about them all the time," Mark chimed in. "I know they love how we're concerned about them, but we have to give them some space."

They all went silent and thought about how true that statement was.

Anna agreed completely. "You worry all the time and they feel it. It has to be taxing on them, feeling you like that. We'll have to learn to back off of them. We have to give them some space. We're so lucky they're in good shape and mentally so strong yet. Let's all try and remember that."

Zac went right over to her, "Thank you, my love, for reminding us that we're *their* children, and they are not ours. I'm sure they know how we feel about them." Then he raised her hand to his lips and kissed it, just like his father always did with his mother.

They all relaxed. Josh and Sarah then told everyone about their conversation with David and Mia the night before, and how they were family now.

Mark told Sarah, "We all felt what was happening and are so happy for you both. Especially knowing how you lost your child all of those years ago. I know it will always hurt Sarah, but I think this is going to help fill that void for you both!"

With that Sarah went to Mark and he held out his arms for her, while the others just smiled from ear to ear.

Zac said, "Are you calling them Mom and Dad now?"

"Yes," both David and Mia said at the same time.

"And our parents Papa and Nana?"

"Yes," again they replied.

"Well, that would make us all your aunts and uncles then." He smiled, like he could not contain himself.

David and Mia just looked at Zac, "Can we call you that?"

Zeke laughed. "He's messing with you. Of course, you can call us uncles and our wives aunts. We would be honored if you did."

Then their daughters all ran to Mia and David. "Finally! We have more cousins! We should all go to lunch today. Just the cousins and their partners."

"Where do you want to go?" Zac asked.

"To Rocco's. Will you call and make the reservation for us, please? It should be ten of us." They all began gawking at both David and Mia, and were so happy that they were now family.

"Margaret, you just assumed they weren't busy. You could have asked them if they wanted to go first."

With that, Mia spoke up. "We're in. We would never pass up a date with our family. We would go anywhere you wanted us to."

Everyone just smiled. Sarah and Josh were so proud, and it was showing on their faces.

61 At Ed's

Chase and Marguerite had made many stops before they reached their final destination, which was Ed's townhouse. Their instructions had been to keep it and give it to the two people who would have their souls. Well, that was one of the instructions.

It had been vacant for the last twenty-three years. It was a nice townhouse too. It had four bedrooms, four bathrooms, and a large kitchen, dining room, and living room. There was even a small yard enclosed in by a big fence.

Every year Mam had flowers, planted in big pots, placed on the deck, where you could also fit a nice-sized table and grill for dinners in the summer. They had paid a cleaning service to come in once a week and keep it in perfect shape.

It was fully furnished, and the big couches were generic, looking like they could fit in any time-frame. They also had the cleaning service change the bedding once a month, and clean the curtains twice a year, to keep it ready for when they finally found Ed and Lilli again.

Everything was in order. They went to the bank and got the safety deposit boxes. One was Ed's and one was Lilli's. They had a new key made, because they only had one and now they needed a second for Mia. They also had the letters, which had been written for the two people who would carry their souls.

They were all set. When they looked at their watches, they saw it was almost five and couldn't believe they had missed lunch and been gone all day. They called home to say they were staying out for dinner. Sarah told them to have a nice time, not wanting to pry.

Back at Sarah's, they were moving David and Mia into the upstairs bedroom. As they were going up the stairs, Mia noticed portraits of Marguerite on her wedding day and Sarah on hers.

Mia asked, "These pictures from your wedding day are beautiful."

Sarah just smiled. Everyone said the same thing and it touched her when they did.

"Look again," she told Mia.

"Oh my God! One is your mother! I thought they were both of you." She stopped in the stairwell, studying the images.

"You wore her wedding gown," she observed. "I can see why. It's just exquisite. That's my favorite style too, off the shoulders …. and those buttons. I see what you mean now. How would you ever get them all undone?" Mia began laughing and so did Sarah.

Sarah's wheels started turning as a thought crossed her mind. She had to speak to her mother first though, so she kept quiet.

Chase and Marguerite went to dinner before heading home, feeling happy and peaceful.

"Do you think we feel so peaceful now because Sarah is finally happy?" Chase asked. "Not that she wasn't before, but now she's truly happy … in her heart too."

"I do feel that," she said. "All of that pain, for all of those years, must have been hard. My heart breaks just thinking about her and Josh, but now they just got the biggest gift from God, and I am so happy for them."

Chase nodded, squeezing her hand and smiling widely at her across the table. "Right now, at my age … at this moment … I shouldn't be thinking the thoughts I'm having about you."

That made the both of them almost fall off their chairs laughing. They just couldn't stop. Chase grabbed her hand again and just held it across the table, smiling at her in pure happiness. If he didn't need that hand to eat with, he would have never let it go.

Multiple people came to the table to say hello, and each time they were gracious and thanked them for stopping by to see them. They were still amazed that people remembered them.

Then they got another shock, when the women who had tried to take Sarah away all of those years ago stopped by to ask if they were Chase and Marguerite Martin. They knew exactly who she was, and felt ice running through their veins.

Chase grabbed Marguerite's hand again and felt her shaking, even knowing that the woman couldn't hurt them anymore. She still had that effect on them.

They'd both moved to stand, but the woman stopped them. "No need to stand. I don't want to interrupt your dinner. I just wanted to come by and say hello."

Chase and Marguerite looked at each other and then back at her.

"I'm really happy everything turned out well for you all," the woman said. "I saw Sarah's picture multiple times in the paper and online, and I know you did a good job with her. You have been the best parents. Anyone looking at those photos can see that. In fact, I just saw all of your pictures again in the paper, from when you were in New York recently. You were all together again. It makes me feel good … families sticking together as you do. It's so rare now."

They were stunned to hear her say that. "Thank you for stopping by," Chase said.

Marguerite nodded. "It means a lot to us that you feel that way."

"I also want to say that I am so sorry for your loss recently. I read about Mrs. Howard passing away. I know your hearts are breaking over her passing."

Chase said, "Thank you again. That was very kind of you, and we appreciate it."

"Please go back to your dinner and enjoy the rest of your evening," she said and left them alone.

Chase and Marguerite just stared at each other. They'd never felt contempt for anyone like they had for her.

Marguerite said, "I think she was trying to apologize. Do you think that too?"

"Yes, I do. I think that's exactly why she came over to see us."

"Amazing." That was all Marguerite could say about the whole encounter.

"This calls for dessert, Mam! What do you think?" Now he was laughing.

"You never have to ask me twice for dessert. I would take it over my meal, any day."

They were both back to smiling and laughing, as if they were in their twenties again.

62. Wedding Dress

Chase and Mam were still laughing when they walked in the door after eight. Even though everyone had been worried, they didn't show it. They just looked at them, smiling. They were glad to see their parent's back home.

Chase said, "There were too many people here, so we got a room for the day!"

Marguerite hit him. "You shouldn't have told them that. Next time we go missing they'll be calling all the hotels in the city looking for us." They both laughed as she pulled him by the hand to their room, where they closed the door and fell on the bed in a fit of laughter.

Everyone's jaws had dropped when Chase said they'd gotten a room for the day, and they were all still just standing there looking at each other. David and Mia started laughing first, and then everyone else joined in and they all relaxed.

David said, "You don't think they really got a room for the day, do you?"

Zeke said, "Who knows. After the week we all just had, maybe we all should have done that. Look what it did for them."

Then they all laughed again and couldn't stop either.

Later after everyone went to bed, Marguerite came out to get some water for Chase and herself. Sarah was in the kitchen getting ready for breakfast.

"Do you want some help, my love?"

"No, I'm done now, but I would like to speak to you for a moment."

"Sarah, it isn't about the room thing your father said earlier, is it?"

"No, not at all. I want to run something by you." She was smiling, just thinking about it.

"Oh, okay, what is it then?" Marguerite had to turn her head so that Sarah wouldn't see her laughing again.

Sarah told her how much Mia had loved their wedding pictures and thought they were both pictures of her. "Mia loved your wedding gown as much as I did. It was so exquisite. Off the shoulders is her favorite style too."

"Sarah, are you thinking she might want to wear it?"

"I thought we could make the offer, and tell her we wouldn't be offended if she didn't want to."

Marguerite was so touched. "Well, let's get it out of storage and take a look at it first. It might not be in good shape after almost sixty-five years."

That made Sarah smile and her mom could tell how happy it made her.

"Let's get it out tomorrow and take a look."

They both went to bed happy.

63

Setting a Date

David and Mia were lying in bed when a thought hit David unexpectedly.

"Mia, I love you and don't want to wait to get married. I want to set a date now."

Mia was stunned that he didn't want to wait to get married, but was thrilled because she felt the same way.

"David, I am so happy you said that. I don't want to wait either. When were you thinking? Sometime this year? Because it's the end of August already."

"I'm thinking next week, while we're still here with our family."

Mia almost fell off the bed. "David, there's so much to do when planning a wedding. I don't want to elope. I'd like a ceremony and reception just for our families. I don't have many to invite, but I have friends I would like to share my day with."

"This is girl thing, right?"

She just smiled and said, "Right!"

David just wrapped her in his arms and said, "Well then, you can have anything you would like Mrs. Allen."

That made her cry, and she just held onto him like she didn't want to let him go. He was pleased.

"Let's talk to Mom and Dad tomorrow," she said. "I know that if anyone could pull this off, it would be them..." Her voice trailed off for a moment and then she asked, "Do you feel funny calling them that?"

"No, not in the least bit, which is how I know it's so right. Now let's get back to the date. How about next Friday?" David asked.

"Eight days away. You're going to make me wait for eight days?" She was now pretending to be annoyed. "I'm just kidding. Next Friday is perfect, and starting tomorrow, we will need to start making lots of plans."

With the date finally set, Mia said, "I love you so much, David. I never thought I could feel as happy as I do now."

David looked into her eyes. "Thank you, Mia. Thank you for agreeing to marry me …. and for loving me."

Josh sat straight up in bed, suddenly completely awake. Sarah felt him move and woke up as well.

"What is it? Are you sick? Is everything all right?"

He just looked at her. "I think David and Mia just set their wedding date. They're both so happy right now." It amazed him that he knew that … and felt it.

Sarah just smiled. "Welcome to my world." Then she wrapped her arms around him.

The next morning after breakfast, Marguerite and Sarah went to the loft bedroom where there was a closet where she kept 'things'. One of those things was her wedding gown. It was professionally packed, so it would not get ruined. The Music Museum kept asking her if she would donate it, so they could place it with other memorabilia from The Band 4. The exhibit was massive and amazing and held, among other things, belongings from all the band members and their families.

For some reason, Marguerite just couldn't part with her wedding gown. Maybe the reason was that it had to be worn again. They both got emotional as they pulled it out. It was Marguerite's favorite dress. It had become Sarah's favorite dress too, and now they were going to see if Mia would like to wear it.

It was in perfect condition. The white had not faded on any part of the gown. The beading was all in place, and it looked like they could have just bought it that week. They were both so happy that it was still in perfect shape. They looked at those one hundred and twenty satin buttons in the back and just laughed.

Sarah went downstairs to find Mia. When she did, David and Mia were telling Josh about wanting to get married next Friday. Josh said, "If anyone can pull off setting up a wedding in a week, it would be your mother."

Sarah hugged and kissed them both and told them they were so happy for them. She then said to Mia, "Can you come with me? I want to show you something. Well, my mom and I want to show you something."

The men knew it was a girl thing, and they both just let them go, smiling because they knew something good was being brewed up.

Before Mia walked into the loft, Sarah told her, "We want to show you something, and we won't be offended if you don't like it or want to use it."

Mia could not figure out what she was talking about, until Sarah opened the door and there it hung. Marguerite's wedding gown. It was the most elegant, gorgeous thing Mia thought she had ever laid eyes on.

Immediately she started crying. She went to the gown and touched the beading on the bodice, and felt the chiffon on the bottom.

She just stood back looking at it, smiling and crying.

Marguerite said, "Would you like to try it on? I already see you love it."

Mia could only nod her head.

Sarah said, "Remember, if you don't like it, or you want your own wedding gown, it's okay. We won't be offended in any way." Marguerite just nodded, agreeing with Sarah.

"I would love to try it on. Will you both help me?"

They got it unbuttoned, took it off the hanger, and helped Mia dress. Once they had her in it, both Marguerite and Sarah got emotional. They brought her over to a big mirror in the corner of the room, and Mia could not stop crying. It looked beautiful on her, and she looked beautiful in it.

"I would be so honored if you would let me wear this on my wedding day," Mia said.

Marguerite and Sarah could only stand there hugging each other. Then they went to Mia, hugged her, and told her how beautiful she looked.

The dress fit her perfectly, and Marguerite told Mia, "The honor is all ours. We are so pleased you want to wear it."

"I can't believe I'm going to wear my grandmother's wedding dress. I am so overwhelmed right now. I don't think I want to do a veil but maybe a pearl headband or something like that will look nice."

Marguerite went back into the closet and found the veil that had the pearl tiara attached to it and showed her. They removed the veil and showed Mia the tiara.

Mia loved it and said, "Nana, can you put it on me?" This made them all even more emotional than they already were.

Planning and More

There were so many preparations to make for the wedding, which was to be held in just one week. Josh and Sarah took them to their favorite hotel, where she, her parents, and her brothers had all gotten married. The affairs they put on were always first class, and the security they provided was excellent.

Mia and David were more than pleased with the arrangements made. The hotel immediately blocked off the top two floors for guests, family, and the wedding couple.

Once they got back home, Mia told David, "We have to make out a list and call everyone." Many of her friends would be shocked, and she knew she would have a lot of explaining to do.

Then she had to think about her shop. It was her business, and at that moment, she was confused about what to do with it. "David, can we discuss where we're going to live and what I should do with my business?"

Marguerite and Chase came in just as they said that. Chase knew it was time to give them Ed's letters.

They called Sarah and Josh and the rest of the family. Everyone sat down around the big table in the kitchen, where all important matters were always discussed.

"David and Mia, do you remember when you let us speak to Ed, and he said it was time to give you the letters?" Chase asked.

They did remember, but had forgotten all about it. It was always so emotional when Ed and Lilli were present, it made it hard to think straight.

"Before you decide anything about where you're going to live and what to do with your businesses, Mam and I would like you to check out this address." He gave them a paper and handed them the key to Ed's townhouse.

"You have more planning to do than you know. Go to this address. There are letters waiting for you both in the house. You will see once you get there that everything will be explained. If you need us at any time, you can call. Sarah and Josh are not aware of what will be happening. We'll tell them once you go."

"I've called for a car with security," Chase continued. "David, I know you have your own security in the States, and I think it would be a good idea to have some here too. Not only to keep you safe but also to keep your lives as private as I think you would like them to be. I've already spoken to our office about this and arrangements are being made. Our office is now your office. Tomorrow we'll go there so you can meet your staff."

David just nodded his head in agreement, shocked about how this had all been planned out for him and Mia. They both couldn't wait to see what was at the address they'd been given. They said thank you and headed off.

Once they were gone, Sarah looked at her father. "Dad, this is so surprising. What's going on?"

"Ed left instructions before he passed, hoping he would come back to find Lilli, and made provisions for the two people who carried their souls. He left them his townhouse. Your mother and I have been keeping it clean and up to date all this time. She planted flowers every year there, and we have visited it often to make sure everything's in order."

Sarah and Josh were shocked, as were all of their sons and daughters-in-law. "How did you do that? Especially without letting us know. We didn't even feel you!"

"Sarah, my love, and all of you," Chase looked around the table at his whole family. "Stop thinking we have to tell you every time we take a wee!"

Sarah became upset, but then remembered what Anna had said the day before. They were placing too much pressure on their parents by worrying and concerning themselves all the time.

As Chase was feeling her hurt and confusion, he continued, "We know you're all worried about us, but sometimes it gets to be just too much. We feel your love for us, and we return it as best as we can. We also know you are all upset because we're so old and could pass any time now. We see it in your faces and feel the sadness coming from you all. We never know when our bodies are going to give up on us, but Ed said we have some time left. I believe him, and your mother and I know that it's not time yet. We feel it in here." He pointed to his heart. "We will never leave you. We will always be in your hearts, so please, stop looking at us like it may be our last day on earth. It is not time yet! Trust us! We so love the way you all care about us. We couldn't have asked for more from any of you. You all have been the driving force in our lives since the day all of you were born. Don't ever forget that. You are the lights of our lives. We are so proud of each of you, and never forget the love we have for you all."

Marguerite then said, "Your father is right. We see the way you look at us and feel the sorrow in your hearts. And those feeling are multiplied by the five of you! Please just love us like we will be here forever. Not like we're going to leave you today or tomorrow. Do you think you can do that for us?"

Mark said, "Mom and Dad ... we are so sorry, and I know you feel it from us. We love you so much, and that's why we always worry about you. We don't know how to stop worrying all the time. Can you help us?"

Matt added, "We just don't know how we're going to be able to say goodbye to you." They all started crying when he said that.

"Maybe we shouldn't say goodbye," Zac said. "Maybe we should say, 'have a good journey,' because we *will* see you again. I know it. In heaven ... we will all meet again. We will all be together again."

Zeke shared his thoughts next. "I'll think about how happy you will be when the time comes. You'll be able to finally be with all of your brothers and sisters again, along with our sister Margaret. We know how much you miss them. We all feel it, and I know you'll still be watching over all of us. I'll think of it as if the webcam was on all the time, like when we were young and had to talk to Dad on it."

Then Sarah looked at all of her family at the table. "That's it! I'll think of it as if the webcam will be on every day, and will always think Mom and Dad are still with us, watching over us ... because they're right. They will still be with us, in here." It was her turn to point to her heart.

Everyone at the table was shaken about the conversation taking place, but Marguerite and Chase knew it was something that had needed to be addressed.

"Thank you all. We know this conversation had to happen, and we knew it would be a difficult one ... so can we all relax now? David and Mia are going to be the ones who need us now. Josh, keep your mind open, because I think you'll be feeling lots of emotions from them both once they arrive at Ed's house."

Josh said, "Dad, can you tell us anything?"

"Ed left the townhouse to David and Mia. He also left all his fortune, which has been collecting dividends for the past twenty-three years. I know David is self-made and has his own money, but this is even greater than anyone could have imagined. Your mother and I managed all his royalties ... all the money he had when he passed away ... for David and Mia. They'll be surprised. Ed was Lilli's husband, so he inherited her fortune as well, and he managed it until he died. Then your mother and I took over once Ed passed away. All of Lilli's royalties, and the money she made from her movie, now belong to Mia. That's where we were the other day. We were making all of those arrangements to transfer the money and properties over to them."

Everyone was stunned and had no idea. The fact that their parents had been able to keep all this from them stunned them even more. They sat there just gawking at them.

All Marguerite and Chase could do was smirk at them, enjoying the fact that they had been able to pull it off.

65 Surprises

David and Mia got to the address and their security guard/driver Tom opened the door for them to exit the SUV. They both stood outside the vehicle, looking at a very nice townhouse. The landscaping was beautiful and had been kept up. They loved the house, but didn't know why they were there.

David used the key and unlocked the door to enter. Inside, the place was huge and well-kept. There were some dated pieces of furniture, but it was in immaculate shape. They wondered if anyone lived there and called out, but no one replied. They looked around while walking to the kitchen in amazement.

There on the table, in a bucket full of ice, was a bottle of champagne. There were multiple letters as well. One was addressed to them both, and two others were addressed to them individually. There were also what appeared to be two safety deposit boxes. They didn't know what to make of it all.

David said to Mia, "Let's start by reading the letter to both of us first." He was still confused as to who would be writing letters to them. When he opened it, his face lit up in amazement, "It's from Ed!"

Mia couldn't hide her amazement either. "Let's sit down and read it. I think my legs are giving out on me." They both sat and started to read.

To the man who has my soul and the woman who has my beautiful wife's soul.

If you are reading this, then you know it to be true. I am sure Mam and Chase told you all about us. That was their job, to let you know all about us and how our marriage and love was cut short, because my wife was terminally ill. I have been waiting for years to see if a promise she made to me would come true. You are reading this ... so I know she kept that promise.

I have been looking forward to this for a very long time. Can you imagine waiting for someone your whole life and then trying to wait patiently until you die, so you can somehow reunite with them? I know Mam and Chase will reunite with each other in heaven, but Lilli and I didn't have a long life together. She was sure we would come back to continue as we should have. Living a full life ... filled with love in our marriage and love for our children to come. I waited forever to get to this moment, and I know she did too.

I could only hope you were not frightened by what happened, and apologize if you were. It was never our intent. We gave some pretty unimaginable instructions to Chase and Mam, and all of my nephews and my niece. I am sure, when Chase read those letters to them, they must have thought I was delusional at the time I wrote them. I assure you, there is nothing delusional about love. Trust me!

So now that your heads are spinning, let's get down to business. This townhouse you are in now belongs to the two of you. Chase should have the paperwork for you to sign, transferring it to both of your names. I hope you like it. I asked Chase and Mam to keep it up for you no matter how long it took. Knowing my brother and sister as I do, I know the place is in good shape, and if I know my sister well enough, I would bet she has flowers planted all over the backyard. I'm smiling as I write that! Now that your living arrangements are all settled, let's get to the other personal letters, written to each of you.

~ Ed

Mia and David were shocked. They couldn't believe this. They had a house in London now, and they didn't even think about whether they wanted to live in London, or in the townhouse. They just knew it was exactly where they belonged.

"Do you want to go first, Mia?"

She nodded her head, shaking as she opened the envelope.

A Letter from Lilli

Mia was not surprised to tell David, "It's from Lilli."

'My name is Lilli Parker-Mehan. If you are reading this, then you know all about us. Before I tell you anything else, I want you to know that I love Ed with all of my heart. Or loved him, I suppose. Knowing I'm dying hurts so much, because I won't be around to love him more ... or at least until we both get old and die more naturally.

If you two truly love each other, then it can only grow every day. Do not ever take it for granted ... ever. Look what's happened to us. How sad is that?

Now I will get down to business. I made a lot of money on a project I worked on. Ironically, it was a book and a movie about a love story. If I'd only met Ed sooner, the story would have been about us. Anyway, all the royalties and money I've made from the movie now belong to you. Ed is going to manage my accounts as long as he's alive, and give Chase instructions to take them over once he's gone.

I hope you are pleased with what's been set up for you. It was more than I could have hoped for and I want you to be happy as well. Any other royalties or money I make from that book and movie should also automatically go to you now.

I hope you like the townhouse. I did add some of my touches, but didn't want to change it too much. When I die, I don't want Ed to be constantly reminded of the pain of my passing.

I also want to say thank you. Thank you for the love you will share with your man now. Thank you for taking in my soul, which will stay with you forever if you choose to let it. If not ... I will understand, and will just say thank you anyway.

My hope for you both is that you live a very long and healthy life together. I hope you have a family, and if you do ... will you make me a promise? Give your children love from Ed and me, and know that your children will be loved two times over, because they will have our love forever.

Thank you. That is all I can say! God bless you both.
Lilli

In the envelope was a key to the safety deposit box, which Mia opened. There were bank books and other documents. She opened one of the bankbooks and almost fainted when she saw the balance.

There were millions of dollars in that account! She was so shaken that she dropped the bank book and started crying even harder than she had already been, for many more reasons.

David quickly grew concerned by her reaction. "Tell me what you're feeling. Please, Mia, we promised we would always show ourselves to each other."

She showed him the bankbook, and he was shocked, not knowing what to say.

She wiped her tears, shaking her head and trying to put her feelings into words. "I feel so sad for them both, and yet they were so lucky ... that they found each other again. I'm happy and shocked and amazed that they did all of this for me ... someone they didn't even know. Right now, David ... I feel so much love for you. I just cannot believe how much I love you and how fortunate I feel ... my life has been so blessed since the day I met you. I cannot wait to be your wife," Mia said, weeping, overwhelmed and unable to process everything that was happening to her.

David got right up and went to her. He held her and talked to her, telling her how much he loved her. He was just as overwhelmed as Mia was.

After a while, she managed to compose herself, and said, "I think it's time to open your letter."

They both braced themselves as David opened his letter, which he now knew would be from Ed.

67
Ed's Letter

By now you know our story. I cannot tell you how much I loved my wife. I got to call her my wife for only a very short amount of time, but all the years we were not together, I always thought of her in that way. As my wife...

First, I have to say thank you. Thank you for not wanting to commit Chase and Mam. When they finally found us, I bet you thought they were just plain crazy. What I've asked them to do for Lilli and me was crazy, but they believed in me. They believed in us. They believed in love, which is the bottom line I guess.

If I know Mam and Chase as I think I do ... they have already welcomed you into their family. Please do not ever take that for granted. Being in that family is the best experience in my entire life. It was a privilege to be considered a brother to them both, and an honor. If you know them, which at this point I think you must, then you see this to be true. Never take family for granted. You will need them now and in the future.

Thank you for taking in my soul. I have a huge amount of hope for you and your wife, and that is to have a long and happy life together. I wish you a healthy one, of course. I hope you have children and love them for both Lilli and me. We will send your children our unconditional love and just know you will feel it too. This I will promise you.

Now, in the envelope is a key to a safety deposit box. Chase and Mam have been managing my accounts for you. Everything in that box *now belongs to you. I hope you will be happy with all that was planned for you. You are now my heir, and that is why this all belongs to you.*

Whether or not you choose to let us live in your spirits, we will not be upset. We will be forever grateful to you for finding us and uniting us once again.

All I can say now is thank you! God bless you both and keep you safe.
~ Ed

David was shaking too, as he took the key and opened the box. He took out a bank book—there were many—and opened it. He began crying. Mia went right to him and wrapped her arms around him trying to comfort him just like he had done for her.

Once he started to calm down, he just handed her the book. She was totally in shock, just staring at the amount. The balance in that one account alone was thirty million dollars.

They were both so overwhelmed by what Ed and Lilli had done for them. For almost sixty-five years they had been preparing for this day, and Mia and David could not wrap their heads around how generous they both were and how sure they had been that this would all happen!

Many emotions were going through them at that moment. Mia said, "Let's try and calm down somehow, so we can take this all in."

"Mia, let's stay here tonight. I am going to call Dad though, because I can feel his distress over how emotional we are right now."

Mia agreed. She did not want to leave yet, and she realized that she might never want to.

"David, I'm so glad you called. Your mother and I are frantic over you. I could feel your emotions, and it's driving me mad right about now."

"Dad, I'm fine and so is Mia. I can't even begin to tell you all that's happened over the phone. I know you felt some of it ... I can feel you do."

"Are you all right? Are you sure? Do you want us to come over to be with you both?"

"No, but thank you for that. We're going to stay here tonight. We just don't want to leave. I hope you won't be upset with us for not coming home."

"Of course we are not upset, just as long as you're both fine. That was our biggest worry."

"Thank you, Dad, for understanding. We love you and tell Mom we love her too. Bye."

Then the doorbell rang, and they both just looked at each other. David went down to get it. It was Tom, the bodyguard.

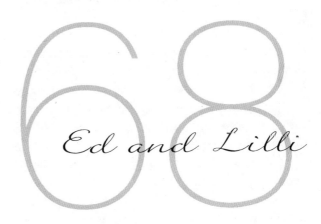

68 — Ed and Lilli

"Mr. and Mrs. Martin sent this for you." He handed David a duffel bag. "They said you would be staying the night. Would you like me to stay or leave? The property is secure, and there is an alarm to set—the security code's in the top drawer in the kitchen—but if you would feel safer with me here, I will be more than happy to stay."

David said, "Thank you, but I don't think we will need you to stay. We'll call tomorrow when we're ready to leave. I'll set the alarm. Thank you for everything."

Mia said, "Who was it?"

"Tom. He handed me this. Papa and Nana sent this, saying they knew we'd be staying here tonight."

He opened it, and saw it contained their clothes and toiletries. They were both amazed. They must have realized they wouldn't want to leave once they started reading those letters. At that moment, they felt so much love for the both of them. It made them so happy.

"Ed said that he felt privileged and honored to be a part of this family and I do too," David said. "I did before and now even more so. We are very lucky. I just cannot believe all that's happened. It *is* spooky!" They both just laughed, because it was either that or cry again.

"Let's open that champagne," Mia said. "I think we could both use it now, don't you, David?"

He nodded his head, but grabbed her around her waist first. "It just occurred to me that I haven't kissed you in a few hours. I think I need one right now."

With that, he planted the most passionate kiss yet on her, and she was more than happy to respond to it with the same enthusiasm. Eventually, they both pulled back and looked at each other, and knew they were both thinking the same thing.

"Do you want them to disappear?" David asked. "Ed and Lilli? Somehow I don't think I want them to."

"David, I was just thinking the same thing. I wonder if they have to give themselves over to us and fade away, or if they could stay ... as they are, I mean. As Ed and Lilli."

"We could ask them, but I have one more thought ... and I hope you won't be upset."

"David, I know what you're going to say and I'm not upset. I want to let Ed and Lilli be together, if you're okay with it too."

They didn't have to say that twice. All of a sudden, Ed was looking at Lilli and Lilli was looking at Ed.

They hugged and began kissing each other, over and over again. Ed finally said, "Can you believe they don't want us to go? What do you think?"

"I think I don't want to leave them either, but we can't interfere with their lives, Ed. We have to let them go. We could stay in the background though, and just enjoy watching their lives together, feeling the love between them, crying during the heartbreaks ... but we can't interfere or they'll ask us to leave. It would all be worth it though ... because we would still be able to feel our love ... through them."

Ed just smiled and agreed. They knew David and Mia heard them, and hoped they approved.

David and Mia were back, and they had heard them. They were thrilled.

"They don't want to leave us!" Mia said. "I am so happy. Are you okay with it?"

"Yes, I think this is the way it should be."

"David, let's let them make love. Will that freak you out?"

"Let's give it a try and see. This is something I feel we have to do for them, after all the plans they made for us."

Ed and Lilli came back and just stared at each other, almost like they were scared.

"Ed, it's been so long." She was in tears, and his face matched his red hair. He was staring at her with his beautiful blue eyes, which now were shedding tears too.

"How are we ever going to be able to thank these two people?" he asked.

"By just giving them our love to feel."

With that, Ed picked up Lilli and carried her to *their* bedroom.

She started undressing him, and he helped her also. Then he stopped dead, completely shocked! All of her scars were gone! There were no signs of all of the surgeries she'd had. There were no reminders of how sick she was. He touched her skin where the scars would have been, and gently kissed each spot he remembered. Lilli was stunned by his actions, and hugged him tightly, remembering how much she loved him.

They kissed until they could no longer hold back. Ed picked her up again and softly laid her down under the covers, where he joined her. She wrapped her arms around him, holding him tightly.

When their bodies finally connected, it felt like sparks were flying between them. They had waited so long, and now the wait was over. They were truly in heaven. Mia and David let them make love all night. They felt they had a lot of catching up to do. In the morning, they even let them wake up to each other. When Ed opened his eyes, he was looking at Lilli, still lying in his arms, and she was looking at him.

He smiled gently at her. It was time, and they both knew it.

"We have to let them go now," Lilli said. "We can't keep them from each other. I know they're just waiting to make love to each other too."

Ed kissed her once more, feeling every bit of the love they had carried for so long.

David and Mia were suddenly back, and wrapped in each other's arms. David grabbed Mia, kissed her passionately, and slowly made love to her, feeling her loving him in return. Much later, they lay quietly in each other's arms, still trying to process how their lives were turning out, and still finding it hard to believe what was happening.

69
Living Arrangements

David and Mia did not want to leave each other's arms, but knew they had to get up. They had a wedding to plan, and it was only days away. If anyone asked them at that moment, they would have just gone right to city hall and gotten married that very morning.

"Come on; we have to go. We have many phone calls to make, and I know everyone is just waiting for us back home," Mia told David, shaking him to get him moving. David had a tight grip on her and did not want her to leave. It made her smile and snuggle into him closer.

"Okay, I am trying to release you," he said, smiling at her, "but I can't seem to get my arms to agree and let you go."

They both lay back in bed, staring at the ceiling and remembering the night they'd just had.

"Can you even believe what's happened to us?" David asked. "It's almost like we've lived a lifetime in the course of a week."

"That's exactly how it feels. In the course of one week, we inherited a whole family of twenty-two people, slews of bank books filled with money, and a house, we rescued a couple waiting to see each other for almost sixty-five years, fell in love, and are now planning a wedding!"

"Just another day in paradise!" David laughed, which made her start too.

"We should start that autobiography," she said. "I know it will be a best seller."

They both got up and called their driver to come get them. Mia was still amazed that they had a driver/bodyguard. Chase had taken care of everything. He said he would and he did.

"Aren't we supposed to go to our office to meet everyone?" Mia asked.

"Yes, I imagine that, once we get back home and tell everyone what happened, we'll head out then. I have to admit that my head is still spinning. I'm trying to grasp everything, but I know I'm probably missing out on some things going on ... or that went on before."

"Well, we have to try and take one step at a time, one thought at a time, one issue at a time, and one plan at a time. Let's try and do it like that."

"You are so right, Mia, and that is why I want you to be my wife. Someone has to be in charge of me."

David's face lit up as he looked at her. Every time he called her his wife, he smiled and sighed happily.

They headed back home to see everyone, with the safety deposit boxes in hand. They were not letting those out of their sight until they could talk to their parents about what they should do. Now they knew why Chase had told them not to make any plans yet. He knew they would just be changing them once they read the letters and saw what was in store for them.

Everyone was waiting for them. Their parents, aunts and uncles, cousins, and grandparents quickly greeted them with huge hugs, as soon as they walked in the door.

Josh told his son, "You must be so overwhelmed right now, after everything that happened last night. Your mother and I were so worried."

Everyone in the room smiled hugely when he said the words "Your mother and I."

"Dad, not only last night but this whole week has been crazy. Mia and I were talking about everything that's happened to us in the course of a single week. I think I'm actually amazed that we're handling it as well as we are."

Mia nodded her head. "I told David we have to take one step at a time. That's the only way I think we can take it all in."

Mia went right to Sarah, who embraced her and it seemed to calm her right down.

"Do you want to sit and tell us how you feel? Everyone knows what was planned for you by Ed and Lilli now. I was able to tell them last night, finally," Chase said. David and Mia noticed that he was standing there with his arms around Marguerite, which gave them warm feelings.

"We don't have a problem with everyone being here. We have to decide what we're going to do after the wedding, and we want you to hear us out. We could probably use the advice," David said, looking at Mia, who was nodding her head in agreement.

Ari smiled. "Thank you for wanting us all to be here, but why don't you just talk to your parents and grandparents now. We don't need to hear everything. We will know anyway, once the boys all feel Sarah." She shrugged. "I hope you're not offended, but there are just too many of us. We just think the six of you should speak about whatever you want to tell them or ask them."

Mia and David went to every aunt and uncle and hugged them, thanking them and telling them they loved them. The sentiment was returned wholeheartedly, while they watched their parents and Sarah and Josh smile approvingly at David and Mia.

Once the room cleared out a bit, the six of them sat at the big table, while David opened up the safety deposit boxes. Sarah and Josh were shocked and stunned at the amount of money the bank books listed. Chase and Marguerite just smiled, because they knew exactly what was in them, having managed the money for years.

Then David told them that Ed and Lilli didn't want to leave them, and had asked to stay. David also talked about the letters left to them by Ed and Lilli.

"Mia, did you notice that they both said the same thing about our children in their letters?"

"Yes, they both said that when we had children they would send all of their love to them, and we would feel it too. I was amazed and picked up on it immediately. They both wanted the same thing for us. Somehow, I just know they would do that ... and not only will we feel it but I think our children might too. Does it sound strange to feel that way?"

Marguerite jumped right in. "After everything that's happened this week to you both, and to us all ... if that is the only thing you think is strange..." She chuckled and shook her head. "No, it doesn't sound odd at all, and I am proud of you both. It's clear that you can cope with this."

Mia got up and went to her grandmother, hugging her. Everyone felt the warm moment between the two of them. Chase was sitting next to his wife, beaming at them.

Josh asked, "Did you make any decisions yet?"

David looked at Mia, "I think we should live here in London in our townhouse and near our family. I feel this is the right thing to do, and I'm happy and content with that decision ... if you agree." He looked at Mia.

"Yes, I do agree. We will have to talk about my business though. I love my gift shop. It took me so long to build it up. I don't think I want to sell it."

Sarah chimed in, "You don't have to sell it. Keep it, and open another one here in London. You could ship things you find here to your shop in the States, and then ship things you find in the States here to your shop in London. It will be different, carrying things from each country. I'm sure you can find someone to manage it there, right?"

Mia's wheels started turning. "What an excellent idea, Mom! Will you help me run the shop here? You and Nana, I mean." That filled both of the Martin women with joy. They both were so pleased that they would be working together.

"I want to talk about my house in Pennsylvania too," Mia said. "I love Pennsylvania. I would like to keep my house there. When we travel home to the states, we could live there and I could work in my store there. What do you think David?"

He grinned in obvious agreement.

Sarah had a thought. "You know, from what you've told us, your house is probably only about thirty miles from ours in Pennsylvania, so we'll still be close to you, if we're all visiting family there. That's another thing. You already have new family right near you, in Pennsylvania. You fly into the Wilkes-Barre/Scranton airport, right?"

"Yes, that's exactly where we would fly into. How strange is this? Again! Everything is falling into place like a puzzle ... with each piece taking its position where it should be." She then looked directly at David.

It was his turn to settle his affairs. "I just bought the condo in New York a few months ago. Maybe we can keep that as well. If we ever wanted to go into the city for any reason, like more art shows, we could use it." He smiled. "I've been getting calls all week. My paintings are flying off the walls there, and they're running out of them, so I'll have to get back to work soon. I have so many thoughts right now on what I want to paint. Most of them are because of my feelings for Mia, and of course, my feelings for all of you too. I can't wait to start up again."

Everyone was smiling and clearly proud of him, Josh and Sarah especially.

"David, are you set on your condo on the twenty-seventh floor?" Josh asked. "Why don't you buy the penthouse? For one, it would fit us all if we all ever decided to travel to New York again, for your shows or just to visit you both or the city. It has a terrace too, which might be excellent for you when you're painting. Your mother and I would give you the difference between what you could get for yours and the cost of the penthouse. We both loved it there."

David was stunned to hear about the generous offer. Mia was just as shocked.

"Of course," Josh added, "if you would rather we stay somewhere else, you could just take the penthouse and we could buy the condo from you. We won't be offended."

David went to Josh and hugged him tightly. He was once again feeling honored to be his son. "We don't want you staying anywhere but with us when you decide to come to New York." He then looked at Mia again. "Is that okay with you? Purchasing the penthouse, I mean? Did you see that terrace?"

Mia could easily tell how excited David was about it, and so was she. "It's more than okay. My mind is already thinking about what I could do with the terrace, so that is a big YES, Mr. Allen!"

David grabbed Mia's face and planted the biggest kiss on her lips. "Thank you, Mrs. Allen." Everyone was pleased everything was going well. Their living arrangements were all set, and they felt better about everything.

Chase said, "I know you didn't think about this yet, but we have a house in Italy on Lake Como. Would you like to take your honeymoon there? You can stay for as many days as you want or can spare. When Nana and I got married, we had two days. We got married on a Tuesday and then had to be back on Thursday night, because we had a concert at the o2 Arena on Friday. It was very short."

"I always wanted to go to Italy. David, can we please?" Mia sounded like a child asking for a piece of candy.

David and everyone laughed. "We can go wherever you would like." He leaned in to kiss her again.

"So basically," Chase said, feeling very pleased, "you now have a residence in Italy as well." They were family after all, and could share in anything they owned.

Josh could see them becoming overwhelmed. "Why don't we take a break and go to lunch. Then we can go to the office and introduce David and Mia to everyone. Bring your safety deposit boxes you two, because your account manager will be there and she'll need all of the bank books and documents you have."

They all thought that was a good idea and went to lunch down the street at their favorite restaurant, entering through the kitchen, where Rocco Jr. met them with warm smiles and hugs. He sat them in the private dining room, so no one would bother them. Josh proudly told Rocco about David and Mia, and how they were his son and daughter now, while Sarah and everyone else sat smiling happily at them.

70
We're a Corporation

David and Mia met everyone at the office, which had about twenty people in it, who did everything you could imagine for them.

There were accountants, to manage the funds and pay the bills, as well as a security team for body guards and drivers. Of course, there were press personnel to control the media, and assistants to arrange all doctor visits, shopping trips, lunch dates, and travel plans. Every family had their own assistant, one for each of the uncles and their families, for Sarah and Josh, and for Chase and Marguerite.

David and Mia were shocked. Each family was a corporation, and now, so were David and Mia.

"David, if you don't feel comfortable using our staff here, you can hire your own personnel," Chase mentioned.

David looked at Josh. "What do you think we should do, Dad? All of these people work for you. Are you pleased and satisfied with them? Being that they take care of the whole family, I don't think we would mind adding our affairs to their portfolio."

Josh was more than thrilled. "Yes, we are happy with the way they handle everything. We would be honored if you wanted to keep your accounts with them."

"Well, this is where my whole family is managed from. Yes, we'd like to stay here also. Mia, are you okay with this?"

"Yes David, more than okay. I think it's the right move for us."

With that confirmation, Chase took them right over to meet their assistant, Dana. She immediately took charge, which was her job. She sat Mia and David down and gave them the run-down on what she would be doing for them. "I know you have a wedding coming up in seven days, so the first thing I would need is your list of guests. I can start making phone calls, inviting them to the wedding. I will make all of the room arrangements and get a plane to Pennsylvania to pick them up. David, I will send a plane to New York to retrieve your people as well as arrange lodging for them."

Chase interrupted. "Excuse me, but Dana, please pay the plane and room fees through Mrs. Martin's and my account. Now, we will leave and let you all get to it." They knew it was going to be a long afternoon for the young couple.

David and Mia just looked at them both, amazed. Sarah laughed. "Don't even argue with them. You will never win."

David and Mia got up and hugged both of their new grandparents. "Thank you so much, Papa and Nana. You have done so much for us already," David said, "I cannot tell you how much we love you. I don't know if there are enough words to say it."

David and Mia took a long time sorting things out there, and Sarah and Josh stayed with them, guiding them all the while.

On the way home, David said to Josh, "I can't believe they already knew so much about us. They knew where to send the plane and about the wedding already. Dana even asked if we wanted her to call Jim the photographer to take our wedding pictures. They knew about Mia's business in Pennsylvania and all about her employees."

Josh said, "That's just the beginning, and it's their job. They have to already be one step ahead of you all the time. When you decide that you want children, Dana will research to find the right obstetrician, and accompany you to all appointments, along with your security. She would have already spoken to the doctor and the office staff to make sure they do not disclose any information about you to the public. She will most likely have them sign waivers, committing them to being discrete. It will be a different life … and David … now that you're even more popular, because of the successful showing you just had, you'll be thanking her for all of it. You two will certainly need it. Trust your mother and me on this one."

Mia and David had not even thought of that part of the lifestyle they were to have, and at that moment, they were very happy they were being helped.

"Where do you want to be dropped off, my loves?" Sarah asked. "Your townhouse or are you coming home with us? It's fine if you had too much today and just want to go home to relax."

Mia spoke straight away. "Can you drop us at our house?"

David smiled at her, and both parents laughed at his mischievous look.

"Tom, take us home and then take David and Mia home." Sarah turned to Mia smiling. "Did you want to come and take more of your things with you?"

"We'll get them tomorrow when we come over." They were smiling at each other. They just wanted to get home, and they were in a hurry.

71 Back to Wedding Plans

The next morning, Mia and David had to head over to the office to give Dana their wedding lists. Mia wanted to make some calls herself, but before she did, Dana went over the schedule with them so they would be able to tell their friends and family when they should be at the airport and what to expect once they landed in London.

Marguerite had already called her family in Pennsylvania and told them all about the wedding. Ashley, Marie, and Kristen were thrilled to be coming back to London for the wedding, as were their children, Maria, Giovanna, and Elizabeth, who were also able to make it. The reunion was going to be bittersweet, because in the past, they'd always traveled to London with their mothers, Donna and Sue. This was the first time they would be traveling there since their passing. Marguerite also told them about Mia living only thirty miles away from them, and about her gift shop. Proving that it was a small world, Kristen told her cousin that she had been in that shop. She shopped there frequently, because Mia carried unique items in her shop. Now they couldn't wait to get there to see her and to meet David.

Mia called her friend Judy to tell her everything that was going on. Judy was already aware of some of the things Mia had been doing that week, partly thanks to a few brief updates from her friend, but mainly because Mia's picture and name had been all over the papers—in an article about David's art show, another about the Martins, and then again in London for the funeral of Mrs. Howard. Judy was just stunned, and couldn't wait to talk to her. When they finally got each other on the phone, the conversation lasted two hours.

David was just pacing, waiting for her to finish. She noticed that he was lingering, so she told Judy that they would continue the conversation later. When she hung up, David grabbed her and picked her up, taking her to bed, where he made love to her.

"I thought you were never going to hang up that phone," David said afterwards, as they were lying with their legs and arms wrapped around each other.

"Well, we need a sign then. If you want me to stop doing something, because you want to make love to me, give me a signal, and I will gladly run right into your arms and let you have your way with me." They both laughed at this.

"So, what do you want the sign to be?" Mia asked.

"I'll put my hand over my heart, and that will mean, I love you and need you now."

"I love that sign. There you have it. When you do that, you'll see the smile on my face and know that I love you and need you too. NOW!" Mia leaned over and kissed him.

Right about then, Dana called and told them that Josh was coming to get David, because they needed to get him a tux for his wedding on Friday. She asked if Mia wanted to go with them.

David ran it by Mia, and she said that she wanted to be surprised.

Dana asked him if he knew who his best man was going to be. "I'll need to make arrangements with him as well, to meet us at the tuxedo shop."

"I have an idea and will call you right back, Dana."

He hung up and looked at Mia. "Dana wants to know who my best man is. I want it to be Josh. Do you have someone you want to stand up for you?"

"Well if Josh is going to be your best man, then I would like Sarah to stand up for me." Then all of a sudden it hit her.

"David, do you think Papa would give me away?" Tears began running down her face as she asked that.

"Oh Mia, I think he would be incredibly honored if you asked him. Do you want to ask him alone or do you want me to be there with you?"

"No, I'll go and ask him. I'll run it by Mom first though."

David called Dana and told her what was going to happen, but told her to wait until they'd asked them all before she shared it with anyone.

On the way to the tuxedo shop, David turned to Josh. "Dad, I was wondering if you would be my best man?"

Josh was surprised and happy. "David ... are you sure? Do you have a best friend you would rather ask?"

"I just did ask him."

Josh was overwhelmed by what David had just said to him. He lowered his head, shaking it in disbelief, and answered in a very quiet voice, "I would be honored to be your best man. How can I ever thank you for making our life so complete?"

They hugged in the back seat of the SUV, while Tom the driver watched them in the rear-view mirror, smiling at them.

Mia called Sarah and told her what David was going to do, and asked her if she would be her matron of honor. Sarah cried and happily accepted. Then she told her about asking Chase if he would walk her down the aisle. Sarah loved the idea

"I will be over tomorrow morning and ask him then," Mia said.

Sarah couldn't wait to see her dad's reaction. She knew that he would be more than happy to do so.

72
Can This Happen?

Mia could not wait to get over to her mother's place to speak to Chase and ask him if he'd walk her down the aisle. It was almost too much for her to handle. She was nervous, excited, and worried about what he would say.

David saw the condition she was in and tried to calm her down. "Mia, think about it. Do you think he would say no? After everything that has happened, you still have doubts? If he still had the strength, I think he'd be doing somersaults when you asked him. Knowing them, everyone will be crying when they find out. Honestly, I don't think you have anything to worry about."

"I don't think I'm worried about him saying no. I think I'm just anxious about asking him and hearing what he says. Does that make any sense?" David pulled her in for a kiss and hugged her like he didn't want to let her go.

"Don't ever stop hugging me like that, David. Like you don't want to let me go. That's how I know you love me. It's almost like when Papa takes Nana's hand to kiss it, and then brings it to his face to feel her touch. That's the most intimate act of love I think I have ever seen. Can this all be really happening to us? Can we be this lucky? Is our bubble going to burst soon? Am I going to wake up and find that I'm still in my bed in Pennsylvania? My heart breaks just thinking of it ... how I would ever cope if I wake up tomorrow and none of this happened."

"Mia, what's bringing this on? I will tell you what is happening, *right now*! We have found each other by accident, and we should thank that big rain cloud you saw that forced you to run into the gallery. From the moment I saw you, my heart has been skipping beats. And yet I feel so calm when I'm with you. That's what you have done to me. You trusted me right from the beginning, and I am telling you, right now, when our daughter comes home and tells us she met someone the way we did … she will not be allowed to leave the house ever again."

He grinned at her and then continued. "Why do you think you can't be lucky or that *we* can't have any luck? Anyway, luck has nothing to do with what has happened to us. Think about it! Our lives have been planned out for us starting almost sixty-five years ago. That's how I know we're supposed to be where we are right now. As far as waking up in Pennsylvania, we *will* wake up together in Pennsylvania, and in New York, and in London, and in Italy. We will wake up in all of those places together. This I can promise you! Have you heard what Papa tells Nana? Do you know his term of endearment for her? He tells her, 'You are the very air I breathe' and she replies the same or just says 'And you are mine.' Without even asking them why they say that … I could guess. Because just saying 'I love you' isn't strong enough to describe the feelings they have for each other. That's how I feel about you. There are not enough words to let you know how much I love you."

David then gently held Mia's face. "I see your tears now, and know they're happy tears. Please, no more doubts about why this has happened to us. Our lives are so special to us, and to so many other people now. It was planned out for us many, many years ago. I thank God he chose us to carry Ed and Lilli's souls. Now we have to honor those souls and give them and us the best life possible, filled with more love than our hearts could ever hold. Please tell me you feel the same."

With tears streaming down her face, Mia said, "Yes, I feel the same … and want to have the best possible life with you, filled with so much love … and children. I want to be a mother, David, so I can give back to our children what everyone just gave to us."

David could not believe she'd just said that. He was blown away at how she felt. "I feel the same way. I want to be a father for that very reason, and because it's the ultimate gift we could give each other, showing how much we love each other."

He grabbed her again, hugging her tightly in an attempt to show her that he *didn't* want to let her go. They both smiled, holding onto each other until the doorbell rang. They knew that it was Tom. He was there to take them to the Martin house.

73 Papa

Once they got to the house, Sarah and Josh were waiting for them. Sarah had the biggest grin on her face. They knew why they were there, and could not wait for her to ask their father about walking her down the aisle. Sarah had been trying all morning to mask her feelings, so her parents would not feel what was going on.

Once they settled down in the kitchen, Chase and Marguerite arrived, having been out for a walk to the grocery store down the street. They came back with some things they had bought for lunch and saw everyone sitting around the table, looking at them with the funniest-looking grins on all their faces.

Marguerite asked, "What's going on? Why are you all grinning like you know something I don't?" They smiled and all got up to leave except for Mia.

"Papa, can I speak to you for a second?" she asked hesitantly.

Chase and Marguerite just looked at each other, not knowing what this was about.

"Your granddaughter wants to speak to you," Marguerite said, "so I will just be in the family room with everyone else." Smiling, she kissed him and left the room.

He still didn't know what was going on and couldn't imagine what was coming next.

"Papa, I want to tell you how much I love you first." Being as sentimental as Chase was, his eyes welled up with tears.

She continued. "I would like to know if you would do me a great honor and walk me down the aisle when I marry David on Friday."

Chase didn't expect that, and David had hit the nail right on the head. His age was the only thing holding his excited enthusiasm in check. The family were all eavesdropping from the family room, and started crying.

He held his arms out to Mia and she walked into his embrace, as the tears rolled down her cheeks. Mia cried as he held her, and then Chase said, "I would be so honored to walk you down the aisle, Mia. You and David make your grandmother and me so happy, and we feel very proud of you both. I would do anything for you." He kissed both of her cheeks, and then held her close and kissed her forehead.

Everyone came out then, as they couldn't wait to congratulate them. A beaming Marguerite went right to her husband.

"Can you believe it, Mam?" he asked. "I am going to walk my granddaughter down the aisle."

She was so proud of them all at that moment. Mia giving Chase that honor was amazing to her.

Josh said, "We have to go get you a tux now, Dad." Chase just nodded his head, smiling happily at everyone.

All the plans were made. Everyone was coming in from New York and Pennsylvania for the wedding and had their schedules. Everyone in and around London knew what they needed to do and where to be.

David and Mia did not think Friday could get there any sooner than it did. Thursday arrived, and they met all of their friends and family at the hotel for a dinner they had planned. Marguerite couldn't wait to see her cousins, who all came in with their daughters, Maria, Giovanna, and Elizabeth.

Sadly, they all felt it might be the last time they would see her, and it made them miss their mothers, Donna and Sue.

Judy was especially thrilled to meet David, and when she saw Mia, they just cried continuously. "I can't believe I left you in New York for one day and you come back with a fiancé," Judy said, laughing through her tears.

David put the icing on the cake when he hugged Judy and said, "Now you're my best friend too, Judy." Then he asked, "How's the new water heater?" which made them all burst into laughing.

When everyone saw Chase and Marguerite walk into the party with their children, the room went silent. They all looked at Mia and David, who knew what everyone was thinking.

David spoke up. "I would like you all to meet our family. My parents, Josh and Sarah Martin-Foster, my aunts and uncles, Zac and Anna Martin, Zeke and Ari Martin, Mark and Catherine Martin, and Matt and Cali Martin, and my cousins, Margaret, Mary, Jess, and Amelia Martin. We would especially like to introduce you to our grandparents, Chase and Marguerite Martin.

Everyone went wild. They just kept looking at David and Mia and the entire Martin family. They didn't know what to say, and yet they were all trying to talk to them, to learn how it all happened. Of all the people it could have been! Chase Martin of The Band 4, and his beloved wife, Marguerite!

The Martins went to all of the guests and personally introduced themselves, shaking hands and saying hello to everyone. Most people were starstruck and the rest were just amazed.

Chase and Marguerite spotted Jim, the photographer. They were so happy to see him and went right to him. Jim had brought his mother and they were so thrilled to see her. Chase said, "Hello Angela. Thank you so much for coming with Jim. Marguerite and I are so happy to meet you finally. We're honored you chose to come to our grandson's wedding."

Angela was smiling, crying, and shaking at the same time. Marguerite just took her by the hand, brought her over to a table to sit her down, and began talking to her some more.

Jim was confused. "Mr. Martin, you just called David your grandson. I thought you only met him recently."

"We did and realized he was family. I can't explain how we knew that. Can we just say that my daughter and son-in-law adopted him into their family, making him my grandson? We love both him and Mia, and something made us all want to be together. Then Josh had a connection to David that was so strong. I can't explain it any better than that, so we made them both family, and they are thrilled about this as well."

Jim just shook his head, believing every word Chase said. After being with them for those few days back in New York, he knew how sincere they were, and what an honor it was for them to think of David and Mia like that.

"I hope you know how fond of you we all are, Jim, and we're so happy you're here with us. I think you know by now that you'll be called by my family all the time when something's going on here."

Jim smiled and was pleased to know how they all felt about him. He felt the same way about them.

74 The Wedding

Marguerite and Sarah kidnapped Mia and took her home, along with all of the aunts and cousins. David was staying at his townhouse with Josh and all the uncles. Their job was to keep him out of trouble and get him to the chapel on time. Chase stayed at home, because he had to accompany Mia to the hotel, since he was giving her away.

It was quite hectic in both houses that night. No one thought they would ever get David and Mia apart. It was almost like they were afraid to separate. Josh assured David that it would be okay, and that his mother would take good care of her. Then he had to promise them both that they would get them to the service on time. That was the only way they would leave each other. They already knew neither would be getting much sleep.

The morning of the wedding, Chase did what he always did when he was anxious. He paced back and forth in the kitchen until his granddaughter Amelia finally said, "Papa, if you don't sit down, we will have to tie you down."

Chase smiled and tried to calm down, while Sarah and Marguerite were getting Mia ready to go.

Dana arrived early to make sure everything went smoothly and on schedule.

Mia did her makeup and Marguerite helped get the pearl tiara secured on her head. Then the uncles all sent a beautiful powder-blue garter for her to wear. She loved it so much that she started crying, before Anna reminded her that she had to stop or she would ruin her makeup.

Next came the gown, and they could hardly wait to see it on her. Everyone loved the gown, and now for the third time, it was going to be center stage with the bride. It took forever to get all of those satin buttons closed, and everyone was laughing over the story again. Mia confessed that she had hidden ten pairs of scissors in her hotel room, so no one could try and ruin her wedding night with David. Everyone just kept on laughing and thought she was brilliant. She already knew the Martin men and wanted to be one step ahead of them.

Mia finally came downstairs in the gown, and she took Chase's breath away, along with everyone else's. Jim was snapping pictures left and right. Chase had tears in his eyes when he saw her. "You are one of the most beautiful brides I have ever seen. My daughter was one too, and my wife was the first. Right now … seeing you in that gown… It makes me think of both of them. Thank you, Mia, for that."

Chase then went to Marguerite and kissed her lovingly. "I remember every minute, every hour of our wedding. It was one of the happiest days of my life." He then kissed the ring he'd given her, which she still wore. "I gave you this to tell you that you were mine and you gave me this," he showed her his wedding band, "to tell me I was yours. That day was very special to me. How lucky I felt and still do feel to this day. You were so beautiful then and are still so beautiful now. Thank you for saying you would stay at my house that first night. Thank you for saying you would marry me. Thank you for my five beautiful children." Then he kissed her again, as tears rolled down both their cheeks.

Everyone had just stood there, listening to the exchange of words between them.

Jim finally cleared his throat, and said that it was time to go, or David would think Mia was not going to show up. Off they went, surrounded by security to get them to the hotel chapel safely and discretely.

Back at David's, everyone helped dress him, because he was shaking so much. He wasn't nervous; he was just so happy and excited that he couldn't contain himself.

Josh gave him a father-son talk, and everyone got a good laugh out of it. Even Josh and David found it amusing. He asked him to respect his wife and treat her like she was a fine piece of china that was so delicate he had to handle it with care. After the first few sentences, David drifted off, thinking of Mia and wanting to get to the chapel to be married. Josh realized that was what was going through his mind, but pretended not to notice.

Finally, he called for the drivers and security. It was time to go.

Everyone was sitting and waiting for the doors of the chapel to open, as the wedding planner and Dana fixed Mia's gown so it would flow properly as she walked down the aisle with Chase towards David and Father Holland. They were especially pleased that Father Holland was able to marry them, having taken over for Father Cummings as their spiritual adviser.

The doors finally opened and everyone looked back at Chase and Mia. Chase felt her shaking and whispered to her, "You are so beautiful; I can't wait to see the look on David's face when he sees you. You are an angel." Mia calmed right down after hearing that.

Mia found David, and felt like she was gliding to him ... like she was walking on air. She saw tears streaming down his face and knew that she couldn't wait to pledge her love to him.

Father Holland asked the question, "Who gives this woman to be married to this man?" to which Chase replied, "Her grandmother and I do!" There wasn't a dry eye in that chapel.

Chase then kissed her. "Your new family will always be here for you, no matter what, no matter when, no matter where. You will always be a daughter, granddaughter, niece, and cousin to us. We all love you." Then he took the hand she had placed on his arm and handed it to David, whom he also leaned over to kiss. David was beaming with love for them both.

The whole day, from the ceremony to the reception, was incredibly emotional for everyone in attendance and went off without a hitch. When it was all over, David swept Mia off her feet and ran out of the banquet room with her, kidnapping her for the night. Everyone cheered in approval.

Then Chase and Marguerite said goodnight to everyone. They were tired out; it had been a long day. Once they got to their room, they just stood there looking at each other, each knowing what the other was thinking about.

"You were so beautiful when we got married," Chase said. "I couldn't wait to finally make love to you. Remember all the love we felt before we married, and how it was nothing compared to what we felt that first night together? Remember how we felt each other's joy and passion? What a gift from God our connection to each other was. I'm not only talking about sex either. How lucky we are ... and why us? Did you ever wonder? Why did God give *us* that connection ... that gift?"

"Chase, we must have been worthy of it. That's what I always thought, and we were lucky and are still lucky. We're blessed to still be so in love with each other, in love with our children, and in love with all of our family."

"I want to hold you, Mam. I want to feel your body melt into mine like it always does."

"I want that too. Come to me now then." She held her arms out for him.

Once under the covers, he turned and held her like he always did, and got what he wanted. He felt her body relax and melt right into his, while he buried his head in her hair, taking in the soft smell of her skin. They remembered when they were young and couldn't get enough of each other.

"I finally know why we had all of that sex when we were young," Chase said. "Remember Mam? When we couldn't get enough of each other? Well, we were making up for when we got old, like now ... when it's practically over for us." They both started laughing and couldn't stop.

"If I'd had any idea *that* was why, I would have made you love me more," she said. Now she was giggling like it was *their* honeymoon.

As the boys were heading to their rooms, they could hear their parents laughing. They all just looked at each other and started laughing too. Their wives looked at them, and it was Anna who finally said, "Well, I hope some of that stamina has passed down to you in *your* DNA!" That made them all rumble with laughter as they practically chased their women to their rooms, to show them what *was* passed on to them by their parents. It sounded like a challenge to the Martin men, and they fully intended to meet it.

75
New Life

Everything calmed down after the wedding and honeymoon for David and Mia. David couldn't wait to start painting again, and he set up a room in their townhouse where he could work from home.

Mia and Sarah found a building where she could open a gift shop in London, and they got started immediately, setting it up by filling it with unique items for sale. Sarah loved working with her and helping her out. Everyone was right when they said that David and Mia would fill the void left in Josh and Sarah's lives when they'd lost their child so many years ago. Everyone was thrilled for them.

One morning Mia got up and her stomach turned. David was watching her, as he always did, because he loved her so much and could never take his eyes off of her, and became concerned. He saw the color in her face turn also, which alarmed him. The feeling passed, but he asked her about it to make sure she was feeling right.

"Do you want to take the day off today and go do something? You've been working so hard setting up your shop lately. Maybe you should take a day and just rest."

Mia was always so touched when David was worried about her. She was lying next to him smiling.

"Why are you smiling like that?" he asked. "Do you want me to make love to you? Right now? Because I would be very much up for that." He laughed.

Mia got out of bed and pulled him with her into the bathroom, where she pulled a box containing a home pregnancy test out of the drawer. David nearly jumped out of his skin, he was so excited. He grabbed her and picked her up, swinging her around like she was two years old.

"Put me down!" she laughed. "I want to take the test first, and then you can have your way with me."

They read the instructions, and she followed them. It was the longest five minutes they had ever experienced. When the time was up, she was almost afraid to look, so she told David to do it.

"What color is it?" She was now holding her hands over her face.

"Is pink good?" David said to her.

Mia started screaming, then crying ... and then she started jumping up and down. "Yes! Pink is good!"

David's eyes teared up, and he joined her in jumping up and down. They were both elated and didn't know how they were ever going to calm down.

Back at the homestead, Josh felt David and started crying at the table, where Sarah and her parents were sitting, having breakfast together.

They all saw that he was emotional and couldn't imagine why. Then he took Sarah's hands and looked into her eyes and said, "We are going to be grandparents."

All of their jaws dropped and Sarah began crying. Marguerite and Chase also became emotional.

"I felt David; he is so overjoyed right now. They just took the test. I'm sure of it. I can't believe I felt his joy like that. It is so amazing," Josh said proudly.

Chase and Marguerite were incredibly happy for Mia and David, but they were overjoyed for Sarah and Josh.

"They will probably call you later," Chase told his daughter. "When I found out your mother was pregnant, I didn't let her out of our room the whole day."

Marguerite rolled her eyes and blushed. "Sometimes you share too much, Chase." Then she laughed at him, and laughed even harder at the expressions on Josh and Sarah's faces.

Back at David and Mia's place, David said, "I know Dad and Mom know. He felt me, and I know he felt why I was so happy. We will have to call them later though, because right now I'm not letting you out of this bed."

That pleased Mia, because she didn't want to let him out of their bed either.

"Do you want to let Ed and Lilli talk about it?" Mia asked.

"Would you let them? I was thinking that just now, and remembered how they told us they would send all the love they had to our children. I know it sounds funny, but can't you just feel the love they have for each other too? They did tell us that we would feel their love too, and they were right."

"I do feel it, and it's so strong. That's how I know it's them. Let's let them share in our joy, because it's their joy as well."

All of a sudden, Ed was looking at Lilli as they lay in bed together. "Can you believe it, Ed? They want us to go through this with them, together. I am so happy for them. We have to make sure we take care of Mia for David. I know I'll protect her and see to it that she's feeling all the love I have for her." Tears were rolling down her cheeks.

Ed's face was all red, because he was also overjoyed at the news they'd just received. "I'll make sure you're both safe, or *all* safe. You, Mia, and the baby."

"I want to give them a gift, Ed. I'll say we will send the *babies* all the love we have for them." And then they kissed each other, happily.

Mia and David were back, and just staring at each other.

"Mia, I just heard Lilli say, 'babies'! Did you hear that? What does that mean?"

Her eyes were very wide. "She said she wanted to give us a gift, and I think that gift was her telling us we're having more than one baby. Maybe twins!" They were both amazed at what was just revealed to them. "Can you imagine that?" Mia was now looking at David in shock. "Twins!" She repeated it, not believing what she heard. "We will have to see if that's really what they meant once I get a doctor's appointment."

David got all smug, and said to Mia, "Well you do know ... twins ... they run strongly in my family!" They smiled, cried, and laughed, feeling completely blessed.

"Thank you, Ed and Lilli," David said. "We love you so much." He looked at Mia and grinned. "Let's tell my parents. I can't seem to wait to share our news..."

Epilogue

Security was tight at the hospital, where everyone was patiently waiting for news on the birth of Mia and David's twins. The waiting room was blocked off to keep the press, or anyone else, from seeing them waiting. The whole Martin clan was there, and their excitement couldn't be contained. Sarah and Josh were there alongside her brothers and sisters-in-law and all of the cousins. The electricity in the room was amazing. David and Mia drew out the suspense by not telling anyone if they were boys or girls. They wanted to surprise everyone, which made them all the more anxious.

Marguerite and Chase were home waiting for the news. They felt they would see them once all the commotion was over and everything had calmed down. Chase did what he always did when he was impatient, pacing back and forth until Marguerite finally told him she would have to tie him down if he didn't stop.

Then the nurse came out with David, who had a grin on his face that looked big enough to split it open. He was in scrubs, and he was crying. They all got nervous seeing that, until he said, "Mia is fine and so are my son and daughter."

Everyone screamed for joy.

David enjoyed the reaction for a moment and then continued. "It's a boy and a girl! We have one of each!" he said proudly. They were all crying and hugging him. The men were patting him on the back. The uncles had been especially pleased to learn of them having twins. When they'd first found out, they had thought, *Well, twins do run in the family!*

Chase and Marguerite got a call from Sarah right away, and they just cried on the phone. They were so moved that they had to hang up. As long as the mother and babies were fine, they were fine too.

Chase took his wife's hand and kissed it, while bringing it to his face so he could feel her. They were overwhelmed, staring into each other's eyes and remembering when their sons were born ... and when Sarah came to them. They never forgot how blessed they felt they all were.

Once Mia was ready to be seen, everyone ran to see the babies, and congratulated the new parents. They didn't want to stay long, because they all knew she would be wiped out, but they didn't want to go until they had told her how much they loved her, and how happy they were for her.

Mia and David were very happy to see everyone there. They wanted to tell everyone what they had named the babies, but not before they called their grandparents. David shooed everyone out into the hallway, and got Chase and Marguerite on the phone. Both of them were very pleased that they had called.

"Nana and Papa ... we want to tell you what we decided to name our children before we told anyone else," David said.

"What did you decide on?" Chase asked.

David told them, and they were delighted. He was relieved. "We're glad you're pleased. Mia and I felt the choice of names were very well-suited. We didn't think of any others."

Chase and Marguerite were beside themselves. "We are both so proud of you, and cannot wait to come and meet our new great-grandchildren."

The new parents called everyone back in. David had his daughter in his arms and introduced her. "I would like you to meet my daughter, Lilli."

Mia was holding her son. "And I would like you to meet my son, Edward." The whole room lost it. Everyone was crying, and trying to go over to see the twins.

They noticed immediately that the babies both had strawberry blond hair. The blond hair was clearly from their father, David, and the red cast ... well ... that was from Uncle Ed.

A LETTER FROM THE AUTHOR ABOUT ED,

Once again, I am so honored you chose to read the second book of The Band 4 trilogy – 'Ed.' When I finished the first book, I had no idea I would continue the story. At the time, my mind was just blank after concentrating for so long on 'The Air We Breathe'. I had no idea I even wanted to write a second book, and now find that the third is almost ready to go.

When I wrote the part of Ed, it was mostly because I felt Chase and Marguerite needed another friend, outside of the group Chase belonged to. I made him so special to them, as well as to their five children. I didn't know why I wrote him like that at the time, but maybe subconsciously, I thought all the while that he should have his own story ... and what a story it is.

I hope no one got confused with the supernatural aspect of Ed's life. I was nervous readers would get lost with his story-line about himself, Lilli, David, and Mia. I am a fan of the unusual though, and this story is very unusual.

Another secret I will confess to, about Ed, is that I love red hair! That's why I gave him that description. So, now you know...

I find that I cannot stop thinking about Chase and Marguerite and all of their children. While I painted the boys as angels in the first book, let's face it, they were boys! All four of them! That is some of what the third book will be about: how they tested both parents. Even our beloved Sarah had her moments. I also wanted to highlight what a difficult time Marguerite had with Chase being gone so much. He left her home with five children, and it took a toll on them both.

While I cannot decide on a name for the third book, it will be about Marguerite and Chase, remembering stories from their past ... and what stories some of them were!

Again, I will ask you to go back and read Ed again, so you don't miss anything.

I hope you all loved reading this book as much as I did writing it. I did it for you!

Fondly,
Marguerite

CHARACTERS

Chase Martin — From London - One-quarter of the most popular band on the planet 'The Band 4'. Father of twins, Zac and Zeke, and Matthew and Mark, and daughters, Margaret and Sarah.

Marguerite Angeli Martin — Originally from Pennsylvania in the United States - Wife of Chase Martin. Mother of twins, Zac and Zeke, and Matthew and Mark, and daughters, Margaret and Sarah.

Zac Martin — Eldest son of Chase and Marguerite Martin. Twin brother to Zeke.

Zeke Martin — Twin brother of Zac and second son of Chase and Marguerite Martin.

Matthew Martin — Third son of Chase and Marguerite Martin. Twin brother of Mark.

Mark Martin — Fourth son of Chase and Marguerite Martin. Twin brother of Matthew.

Baby Margaret — Firstborn of Chase and Marguerite Martin. She died at birth.

Sarah Martin Foster — Second daughter of Chase and Marguerite Martin. Adopted when her mother left her on the Martins' doorstep before she passed away.

Ed Mehan	Best Friend and brother to Marguerite and Chase Martin. Singer/songwriter. Winner of six Grammy Awards and One Oscar. Husband of Lilli Parker-Mehan
Lilli Parker-Mehan	Wife of Ed Mehan. Author, screenplay writer, producer. Passed away from cancer.
David Allen	Artist. Adopted son of Josh and Sarah Martin-Foster. Harbored the soul of Ed Mehan.
Mia Addison Allen	Wife of David Allen. Gift-shop owner. Harbored the soul of Lilli Parker-Mehan
Margaret Martin	Daughter of Zac and Anna Martin.
Mary Martin	Daughter of Zeke and Ari Martin.
Jessica Martin	Daughter of Mark and Catherine Martin.
Amelia Martin	Daughter of Matt and Cali Martin.
Anna Martin	Wife of Zac Martin
Ari Martin	Wife of Zeke Martin
Catherine Martin	Wife of Mark Martin.
Cali Martin	Wife of Matthew Martin.
Jim	Photographer befriended by all the Martins.
Blake Thomas	One-quarter of The Band 4. Brother to Chase, Drew, and Quinn.

Drew Bishop — One-quarter of The Band 4. Brother to Chase, Blake, and Quinn.

Quinn Howard — One-quarter of The Band 4. Brother to Chase, Blake, and Drew.

Abbey Thomas — Wife of Blake Thomas. Sister to Cara, Jeanine, and Marguerite.

Cara Bishop — Wife of Drew Bishop. Sister to Abbey, Jeanine, and Marguerite.

Jeanine Howard — Wife of Quinn Howard. Sister to Abbey, Cara, and Marguerite.

Colin — Family Lawyer of the Martins.

Peter — Manager of 'The Band 4'.

ABOUT THE AUTHOR

Although Ed – For Love and Hope actually begins a short time before her first novel, The Band 4 – The Air We Breathe, it is very much its sequel. With it, the author is thrilled to have had the opportunity to breathe life into one of her favorite characters, who definitely deserved a spotlight of his own.

Marguerite Nardone Gruen is currently living in Northeastern Pennsylvania with her husband of 36 years.

Printed in Canada